RIDERS OF PARADISE

ROBERT J. HORTON

LEISURE BOOKS NEW YORK CITY

A LEISURE BOOK®

June 2007

Published by special arrangement with Golden West Literary Agency.

Dorchester Publishing Co., Inc.
200 Madison Avenue
New York, NY 10016

"Riders of Paradise" by Robert J. Horton first appeared as a seven-part serial in Street & Smith's *Western Story Magazine* (10/3/31–11/14/31). Copyright © 1931 by Street & Smith Publications, Inc. Copyright © renewed 1959 by Street & Smith Publications, Inc. Acknowledgment is made to Condé Nast Publications, Inc., for their cooperation. Copyright © 2006 by Golden West Literary Agency for restored material.

ISBN-10: 0-8439-5895-2
ISBN-13: 978-0-8439-5895-9

Visit us on the web at www.dorchesterpub.com.

RIDERS OF PARADISE

CHAPTER ONE

Andrew French sat in a stout rocking chair on the broad front porch of the Two-Bar F ranch house and looked out over the green, fertile acres flowing down to the timbered banks of the Teton. Far off, the river wound, twisting and turning, appearing and vanishing, until the effect was that of silver tassels against a purple velvet field. The afterglow of the sunset stained the buttes with pink reflections. A universe swept out from the ranch house just where Paradise Valley widened and merged with limitless plain. And such was the domain of the rugged man who rocked slowly in the chair on the porch.

With the cattle baron, in an armchair on his left, was a friend, Norman Webb, come up from the town of Conroy, to visit him overnight on a matter, so he had said, of personal business.

They were large in build, both these men, and about the same ages—around sixty—but French appeared the younger of the two. He had bushy black brows in direct contrast to his gray hair, was clean-shaven, round of face, well tanned, with deep-set dark eyes and a fine network of thin wrinkles at their corners.

Webb's face was ruddy and suggested good living. His eyes were blue and seemed set in a perpetual twinkle. He wore a close-cropped gray mustache. He was as wide of shoulder as French, but his manner did not carry the authority and suggestion of power that French could display in a single gesture.

Both men had pioneered on the north range, and, while French had remained in possession of his vast acres and breeded herds, Webb had sold out his ranch holdings, retired from stock raising, and moved to town.

"You were sayin' things are quiet in town, Norman?" said French. "Well, they would be with spring about done and summer in sight."

"Pretty quiet," said Webb, clearing his throat. There had been a long silence. " 'Course, there's some places that're always more or less lively down in Conroy, as you know."

"Yes, I know." French's voice rumbled in his throat. "The Stampede is one of 'em, and it wouldn't hurt my feelings none if an earthquake struck it into the ground tomorrow."

"I'm with you there," said Webb. "It's got to be nothing but a gambling hell . . . that's all it is. The sheriff knows it, but what can he do? The people seem to want it . . . think it brings trade to town. It does bring in money, but . . ." He suddenly fell silent.

"And Red Tower gets it!" French exclaimed. "Lot of good that kind of money does a town. How's Pansy?"

Webb cleared his throat again. "She's well," he answered.

French turned his head to look at him. "Norman, did you come up to tell me that Clint's been bothering around again?"

"Well, there's no use of chasin' a horse around the corral, Andy. We've been friends a good many years and there's no reason why I shouldn't be frank with you, and you with me. I came up to talk about Pansy and Clint, but we don't want to let those two young folks get the idea that we're doing anything behind their backs or they maybe'll both lose their heads entirely."

"Has Clint been cutting up pretty bad?" asked French with a scowl. "Tell me the truth, Norman. Don't try to hide anything or spread on any syrup just because he's my son. I know Clint's wild."

"I didn't come up with any complaints about Clint, exactly," said Webb. " 'Course, he's wild, and my girl's wild, too, in her way. Sometimes I think it would have been better if I hadn't sold the ranch after my wife died. I seemed to think it was no place to bring up a girl with her mother gone. But that's all past. We're used to town now and I'm too old to go back to ranching on another place. And it wouldn't do any good, anyway."

"No, it wouldn't,". French agreed. "Well, what about Pansy and Clint? Talk right out plain, for I'm listening. I know that the way things are, you don't want Clint hanging around Pansy. He's been running pretty wild, and I've been trying to figure out how much of it is my fault."

"Clint's all right at heart," said Webb, "and I can't see how anything he's done is any of your fault. Of course, he isn't the same as Dick. . . ." Webb halted. "I mean he isn't . . . hasn't got the same ideas as Dick," he added hastily. "I think he's going to come 'round all right, Andy, and I'm wondering if there isn't something both of us can do to help him. That's why I came up to see you."

"Yes, there's a difference between Clint and

Richard," French said in a brooding voice. "A big difference, Norman."

It was notable that while he spoke of one of his sons as Richard, he abbreviated the other son's name. He never spoke of the one as Dick and the other as Clinton. The boys were twins. After the death of their mother, French had sent them away to school. It had been his wife's last wish that the boys have an education.

Richard French had liked school and had stayed. Clinton French, with the wild blood of the ranges ever uppermost in his veins, had run away from school and had taken up with a band of near outlaws. His father had brought him back to the ranch, deciding that was the best place for him. But young Clint, as the boy always had been known, "wouldn't stay put," as the cowhands had it.

He was tall, slim, and handsome, and became one of the most proficient riders on the range, winning prizes at rodeo meets, breaking wild horses, flashing his reckless, boyish smile in the face of danger. But more dangerous still, he had become absolute master of his gun—quick as darting light on the draw, perfection in his aim. No man in the outfit could outride him or outshoot him. "Thank the Lord, he hasn't killed anybody yet," Andrew French had said on more than one occasion.

Richard French had gone through school and had graduated from a great university in the East. He became nationally known for his feats as an athlete. He took on polish and that intangible manner of culture that in time came to awe his father into dropping the Dick and calling him Richard. His father was proud but puzzled. After the university, Richard had traveled abroad. He was as much at home in Paris or Cairo as he was in Conroy, twenty

miles from the ranch where he had been born—
possibly more. He, too, was handsome, tall, and
slim, and so like his twin brother in features that
few could distinguish between the two when they
were together.

Between the twins, now twenty-five years old,
there always had existed an unfailing bond of affec-
tion. Each respected the other for his peculiar talents.
But while Richard had seemingly drawn farther and
farther away from the West, Clint had become a part
of its body, soul, and spirit. Of late years, Richard's
visits home had been few and of short duration. The
brothers, never quite understanding each other as
brothers should, had drawn apart until they were almost uneasy in each other's company.

"Why don't you stay home more, Richard?" Andrew French had asked his son three years before.

"I will if you want me to, Dad," had been the
youth's answer. "It isn't that I don't want to be here
with you and Clint, it's just that I like . . . that I've
had training different from most of the fellows
around here. I don't like ranch work, and I don't
know much about it. Someday I'll have to learn. But
can't that come later? I don't want to tie myself
down right now. I have so many friends in the East,
and they're different from these fellows, too. You
know me well enough to know that they could not
educate me into a snob. It's just . . . well, it's hard to
explain, Dad, now that you pin me down to it. But I
want to see something of the world. I thought we
could afford it, but. . . . No, I didn't mean that. But if
I'm going too strong, Dad, just give me a hint."

"Thunderation!" his father had exclaimed gruffly.
"Your drawing account at the Stockman's Bank is
unlimited. Do as you please, but keep clean. And
don't worry about shorting me none."

And Andrew French had let it go at that.

These thoughts all passed through the old stockman's brain after he replied to Webb. Now he spoke again. "You say you're wondering if there isn't something both of us can do to help Clint?" His tone was rather cold, and his friend noticed it immediately.

"Now I didn't come up here to try to butt in on your private affairs, Andy," he said quickly. "You know Pansy and Clint, yes, and Dick, practically grew up together till the boys went away, and I sold out. And Pansy and Clint have always been good friends. It's natural I should be interested in him . . . can't you see that?"

"Yes, I can," said French soberly. "And seeing that Pansy and Clint seem to think quite a bit of each other . . . at least Clint thinks a lot of Pansy . . . you want to see him settle down. Just what kind of an idea did you have in mind?"

"I don't know as I have the right to say what's in my mind," said Webb doubtfully. "It's . . . it's too big a proposition, maybe."

"Proposition?" French's tone was puzzled. "No proposition is too big for me in this country, Norman."

"But it doesn't involve money," said Webb. "If it was just a question of money, it would be easy. And I'd put in with you in a minute. It . . . it concerns Dick, Andy."

"Richard?" said French, more perplexed than ever. "Well, let's have it, Norman. We're not gettin' anywhere as it is."

"I was going to suggest that you send for him," said Webb. "I believe if the two boys were together for a while, not just a couple of weeks or so, but for quite some time . . . so they could get acquainted with each other again . . . it might have some effect on Clint. Anyway, it would take up his attention. I think . . . now you can get mad if you want, Andy . . . I think that the boys have been separated so long that they're almost like strangers. And I think Dick . . . er . . . Richard would have a good influence on Clint. I believe if Richard knew, he . . ."

"Richard knows all he needs to know," French broke in sternly.

"Maybe he wouldn't think so, if he knew everything," said Webb.

"There's no use bothering him with Clint's troubles, or mine," French retorted in an angry voice.

"Just as you say," said Webb quietly. "It came into my head, that's all, and I kept telling myself on the ride up here that I was making a fool of myself. Well, it isn't the first time I've done that."

"Now just keep hold of yourself," soothed French. "I'm glad you came up . . . darned glad. I'll tell you something now. I'm worried. Richard's coming home the end of this week."

Webb gave vent to a smothered exclamation and straightened in his chair. "That's good," he said finally. "Did he say how long he intends to stay? I don't see why you should be worried, Andy. Looks to me like the best thing that could happen right now."

"Said in his letter he would stay all summer," said French. "I'll certainly be glad to see him, but . . . how will he and Clint get along? That's what worries me. Like you say, Richard and Clint ain't seen much of each other these last few years, and, when Richard hears about some of the wild stunts Clint's pulled, he'll . . . well, what will he think? And . . . maybe Clint won't be here." He finished in a low, troubled voice.

"So far as what he'll think about Clint, you needn't worry," Webb assured him. "Dick . . .

Richard's as loyal and sensible as they make 'em. 'Course, he's a little high-toned, as we might say out here."

"No, we won't say any such thing," French interrupted. "There's nothing stuck-up about Richard. He's . . . he's had a different training, that's all. He's been around a lot and got the rough edges worn off, but that's all. Maybe he'll be sore at me for not telling him how Clint was carrying on. And if Clint ain't here, he'll go looking for him."

"Why won't Clint be here?" asked Webb in a suspicious tone.

"Well . . . you know how he roams around," French evaded.

"Andy, look here," said Webb sternly. "Look at me! It isn't so dark but what I can see your face. Have you made a fool of yourself and ordered Clint off the ranch?"

"I'm taking stern measures," French declared guardedly. "I haven't exactly ordered him off the ranch, but I've told him a few things. Do you think I'm goin' to have this thing run on forever?" The stockman was becoming angry.

"Don't you know that to turn him out will only make matters worse?" Webb demanded. "Now I've got some rights here, Andy French, and don't you forget it. Clint's been going, or trying to go, with Pansy for a long time. He's asked her to marry him! Now, do you think I'm sittin' on this porch talking to you for amusement? They . . . the two of 'em . . . had a fuss a day or two ago, and Pansy's been in a huff ever since. I won't have it. If Clint wants to come around my place, he's got to go straight, and I mean it. He's acting like a devil-may-care fool kid, and he's too handy with his gun not to walk into real trouble one of these days. I've heard in a round-about way that Jake Burness has it in for him. So he's done something to rile that cut-throat, and Burness is as bad as they make 'em. You turn him out and he'll run hog-wild and step into a real gun play in a month."

French was gripping the arms of his chair. "Why didn't you tell me this in the first place?" he asked hoarsely.

"Because you began to get peeved," was Webb's sharp retort. "You didn't come clean with me and I was trying not to hurt your feelings, for one thing, and make it as easy as I could for another. And, now that you know, I'm washing my hands of your end of the business here an' now!"

"Wait . . . not so loud," said French, pointing to the road.

Webb looked and saw a horseman approaching. The twilight was merging into night, but he recognized Len Miller, foreman of the big Two-Bar F Ranch. With calves still being branded, it must be something important that was bringing Miller to the ranch house at this time, he thought.

Miller saw the two figures on the porch and dismounted in the courtyard. He soon appeared around the corner of the house and walked swiftly to the porch steps.

"Hello, Len," French greeted. "Webb's here with me. What's on your mind?"

Webb sensed that the stockman was conveying a warning to his foreman. "I'll go inside, Andy," he said, starting to rise.

"No, no," said French quickly. "Stay here. What is it, Miller?"

"Why . . . there's ten head missing on the lower

creek range," said Miller evasively, as if trying to signal French that he wanted to speak to him alone. The foreman took off his hat and thoughtfully scratched his head.

"You don't have to come to me about any measly ten head being missing," said French in a growl. "There ain't been any rustling on this range for quite a spell, Miller. Come to me when a hundred head are missing. Now, what is it?"

"Clint's down at the lower camp," said Miller promptly.

For a space there was silence. Then: "All right, is he?" asked French.

"S'pose so," drawled the foreman. "Dropped in late from somewhere over southwest. Didn't say where. You told me . . . I mean what'll I set him doin'?" It was plain the man realized he had made a slip of the tongue, but French ignored it with his next remark.

"Tell him in the morning that I want to see him up here," he instructed. "Is that all, Miller?"

"Reckon that's all," was the answer. "Everything's in good shape. Ten head have strayed, but we'll find 'em. I'll be slopin' back now. Glad to have seen you, Mister Webb."

"Always glad to see you, Miller," said Webb warmly. "I've liked you ever since you turned me down when I tried to hire you away from Andy. Anyway, I knew a good foreman when I saw him, and now I don't need any." There was a trace of regret in his tone.

Night had fallen and the stars were breaking out in clusters like the fire showers of rockets. "Let's go in the house, Webb," said French, rising.

"Say we do," Webb agreed. "I'll be ridin' home in the morning, Andy, and tonight I want to beat you a few games of cribbage, just to show you that I haven't lost my knack by living in town."

"For every game you beat me, Norman, I'll. . . ."

They went into the living room, joking, as the housekeeper lighted the big lamp on the center table.

CHAPTER TWO

When Len Miller reached the camp on the lower range, he found some of the men still up, sitting by the open fire near the chuck wagon. One of these approached him before he could join the group after turning out his horse. He was a dark-faced youth, tall and handsome, with eyes that sparkled in the starlight.

"Anything new up there, Len?" he asked in a pleasant voice that carried a slight drawl. "I saw you ride away, and I guessed the rest."

"No, Clint," Miller evaded, looking keenly at the youth. "I went up to report the missing cows."

"Don't make me laugh, Len, not right out loud," said Clint French. "You worry about ten cows? If the old man caught you goin' in to report ten cows gone, he'd fire you on the spot and you know it. Come on, Len . . . let's hear the news. You went up to tell Dad that I was here. What did he say?"

"I was obeying orders, Clint," said the foreman gravely.

"Sure." The youth nodded. "Do you think I'm blaming you for that? It's quite a compliment to know the old man is interested in knowing where I am. Told you to run me off, did he?"

"No." Miller scowled. "He told me to tell you in the mornin' that he wanted to see you up at the house. And I did report the missing cows . . . for an alibi, because . . ." He ceased talking abruptly.

"Now be careful, Len," Clint teased, with laughing eyes. "You had to have an alibi, you thought, because old Norman Webb is up there. See how smart I am? You can't keep anything from me."

"I have at times," said Miller wryly. "How'd you know Webb was up there?"

"I wouldn't keep anything from you, Len. I saw Webb ridin' up from Conroy, and where else would he be goin' up this way? Did he have anything to say, and what was the general layout? This all concerns me, and you've always been my friend. I don't see why you should have anything to conceal."

"Webb didn't have a thing to say except give me a tumble," replied the exasperated foreman. "Sure we've always been friends, but you make it hard for me at times without knowing it. They were sittin' on the porch, and your dad made me tell him what I'd come for right in front of the honored guest. Then he gave me the message for you, and I beat it back. Now you know as much about it as I do."

"That's fair enough," Clint decided. "Didn't overhear 'em talking or anything? No, of course not. Well, Len, old hoss thief, that old he-bear of a Webb ain't up there trying to plug my stock up any, and, what's more, he's up there on account of me. I'd bet on that high, wide, and handsome. What do you suppose he's got up his sleeve?"

"Don't ask me," Miller answered in a helpless tone of resignation. "This whole business got past me long ago. But I don't think Webb has anything against you, Clint. I don't, for a fact."

"No? Well, he isn't wearing the shoes off any horse carrying good news about me, Len," said Clint with a grim note in his voice. "He has never said anything against me to my face, but I know he doesn't like my style. He doesn't like it because Pansy and me are good friends. You don't have to be told that."

"No, and what's more, it ain't any of my business," declared the foreman. "I'm your friend and all that, Clint, but I've got this ranch to look after, and it's no sweet job. I'm laying off everything else."

"Don't blame you a bit, Len," said Clint cheerfully. "I've thought of laying off the whole thing myself, only in a different way. I would if it wasn't for Pansy. But I'm not talking about her to anybody. I'm trusting you, that's all, and trusting you hard. You say Dad said to tell me in the morning that he wants to see me at the house?"

"That's what he said," Miller affirmed.

"All right, Len. Now you do just what he told you to do. You tell me that in the morning, understand? That's what you're supposed to do." With this, Clint turned and walked rapidly away.

The significance of what he had said was not lost upon Miller. Tell him in the morning. And in the morning Clint would be gone. The foreman made a step as if to follow him, but stopped short. He had said he was laying off and he was. He joined the men at the fire.

Clint saddled his horse, tied a light pack on the saddle, and rode swiftly away from the camp. Instead of riding toward the ranch, he raced for the road and turned east toward Conroy, twenty miles away. With Norman Webb away, he had business, important business in town. He hummed gaily as he rode, and none could have suspected the serious determination that was in his mind. If it wasn't for Pansy.

His thoughts reverted to the ranch house. Webb certainly wouldn't attempt the ride back to Conroy that night. His father wouldn't hear of it in any event. Webb was no longer used to the saddle. And Clint French knew the rivalry that existed between his father and the former stockman at cribbage. They would play all night, and Webb would ride back in the morning after a hearty breakfast. Clint kept a fast, steady pace and, by midnight, the lights of Conroy showed like yellow lanterns in a bend of the river straight ahead. He indulged in a burst of speed, slowed his pace, and trotted into town by a back street. He had no wish to be seen by too many people, and there were some he wished to avoid entirely. At the livery he merely signaled to the night man as he dismounted. The man evidently understood, for he came at once and took the horse as Clint went out the rear without having spoken a word.

Clint walked down a side street that was lined with tall poplars. This was the best residential street of the town and boasted a sidewalk on either side. Almost at its end a large, white house was set back some distance from the street. There was a lawn around it, and flowerbeds and trees. It was near the middle of a large plot about which ran a white picket fence.

The house was dark, but Clint didn't hesitate. He opened the gate, walked to the porch, and went up the steps. He rapped smartly on the front door and moved about nervously, awaiting an answer to his summons. He was clad in a soft shirt, open at the throat, riding breeches, tall, polished boots with

Cuban heels, and the soft, gray Stetson so suitable to the range. A cartridge belt was strapped about his waist and a gun was holstered on his right. He looked smart in this garb and carried himself with an air that was natural and in no way affected.

After a time, receiving no answer, he rapped again on the door.

"Who is it?"

The voice was cool and musical, but imperative. It came from a window above the porch, and Clint recognized it instantly as belonging to Pansy Webb. He went lightly down the steps.

"It's Clint," he answered, standing in full view in the light of the stars. "I must see you, Pansy. It's . . . it's important."

"Oh!" The girl's voice was startled. "Is it . . . I'll be right down. Wait at the door, and I'll let you in."

In a few minutes, a light glowed in the front room, and then the door was opened and Clint went in. He stood for several moments, staring in mute admiration at the glorious girl who stood in house slippers, with a blue negligee about her slim figure, looking at him anxiously out of wide, blue eyes. Her hair was spun gold with a touch of glowing copper. His tongue was mute as he decided he never had seen her look so beautiful.

"Clint . . . tell me! Is . . . has something . . . is it about father?" she asked breathlessly in a frightened voice.

"It is, in a way," he answered. "Now don't be scared," he added hastily. "Nothing's happened to him, if that's what you're afraid of. Did he tell you where he was goin' when he left town?"

"Yes, Clint," the girl answered quickly, her eyes clearing slightly. "He said he was going to see your father on business. Tell me, please, if anything has happened." Her tone was pleading and caused him to catch his breath.

"Nothing has happened to him," he told her in a soft voice. "He's playing cribbage with Dad up at our ranch this minute. Those two will probably play all night, and he'll come back after breakfast in the morning. There's nothing wrong, but, tell me, Pansy, did he say why he was goin' up to see Dad? I mean did he say anything what the business was?"

"Why, no," replied the girl, prettily puzzled. "He has some business interests with your father, as you know. This is all very mysterious, Clint. Did you just come from the ranch?"

"Yes, Pansy, but I didn't see your dad. I was down at the lower camp where we're branding. It's because he went up there that I came down here to see you."

"Oh, Clint!" said the girl impatiently, stamping a dainty foot. "You came, and at this hour of the night, because you knew Father wasn't here. You know you can come when he *is* here." Her face clouded suddenly at recollection of their last misunderstanding. "I would call this a silly visit," she said with dignity, tossing her head.

He stepped closer to her. "It isn't silly, Pansy," he said in a low, earnest voice. "I had to come, regardless of the time of night. I'd have come through a blizzard or fire or water. You know I . . . I believe your father went up to see Dad about me." He flushed. There. It was out.

Pansy merely lifted her brows in surprise. "You sound so terribly serious, Clint. I don't see why Father should go up there about you. Maybe you're thinking too much about yourself."

"I'm not thinking about myself that much." He snapped a thumb and finger. "I'm thinking about you, Pansy. Maybe I'm talking foolish and acting foolish, but it doesn't seem foolish to me. I've got a hunch, Pansy, that something is goin' on behind our backs and . . . well, it isn't fair, that's all."

"Now, Clint, you're not coming here in the middle of the night, or any other time, to hint things about Father," she said, raising her voice.

Clint struggled with the impulse to gather her into his arms and smother her with kisses. He had kissed her, but something told him he should not, and would not, kiss her this night. He suddenly became cool and his fine features paled a trifle.

"Pansy, listen to me, please," he said soberly, putting his hat on the table. "I haven't come here to hint things about your father . . . or mine. I like one of them, and I guess I . . . well, I think a whole lot more of Dad than he knows. There's just one reason why I'm here, Pansy."

The color came into the girl's cheeks, but faded instantly. "I suppose it's . . . that I'm supposed to ask what your reason is," she said, simulating weariness.

"It's because I love you," he said frankly. "Dad and I had a few words the other night, and I left in a huff. When I showed up at the lower camp this afternoon, Len Miller left. He had been ordered to report to Dad when I showed up. When he came back, he said our dads were sitting together on the porch, and that my dad wanted to see me at the house in the morning. It has something to do with you and me. I'll trust my hunch for that."

His seriousness sobered the girl. "You know the old trouble, Clint," she said in a tremulous voice. "It's the way you carry on. You can't expect . . . you can't expect. . . ."

"Can't expect to have you," he supplied. His face went white for a moment. "Pansy, I'm not bad . . .

not really bad. Don't you think that things might be different if we . . . well, I can't seem to get it out."

She was looking at him steadily. "I believe I know what you mean, Clint, so you might as well say it. Things might be different if we. . . ." She nodded to him.

"If we were married," he said boldly, tilting his chin.

The girl shook her head, although she looked at the floor. "It would be cowardly," she said slowly. "It would be cowardly on your part, for they would say I married you to reform you. And it would be cowardly on my part because . . . you won't understand . . . I'd be taking advantage of you. And why do you think I would marry you? I ask this because I assume you are . . . proposing."

"Pansy, we've always expected to get married someday, haven't we? You know I've always loved you and you've told me you loved me. I've thought for some time that we were the same as engaged and. . . ."

"Well, you had no right to think that, Clint French," she interrupted. "And I haven't told you lately that I love you."

"But you do, do you not?" he asked in genuine surprise.

"I don't have to stand here answering questions. You take too much for granted. I suppose if we were engaged, you'd suggest that we run away and get married tonight or tomorrow, and then. . . . What then, Clint?"

"Then . . . we'd be happy," he floundered, looking helpless.

"The thing for you to do, Clint, is catch hold of yourself. I know you had some wild idea about us when you started to talk tonight. Do you think it's fair to keep me here talking about something that is foolish and utterly impossible?"

Clint didn't answer at once. There was a queer look in his eyes that she didn't like. It was as if he were deciding some big problem in his mind without any intention of telling her about it. She started to speak again, but he held up a hand.

"I'm wondering, Pansy, if there's anything between us after all," he said in his low, vibrating drawl.

It seemed to her that his words carried a disconcerting note of finality. "What do you mean by that, Clint?" she asked.

"Just what I said. Maybe you don't love me after all. Maybe I've been making a fool of myself, or . . . you've been making a fool of me. If it'll give you any satisfaction, I can tell you that you're the only girl I ever did make a fool of myself over, and there'll never be another."

"Now you are talking silly, Clint," she said spiritedly. "You talk like the end of the world. What did you want me to do tonight?"

"I wanted you to run away with me like you said. I guess I was excited. I see now that it wouldn't be such a smart thing to do. There are two trails left for me to take . . . at least, there were two trails. Now there's one. The world can turn over on its back in a minute."

"One trail?" she said with concern. "You're not planning to do anything rash, are you, Clint? You know I'll worry about you if you go away in any such frame of mind."

"I shouldn't have said that," he said with a frown. "No, I'm not goin' to do anything rash. I suppose you're afraid I might take it into my head to kill myself or something." He laughed. "No such compliment for you, girlie." His eyes flashed.

"Then follow your trail, Clint," she said, nodding. But there was a light mist in her eyes. He saw it and stepped close to her.

"Let's go back to where we stood before I came, Pansy," he said softy. "I'm just Clint French and I can't be anybody else, it looks like. I can pull more fool stunts than anybody on this range, but I don't like to pull any of 'em on you."

Her eyes were wet when she looked up at him. Then he took her in his arms, her warm body pulsating against him under the silk thing she wore. He held her, but when he would kiss her, she drew away, her eyes deep wells of accusing light.

"You better go, Clint," she said, "and, if you take the right trail, I might . . . meet you at the end of it."

"And that would be just the beginning, Pansy," he said with a flashing smile. "I don't care what anybody does, they can't cheat us. Just remember that and forget the rest of it." He took up his hat and went to the door, passing out swiftly, with a—"So long."—flung over his shoulder.

Pansy Webb put out the light, locked the door, and hurried upstairs. She looked out of the window in time to see him vanish in the shadows up the street. Then she saw another figure steal out of the trees, run across the yard, and vault the white fence.

There had been an eavesdropper!

CHAPTER THREE

When Clinton French had quit the Webb house, he
did not appear as calm and confident as he had just
before he left. He hadn't wanted to leave Pansy angry, and he realized that he had very nearly caused a
breach between them. But he had left her with a
false impression. For Clint was certain pressure was
being brought upon her to throw him over completely. Webb, more than likely, had gone up to the
ranch to tell Andrew French that he, Clint, had worn
out his welcome around the Webb domicile. If this
was true, Pansy's father must have told her a thing
or two before he started. The girl's attitude con-
firmed this in his mind. It roused the youth's anger,
and he walked about in the cool of the night for
nearly an hour before he cast his brooding aside
with a shrug of his broad shoulders and sought the
great emporium of chance and refreshment known
as the Stampede.

However dull the season, there always was life in
this notorious resort that Conroy maintained was a
necessary evil. Every game and device of chance
was represented in the big room with its long bar, its
hanging lamps, its tables and layouts and wheels,

and its customers who now and then chanced their very lives in serious altercations.

Clint French was not unknown here. Indeed, he commanded more respect than his years would seem to warrant. His well-known proficiency with his gun was backed by the formidable reputation of the Two-Bar F outfit and the fact that he was the son of Andrew French, the most influential stockman on that range. But Clint never courted prestige except in a strictly personal way.

Red Tower, owner of the resort, frowned when he saw him come in, and then advanced to greet him graciously. "Back so soon, Clint?" he said in an off-hand manner, as if the youth's arrival was neither expected nor unexpected.

"How do things stand, Red?" asked Clint bluntly as they leaned against the upper end of the bar. "I came back on other business."

"Well, you know I keep my hands off trouble unless it starts in my place," said Tower, lighting a cigar. "I hear things, naturally, but I don't usually pay any attention to what goes on outside of the Stampede."

"Maybe that's why you know so much," Clint remarked with a shade of sarcasm in his voice. "Has there been much talk about my run-in with Blunt Rodgers the other night? You know I've never deliberately started any trouble in your place, and I didn't start that. But after it did start, you couldn't expect me to side-step it and let the crowd boo me, could you?"

"No," said Tower, frowning, "you couldn't very well slide out of it without leaving a wrong impression, but . . . well, it's just my hard luck, that's all. Any number of these hit-and-miss hoodlums could shoot themselves to pieces in here, I suppose, and I could still run. But if there was real trouble between you, say, and one of the Burness outfit, I'd be in for it. Your dad's a big man. . . ."

"Leave him out of it," Clint broke in sharply. "Listen"—he lowered his voice—"is Blunt running with the Burness gang?"

"I'm not sayin' so out and out," grumbled Tower. "You ought to know more about these things than me, Clint. You get around on the outside, and I don't. And I have to be careful what I say."

"Not with me, you don't," Clint said stoutly. "You know me too well, Red. If they're gunning for me, I'm entitled to a tip."

"You mean you're entitled to a hint," Tower corrected in a low voice. "You've already got that, and I never give tips."

"That's an easy way of putting it, Red, and just as good as any. Now, if there are any of that crowd in here at present, doesn't it look bad for us to be holding a confab here in plain sight?"

"Best way to hold it," declared the resort owner. "Everybody knows you amount to somethin' around here, and that I couldn't afford to snub you. I've got my list of customers who're entitled to personal attention, and you're on the list. Why, I'd have to do the honors if Jake Burness came in here himself."

"And that's social distinction," said the youth, laughing. "I'll buy you a drink and take a cigar myself. That'll make it look better, and everybody knows I don't drink. You might wiggle your mouth like you was tryin' to laugh. That would make a good impression."

Red Tower did laugh, and signaled to the bartender. "That's one point they can't score on you, Clint," he said, chuckling. "You don't drink, and I, for one, am glad of it. You know, Clint, I believe you'll snap out of it yet."

"You people all make me sick!" exclaimed the youth. "Snap out of what? What have I done except get in a few fights and play some high cards, and get a little living out of life like any other cowpuncher? I'm surprised to hear you turn preacher, Red."

"I'm not turning preacher," said Tower, lifting his glass. "But you're not a cowpuncher. You're Andy French's son, and one of the heirs to the Two-Bar. That very thing puts you in the limelight, and folks watch every move you make. It's kinda unfair to you, but it's a fact, just the same. I suppose the average cowpuncher has got your responsibility. And I could say more along another line and make you fightin' mad, but I'm too wise to do it."

"I know what you mean," said Clint grimly, pocketing his cigar and taking out tobacco and papers. "It's in that direction that the big-mouths are liable to get into trouble," he declared, fashioning a cigarette. "But I'll tell you frankly, Red, that I don't want trouble with this Blunt Rodgers, and I certainly don't want trouble with Burness." He snapped a match into flame and lighted his cigarette as Tower nodded in approval of what he had said. "And the beauty of it is that I'm not afraid of either of 'em," he finished, with a convincing flash of fire in his eyes.

"There! Now that's the worst of it," said Tower. "That's what scares me. You're not afraid of 'em an' I don't believe you know just how bad they are. You know me. I'm tough, and I say I'm not scared of any man on earth. But I wish there was some way I could keep that gang out of here. Now forget what I've said, but you can see I'm not as independent as I make out. And you can bet I wouldn't have said what I did if I didn't have good reason. Clint, that outfit could knock off this joint, and this town, if it wanted to. And they're hanging around close."

"But they'd chop their own heads off doin' it," said Clint. "They say this Burness is some smart in his way. He wouldn't be very smart to turn a trick like that."

"I dunno," said Tower doubtfully. "I'm never sure of anything any more. Oh . . . I was wondering. Is your brother Dick comin' back this summer?"

Clint's face clouded for a moment. "I don't know," he confessed. "Last time I heard from him, he was in some place in Maine, fishing for salmon. Guess he's better off there than here."

"Lives a pretty easy life, don't he?" said Tower casually.

"That's his business," Clint said, looking Tower in the eye.

"Sure," Tower said quickly. "I merely spoke about him because I like him and he always drops in here when he visits home."

"He'd be better off if he didn't," Clint snapped.

"I've put in some of them new-fangled slot machines," said Tower, changing the subject. Unknowingly he seemed to have trod on dangerous ground, or delicate, at least.

"And I'm goin' to try one of 'em right now," Clint said decisively. "I'm always ready to try a new gambling rig, hoping sometime I'll run across a square one. What's the pay?"

"There's two kinds," said Tower, strolling down the room with him. "You play nickels in one and get paid in nickels, and you play quarters in the other kind and get paid in quarters."

"Maybe I better start with nickels till I get the hang of it," said Clint with a grin. "I'll get some change." He stepped back to the bar, peeling a banknote from a roll that he took from a pocket. As he edged in, a bulky man swung against him, throwing him against several others at the bar. The man turned, and Clint saw the leering, pudgy features of Blunt Rodgers. And Red Tower hadn't tipped him off! He looked swiftly in the direction of where he had left the resortkeeper, but Tower had disappeared.

"Oh, it's you, eh?" said Rodgers loudly. "Horning in again. Man, I take it that you want it bad!"

There was an immediate cessation of talk at that section of the bar. Several rough-looking characters crowded behind Rodgers. The tenseness spread rapidly through the room.

Clint stepped close to Rodgers. "Listen, Blunt, we're not goin' to have any trouble tonight," he said sternly, his face set. "Get that straight. We're not goin' to have any trouble. If you start it, there's only one way it can end, and you know it."

"Well . . . what of it?" said Rodgers, sneering as his companions shot hard looks at Clint.

"I'm not afraid of you, Blunt, but there's a reason why I don't want it. If you start . . . I'll refuse to draw."

Rodgers stared at him as if he were stunned with astonishment. Then one of the men behind him guffawed, and he broke into a mean laugh. "You won't draw, eh? Who said anything about drawing, kid?"

The way the question was put was an insult, and Clint's eyes narrowed. He struggled with his voice until he could control it. "Any talkin' that you're doing, Blunt, you're doing for the benefit of the crowd," he said. "You were goin' to try to bully me into a draw right here, and you know it. You can't do it, that's all. And I'm not goin' to stand here and talk about it, either."

He flipped the bill on the bar. "Break that up into small change," he told the white-coated servitor.

The crowd held its breath. The spectators sensed

that Clint had in some way turned the tables on Rodgers and had got the best of the encounter. They saw Rodgers's face darken with anger. The man had the reputation of being a killer. They awaited the next move, which was not long in coming.

Rodgers and his companions burst into uproarious laughter. "Listen, kid," roared the gunman, "you quit totin' it around . . . that gun, I mean. You think too much about it. It looks pretty in front of the ladies, but it's dangerous around men."

Clint caught his meaning instantly and his face went white. "You . . ." He bit his lip, and his eyes shot fire. "Listen, Blunt, I'm not taking this from you because I'm scared of you or the crowd with you. But if we ever do mix in a gun play, I'll kill you."

Rodgers thrust out his jaw. "But there can't be any gun play because you won't draw," he said, showing his teeth. "I'm giving you credit right here in front of the whole house for bein' smarter than I thought you was. Pick up your change, kid." He and his companions again roared with laughter. But it wasn't genuine, and the throng looking on knew it.

Clint picked up his change and pocketed it with a smile. "So long, Blunt," he said cheerfully. "You tell 'em about it while I'm gone. You can do it. And give my regards to the audience."

He walked out the front entrance, leaving Blunt Rodgers and his friends laughing and slapping each other's backs to cover their anger and chagrin. Outside, he encountered Red Tower and stopped short.

"Why didn't you tell me Blunt was there, Red?" he demanded.

"I'd just come out of my office and didn't know he was at the bar," replied the resortkeeper. "After it started, I saw you knew how to handle the situation and kept out of it. You can believe it if you want to."

"It isn't what I believe," Clint interrupted shortly. "It's what I know. Red, you're an out-an'-out liar, and you can take it any way from the jack." He looked into Tower's cold eyes for a moment, and then strode away down the darkened street toward the livery.

CHAPTER FOUR

A northwest wind was blowing clear from the Sweetgrass Hills. Clint French turned his face to it as he rode westward under the stars, with the black bulks of the Rockies mounting into the sky ahead. He could have waited until morning, but he did not want to chance meeting Webb returning from the ranch. Nor did he wish to stay in town and risk another meeting with Blunt Rodgers, or some of his friends. Blunt had said enough to bring on a gun play, but Clint was wise enough to realize that, while he might beat the bully to his gun, it would react against him. He was thinking of Pansy. And why had Red Tower lied to him? Clint's lips curled as he considered the answer to this. Tower had told him more than he had intended to tell him, probably. What he had said, coupled with his apparent disinclination to warn Clint and his subsequent disappearance when trouble started, showed that he was afraid of Rodgers and the specter behind him—Jake Burness. Clint dismissed the resortkeeper from his mind. It was of Pansy and Webb's mission to the ranch that he thought most on his ride back to the lower camp.

When Len Miller saw him at dawn, rolling out of his blanket, the foreman stared hard. Then he went over to him. "Reckon you're gettin' that message now," he said testily. "Have a nice ride last night?"

"Not as nice as it might have been, Len," replied the youth soberly. "I went to town for reasons of my own and ran into Blunt Rodgers again. He's hanging around the Stampede a lot these days."

"What happened?" asked Miller quickly, his eyes keen.

"I stopped it from happening," Clint said with a sour smile. "I took something from him and I shot something back. I guess the crowd was wise that I was crawling away from him or scared of him. But I can't afford a bad gun play just now."

"That's sensible," said Miller suspiciously. "Was he lookin' for gun play?"

"He was ready to start it, and I stopped him by telling him I wouldn't draw with him," said Clint with a frown.

Miller whistled softly. "Then he must have rode you to death!" he exploded. "I didn't think it was in you to back down that-a-way."

"He thought he was ridin' me, but the crowd knew better. I didn't exactly back down the way I worked it. If I'd gone for my gun, I'd have killed him, and you know what that would have meant."

"There's many a good gunman that's showed he had a head by backing down," said Miller thoughtfully. "He'll think it's a trick, or else he'll think you're afraid of him. He's bad medicine, Clint."

"Just how bad is he?" Clint asked coldly.

"I've never seen him in action," the foreman confessed, "but I know those who have, and he's one of these wink-of-an-eye men who ain't particular about giving the other fellow even the show of a chance. He's all bad, what I mean, and don't play him any other way."

"Travels with Jake Burness, doesn't he?" Clint queried.

"So they say. But nobody's seen Burness in these parts in years. If he's around, he's keeping low. You don't want to get mixed up with that outfit, Clint." There was no doubting that Miller was deeply in earnest.

"Red Tower's scared stiff," said Clint scornfully. "He was preaching to me at the front bar, and didn't tell me Blunt was around. The crowd was three-deep at the bar, and I didn't see him. Tower's yellow. Looks like he didn't dare tell me. They've got him buffaloed."

"Well, that outfit has got tougher men than Tower could ever hope to be buffaloed," Miller observed. "I'd keep clear of 'em, Clint. It might take more than our bunch to stop 'em, if they got a good start."

"*Humph!* Well, I'm goin' to take on some breakfast and go up to the house," said Clint. "Might as well have it over with."

Miller put a hand on his shoulder. "Take it easy up there, Clint. Before you say anything hot to the old man count three slow. If you do that, you probably won't say it. Let him do the talking."

"Thanks, Len," Clint said, smiling. "You're a good old scout, even if you did get your start stealing horses." With a laugh, he went for his breakfast.

Miller didn't like that laugh, but he could think of nothing more to say.

Clint French flung the reins over his horse's head and left the animal in the courtyard as he went to join his father on the porch of the ranch house. He had waited until he had seen Norman Webb leave, and, when the retired rancher was out of sight, he had ridden up the trail. Now he towered above the stockman in the rocking chair with a faint smile on his lips.

"I dropped into the lower camp last night, and Len told me this morning that you wanted to see me," he said. "So here I am."

"Sit down," said his father, studying his face.

Somehow it was easier to tell Clint what was in his mind than it was to speak in a similar manner to Richard. Andrew French could even cuss at this son, but with Richard it was different. He understood Clint, he thought. But on this clear morning, flooded with sunshine, he wondered whether he did understand him. It was the first time, since he could remember, that he felt uneasy in Clint's presence. This, however, merely served to irritate him.

"Where have you been?" he demanded.

"Dad, when I saw you last, you said you didn't give a whoop where I went so long as I got started," said Clint. "I don't have to answer that question unless I want to. But I don't mind telling you that I've been over Sun River way."

"In some tough spot, I suppose," said his father, frowning.

"In an easy spot, Dad," said the youth cheerfully. "I picked up nine hundred at stud as easy as picking berries from a bush."

"You haven't lost any of your impertinence," snapped French.

"Would you rather have me lie to you?" Clint asked quietly.

"Would you rather run wild and gamble and fight than earn an honest living and learn the cow business?" said his father, flaring up angrily.

"I reckon I've learned quite a lot about the cow

business," was the cool answer. "But you never. . . ."
He paused, remembering Miller's advice to count
three before he made any hot retorts.

"Yes, yes, go on," Andrew French prompted impatiently.

"I reckon that's all," said the son. "I decided not to
finish it."

The older man looked surprised. "If it was another of your disrespectful come-backs, it's the first
time I've known you to lag," he said suspiciously.

"I was never willingly disrespectful," said Clint
slowly. "Maybe I'm too hot-headed. But there's no
sense in our having a quarrel, Dad. I didn't come
here without being sent for . . . so let me have it . . .
straight."

"I've been hearing fresh news about you," said
French. "You're in way to get yourself in bad with
that Burness gang."

"So that's what old man Webb came up here for!"
Clint ejaculated. "I might have known it. Did he give
any orders, Dad?"

"Orders? What do you mean by orders, Clint?"
his father asked sternly.

Clint leaned forward in his chair, turning his hat
by its brim in his hands. "About me and Pansy," he
said, looking his parent in the eye. "He wants me to
stay away from her? Is that it?" His voice was hard
as he finished.

French was staring hard at his son. "He's ready to
help you, if you'll quit kicking over the traces and
show you've got something in you besides dev-
ilment," he said coldly.

"Oh? Well, isn't that nice of him. Do you suppose
I need his help, as he calls it? How's he goin' to help
me? Did he say?"

"He didn't say anything against you," answered

French gruffly. "And I'm not going to talk about it, anyway. But, speaking of Pansy, just how do you and Pansy stand these days?"

"We stand all right," Clint replied airily.

"Then what was the fuss about the other day that upset her so much?" his father demanded.

It was Clint's turn to look surprised. So Webb had told about that, too. And Pansy had been much upset? Then she did care about him! His face broke out in a smile. "That was just a misunderstanding, Dad. Those things will happen now and then."

Andrew French was thinking very hard. "I'm going to ask you a question, Clint, and I wish you'd answer it. How much do you think of that girl?"

"I think enough of her to want to marry her," Clint declared. "And it isn't goin' to do Webb any good to start sneaking around behind my back. If he doesn't want me at the house, he can say so."

"I don't doubt but what the girl will have something to say, too," Andrew remarked dryly. "They usually do. Seems to me, if you think as much of her as you say, you'd try to show her something."

"I couldn't . . . change, I guess you'd call it . . . quick enough," said Clint with bitterness in his tone. "Let's just leave her out of it, Dad, and get down to the business you have with me."

"You'll fool around till you'll have to leave her out of it for good," said Andrew. "She's a right sort of girl, too."

"I'm not crawling to her on my hands and knees," said Clint, nettled. "When I go to her, I go standing up on my feet."

"Well, I'm not going to try to preach to you. I've tried that too often. I've always stood behind you, helped you out of your scrapes, and done my talking to your face without complaining behind your back.

As your father, I thought I was entitled to some consideration from you, but it looks as though I was mistaken. I heard something else after you went away, all heated up the other day, and that's why I sent for you."

Clint was counting again. "I'm not goin' to make any explanations about things people tell you behind my back," he said finally. "I'm gettin' tired of all this business, and I reckon you are, too. If we can't get along, Dad, we might just as well call it quits, and let it go at that. I'll take a chance on gettin' by on my own, and you've always got Dick. That's the way I feel about it, and I might as well say so and have it done with." He met his father's gaze squarely.

"That's fool talk," said Andrew irritably. "And I didn't send for you to talk about anything anybody has told me. I got a letter from Richard, and he's coming home."

Clint's eyes widened. "When's he coming?" he asked.

"He's coming the end of the week," replied Andrew.

"Did he say how long he intended staying?" was Clint's next question. His eyes were blazing with interest.

"Yes, he said he was staying all summer. Maybe he's finally got a little homesick, or is sick or something. Lord knows, I'll be glad to see him. So you see, it wouldn't look any too good for you to be off the ranch, do you think? He'd only set out looking for you, if I know anything about him at all."

"How much does he know?" asked Clint breathlessly. Then his eyes narrowed. "Have you been . . . ?"

"I've told him nothing," Andrew interrupted

sternly. "And I don't believe anybody else has known his addresses of late, but you and me. But he'll probably find out plenty, and then you and me will have to do a lot of explaining or lying, one of the two."

"Dick isn't that kind," said Clint quietly.

Andrew's eyes sparkled momentarily. "I guess you better stay on the ranch, Clint. Suppose you go down and work with Len for a couple of days. We'll have to go to Conroy together and pick him up and get him home before some no-good son-of-a-gun can blat to him. And you'll have to trail around with him. You always got along good, and I wouldn't have it any other way. Don't you think that's the ticket?"

"Yes," said Clint dully, "that's the ticket."

CHAPTER FIVE

Clint was more concerned over the coming of his twin brother than his father suspected. The prospect of his brother's staying all summer was what worried him most. During the past three years, Richard had spent exactly seven weeks at the ranch. Two weeks each summer, and a week at Christmas two years before. That had been all right. Clint had had no trouble in entertaining him—for it amounted to just that—during these short stays. But a whole summer! A lot could happen in three months. The divergence in the paths of the brothers' lives had become so wide that they hardly knew each other. They regarded each other with guarded curiosity. Clint held his brother in respect, and always spoke of him as a square shooter. "Any man that says he's a snob has got me to fight," he had declared upon more than one occasion. And the whole Two-Bar F outfit seemed to like him. They said simply that he was "Eastern" and let it go at that. He had licked two men who thought differently, and his prestige had soared. And none could get away from Richard French's record as an athlete. It was generally conceded that, if he didn't want to live on the ranch, it was his own business. Folks said about him: "Andy French has got lots of money, and he should worry."

Until he learned the news of his brother's impending visit from his father, Clint's plans had been vague, and his thoughts in chaos. But now his work plainly was cut out for him. It was up to him to trail with his brother all summer, and—what would he do with him?

Clint thought of all this and much more as he rode down to where Len Miller was supervising the branding of calves. He had no intention of going to work, for there was no need of an extra hand, which he amounted to if he wanted to look at it that way. One possibility bothered him immensely. There was no question that he was in bad with Blunt Rodgers and his friends. This might mean that he was also a mark of interest for the outlaw, Burness, who he never had seen. And he and his brother looked so much alike. It was possible that Richard might be mistaken for him. And Richard was slow as molasses with his gun. In fact, a score of complications were possible and, if any of them should crystallize into trouble, it would be Clint's fault.

It was night before Clint had a chance to talk with Miller alone. The foreman was curious, expectant, more interested than he let on.

"I've got to hang around a couple of days," Clint told him, "but I'm not promising to be much good as a hand. I've got too much to think about."

"Did the old man tell you to stay in camp?" asked Miller in a tone of relief.

"Yes. What do you think is coming up next?"

"I dunno," said the foreman thoughtfully. "I wouldn't be surprised at anything. I told you yesterday that this business had all got past me, although I'm always with you when you're right, boy, and I'd be with you if you was wrong, against certain people."

"Dick's coming," Clint blurted. "Coming to stay all summer."

"Whew!" Miller whistled softly, a habit when he was taken by surprise. Then: "Well, maybe it's a good thing. I'll be glad to see him, and so will the outfit. He's all right. And it'll give you something to do. You'll have to take him around and. . . ."

"That's just it," Clint broke in grimly. "I'm the entertainment committee. Not that I won't enjoy it, but where'll I take him, Len? I'm liable to run into something wherever I go. An' he'll hear things. Oh, I don't care so much about that part of it, but after this mix-up with Rodgers and one thing and another, he might get involved."

"I wouldn't worry about that," Miller advised. "Keep him away from the Rodgers crowd, that's all. Take him over Sun River way, if he wants a run at cards or something. Take him north. I'll tell you what to do. You said he'd been up in Maine, fishing . . . I guess that's where you told me he was last time you heard from him. But, wherever he was, he likes fishing. All right. Take him up the Teton, over on the south fork of the Flathead, up in the mountains in the Wild River country or the north fork of Sun River, anyplace to get him away from . . . well, you know. I'll bet that's just what he wants. Wants to get away from those . . . the sort of people he runs around with back East and in Europe. Take him up in the hills and be enthusiastic about it. He won't refuse, when he sees you're set on it."

"Might be a good idea," said Clint dubiously. "But there we'd be . . . the two of us alone. We ain't much alike, Len, except in our looks. What would we talk about, what would . . . ?"

"That'll solve itself." The foreman frowned. "Remember, you'll have horses to pack and unpack and look after, and camps to make ... plenty of work. He hasn't been up in these mountains since he was a kid, and I'll bet he'll be tickled stiff. You'll have to guide him. The trip won't hurt you any, either. Good for both of you. There! Your problem is solved ... now, thank me."

Miller's enthusiasm was catching, and Clint brightened. "Dog-gone, if I don't believe that's the ticket," he said. "I'll get a good horse in for Dick and have things ready. Dad won't kick, so long as he hangs around the house long enough for a few talks. I'll rush him into it."

"That's the idea," said Miller approvingly. "And if he wants to run with the outfit a few days, that's all right, too. But spring this mountain trip right at the start and make him think you have been planning it ever since you heard he was coming. Get the pack horses in, and get out the pack saddles and bags and everything. Take along a couple of guns for practice. Your play is to get him all worked up over it right from the start. If you need any help, just call on me. You better let the old man in on it, too."

"Len," said Clint with a grin, "you ain't got any idea how close you came to being a smart man."

Early on Saturday morning, Andrew French sent two men on their way to Conroy in a spring wagon that was to convey Richard's belongings to the ranch. "He won't come home for the summer with just a couple of suitcases, if I know anything about him," the stockman had boomed.

Clint saw that his father was trying to conceal his excitement and expectancy behind his bluster. The rancher had been giving orders right and left since dawn. A French was coming home where he belonged. No one should forget that, and none did. Richard's room was ready for him; Susan, the elderly housekeeper, had seen to that. The colored cook got her instructions to the letter and promptly put her hands on her broad hips and spoke her mind.

"Ah know what Mister Dick wants, and what he wants he gits. And he don't git no fancy vittles. He never asked for 'em befo', and, if he asks for 'em this time, I'll tell him right where to git off at. Me and Mister Dick's friends, we is."

Andrew glared and kept his mouth shut. With the exception of Susan, he was the only person on the ranch that called his son by the name under which he had been christened. "I want Richard to have what he wants," he blustered as he stamped out of the kitchen.

Two spanking grays—Andrew's pride—were hitched to the double-seated buckboard, and two hours after sunup the powerful owner of the Two-Bar F and his son, Clint, were on their way to town.

News of the expected arrival of Richard French had not been circulated in town, for Andrew had told no one except Norman Webb, and Webb had seen fit to keep the information to himself.

In Conroy, Andrew rightfully was a very important personage. He shipped more cattle from that terminus of the railroad than any three other stock-raising outfits combined; he had helped to establish the Stockman's Bank and still held a directorship; he owned property there, and had always been one of the first to respond when civic improvement or funds were an issue. Moreover, he was a pioneer, respected and well liked, and a power in politics. Many times he had been asked to become sheriff, the most important office in that big county. For these reasons as well as others, his infrequent visits to town never failed to cause a stir. And this occasion was, indeed, no exception to the rule.

Clint drove his father to the hotel and left him there, surrounded by friends and important citizens, while he went to put up the team. There was something he wished to learn at once, and, as soon as he had placed the team in the care of the livery, he proceeded straight to the small house occupied by Red Tower.

He rapped loudly on the door. Tower lived here alone except for a man he employed in the double capacity of bartender and bodyguard. It was this man who opened the door cautiously.

"I want to see Tower," Clint announced.

"Why . . . he's still in bed," said the bodyguard.

"Then get him up long enough to speak to me a minute," Clint ordered sharply. "He doesn't have to dress. I won't keep him long."

"Tell him to come in," came Tower's voice. The resortkeeper evidently had recognized Clint's voice, which had awakened him.

Clint went in to find Tower sitting up in bed and looking out the open door of his bedroom. "What is it, Clint?" he asked.

"Is Blunt and his outfit still in town?" Clint demanded.

Tower shook his head. "No, they went out of town the same night you did, and haven't been back since," he replied.

"Listen," Clint's eyes hardened. "Dick's coming on this afternoon's train. You needn't tell that bunch of rotters anything about him. I don't want him mixed up in this business, see? I'm goin' to hold you personally responsible, and, if you cross me again, we'll have it out any way you choose. That's all."

"That's enough," Tower said in a rasping voice. "I'm off you and your affairs. After this, you look after yourself."

"And I'm well able to do that little thing," said Clint grimly. Then he went out. "What I said goes for you, too," he told the bodyguard as he left.

At the hotel he found his father literally holding court in the front sitting room. Andrew separated himself from the others long enough to speak to him. "Norman Webb has invited us up to his house for dinner," he said. "The train won't be in until four o'clock, and I'll have some business to look after later."

"You better go alone, Dad," Clint said soberly. "I'll get my dinner here at the hotel with the boys who came in with the wagon. Tell 'em I'm looking after things, or you couldn't find me or something."

Andrew sensed there would be no use in argument. "All right," he agreed, "but don't get mixed up in anything and miss the train."

"That's not very likely," said Clint. "Anyway, I've got some things to buy that Dick and me will need on our trip. You can tell 'em that, if you want to." He left his father in a very pleasant frame of mind.

The station platform was crowded when the train still was but a streamer of smoke trailing lazily across the sky in the south. Andrew French had not concealed the fact that his son Richard was coming, and the stockman's friends were almost all there. Pansy Webb was there, too, with her father, but Clint found it easy to avoid her in the crowd. He didn't want to see Pansy again so soon.

When the train came to a rumbling stop with the brake shoes striking fire from the wheels, Richard French was first to alight after the conductor. Clint was there to greet him, with the crowd swaying back as Andrew and his friends pushed through.

"Hello, Clint!" Richard sang out as he grasped his brother's hand. "What's all this mob here for?"

"They're the reception committee." Clint grinned. "You're sure lookin' fine, Dick."

The crowd looked on admiringly. For the twin brothers were good to look at, of equal height, broad of shoulders, and slender of waist, looking exactly alike almost, handsome and clean-cut of features. A winter in southern France, the winds of the sea, and the spring months in Maine had bronzed Richard so that his skin was as tanned as Clint's. No weaklings, these two.

Now Andrew French broke through. "'Lo, Richard," he boomed, wringing his son's hand. "Don't mind these folks. They're just curiosity-seekers. But maybe there's some of 'em you know. Here's old Norman Webb . . . and Pansy . . . and . . ." There was a general round of hand-shaking, with Andrew mopping his face and brow with a big bandanna, and Richard laughing and talking to several people at once, answering questions the best he could, and apparently enjoying it all.

"Just a ranch boy," Andrew kept telling his numerous friends. "Born right on the Two-Bar. Been around a little more'n the rest of us, that's all."

But Richard looked like anything but a ranch boy. He had a bearing—a manner. He had an instinctive aristocratic way of holding his head. His smile was spontaneous. He was dressed in a double-breasted gray suit that fitted him perfectly, white shirt, and soft, white collar with a plain, dark-blue tie, black low shoes, and a gray, soft hat that whispered London to the wide prairie wind.

"I've got a mess of luggage, Dad," he said gaily.

"Three trunks and some other pieces that'll make it look as if I were moving in."

"Clint's lookin' after it," said Andrew. "I've got two of the boys down here with a spring wagon, and, if that won't hold 'em, we'll send down a hayrack."

The crowd closed in behind them as they moved to the end of the platform where the grays were stamping and snorting, eager to be off. Clint was already in the front seat of the buckboard.

"You two get in behind," he ordered. "I'll do the driving, and you'll want to talk."

The crowd cheered as Andrew and Richard got into the rear seat. Richard waved his hat, and Andrew held a hand aloft as they drove away and turned into the main street through town. Scores saluted them from the sidewalks and the entrances to stores and other business places. Clint watched out of the corner of his eye as they passed the Stampede. There was a group in front that waved to them. But Red Tower wasn't in sight.

Clint shook out the lines, and the grays pranced out of town into the road that led toward the setting sun.

CHAPTER SIX

As they swung up from the river and crossed the eastern boundary of the Two-Bar F range, Richard French rose in the rear seat of the buckboard and swept his hat from his head in salute.

"Looks good to me, Dad," he told his father as he sat down. "Look at the fireworks the sun is staging for me."

Flames of crimson were bursting through the silver clouds that billowed above the peaks. The flowing purple robes of the mountains trailed in the soft green of the rolling foothills. The bench lands rose gently in long, easy steps to the golden portals of Paradise Valley, with the sparkling waters of the creek scattering diamonds and rubies and emeralds in their wake. In the grass were splashes of color where the pink and yellow blossoms of the prickly pear nestled. Over all, the sky threw its glorious canopy of blue, smiling a welcome to the twilight.

Richard drew in great, exhilarating breaths of the dry, scented air, and spoke again to Andrew French. "I've often wondered why I stay away so much," he said. "Maybe it's because everything looks so beautiful every time I come back."

"We don't notice it so much, being here all the time," said Andrew. "Can they beat this in Europe, Richard?"

"No!" was the emphatic reply. "They can't touch it!"

"I was thinking of drifting over to Paris myself this winter," drawled Clint from the front seat, shaking out the lines.

"I'd have dragged you over there long ago, if I'd thought you would go," Richard said, laughing. "You're real West, Clint, and, while I'm here, I'm going to be real West, too, if possible."

The remark made Clint feel uneasy. It sounded ominous. Did Dick have plans of his own? Real West! Clint smiled rather grimly. His brother would have a hard time of it being "real West" with Blunt Rodgers and his followers, as an instance.

"You'll be real West, all right, before I get through with you this summer," Clint said over his shoulder.

"Now you're talking," sang Richard. "That's why I'm here."

Clint thought his brother seemed different from what he was on his last visit the summer before. He was more lighthearted, more ready for give and take in repartée. Well, why wouldn't he be jovial? Hadn't he spent the winter in Europe and the spring in Maine? Wasn't he free to start for London or Singapore or Buenos Aires as soon as his vacation was over? Vacation! Why, life was just one long vacation with him. And there was not an iota of resentment in Clint's heart.

"Clint's got a great trip planned for you, since you're going to stay a while this time, Richard," his father boomed. "You haven't been in the mountains to speak of since you was knee-high to a grasshopper, and Clint figures you and him will take a jaunt into the high hills after trout and grayling, and maybe do some mountain climbing. Soon's he heard you were comin', he started to get things ready and, from the looks of the outfit, he figures on crossing the Rockies and the Cascades both."

"Maybe we will . . . if we feel like it," Clint chimed in.

"That's fine!" exclaimed Richard enthusiastically. "I've got half a dozen new rods, too, and I'll split them with Clint.

But, first of all, I want to get acquainted with the old ranch again. Are you still branding?"

"Will be for another month, the way it looks," said Andrew. "You don't figure on working, do you, Richard?"

"Never can tell." Richard laughed. "I guess I'll have to learn this business some time. Clint's got a big start on me, you know."

Both Andrew and Clint were wondering. Could it be possible that Richard really intended to work on the ranch? Both were thinking the same thing: if he did turn his hand at work, it would keep him from the towns. But they thought they knew Richard better than that.

"Don't cheat me out of a vacation, Dick," warned Clint. "If you work, I'll have to work, too. And I'm stuck on taking this trip to the hills."

"You can work later on if you want," said Andrew. "And don't forget that the old man, here, wants to get acquainted with you again. I'm not goin' to chase you around the range, Richard."

"I lose," said the visitor. "I know when I'm licked. But you don't expect to follow us into the hills, do you, Dad?"

"No, but I don't care about you working with the men, either," said Andrew. "Wait a minute"—he spoke hastily as he caught his son's look—"for my reason isn't what you might think. The boys all like you and would be glad to have you ridin' with 'em, but I . . . well, I want you to get the smell of the grass back without the dust. This'll be the longest you've stayed with us since . . . for a good many years. I want to rouse the old West that's in your veins, boy, and workin' from daylight to dark in a cow camp won't bring back the old love of the land. Now maybe you get what I'm driving at."

"I see." Richard nodded gravely. "Have it your own way, Dad. To get right down to cases, as we used to say, I'd be a nuisance around a cow camp, anyway. Look! There's a bunch of the boys now."

Andrew looked and saw Len Miller and some of the hands from the lower camp riding toward them. Well, the foreman had known Richard was coming and he was bringing the men along to welcome him. Not a bad idea at all, the cattleman decided.

Clint pulled up the team as the riders circled in about them. "Hello, Len," he called loudly. "Well, that's Duke there in the back seat."

Miller scowled at him as Richard smiled broadly. He knew, Richard did, that many of the men called him Duke behind his back. But it was all in good humor and with no thought of belittling him.

The foreman spoke to Andrew and leaned from his horse to shake hands with Richard. "Don't let this kid brother of yours put anything over on you, Dick," he said heartily. "We're all glad to see you. Guess you know most of these boys."

"I know them all, but I wouldn't want to bet on having all their names right offhand," said Richard. "Come on up, boys, and shake hands." As the men closed in by the buckboard, he shook hands with them, one by one, with a cheery salutation for each.

"Ten more head gone . . . missing, I mean," Miller was saying to Andrew in an undertone. But Clint heard him and pricked his ears.

"What's that getting to be, a password?" snorted Andrew. "It's your job to find 'em."

"Sure, I'll find 'em," said Miller confidently. "Just wanted you to know I'm keeping count."

"Think up something more cheerful next time you see me," said Andrew. "Richard looks pretty good, don't he?"

"Looks fit," Miller agreed. He was looking intently at the newcomer. "Dead ringer for Clint, same as ever . . . in looks."

Andrew frowned. "Len, what have you got on your mind?" he asked crossly.

"Not a thing," replied the foreman. "But any time I do get something on it, I'm comin' straight to you. Tell Dick to ride down and see us." He drew away as Richard finished greeting the men.

Clint started the team. He was pondering deeply over what Miller had said to his father. He knew Miller lied when he said he had nothing on his mind. Maybe he could get the foreman to talk.

"So long, Miller!" Richard called. "Don't let anybody tack the wrong brand on any of those doggies for my expenses are going up."

Miller's grin was followed by the laughs of the men. They liked Duke's frankness. He didn't attempt to conceal his distaste for ranch work and made no apologies for his mode of living. Even Andrew French smiled. He liked his son's frankness, too. Nevertheless, the remark left him dissatisfied. He was hoping wistfully for the day when Richard would come home to stay.

They drove up the road to the house in the gathering twilight. Susan Enfield, the housekeeper, met them on the porch. She greeted Richard cordially and addressed him by that name.

"And I'm really glad to see you, Missus Enfield," he responded. He never called her Susan, a name that Clint was apt to abbreviate to Susie, to her discomfiture. "And there's the chef." He shook hands with Hannah, the colored cook.

"I'se sho glad to see you, Mister Dick, and don't you go askin' fuh no fancy vittles, fuh you ain't gwine git 'em."

"You know what I like, Hannah." Richard laughed. "And you give me plenty of it, that's all."

He put his hat on a hall rack in the rear of the big living room and looked about him. He was home. And at this precise moment that old intangible barrier rose silently between him and his father and brother. All three men seemed conscious of it. None spoke. Andrew took up his pipe. Clint dropped into a chair. Richard stepped to the table in the center of the room. Susan broke the short, awkward silence by announcing that supper was ready.

"Let's go!" Clint exclaimed. "Dick, you look like you had a regular appetite."

"It hasn't failed me yet," said Richard as they went into the dining room.

Andrew sat at the head of the table with Mrs. Enfield at the foot and the boys on either side. "Pansy asked why you didn't go over to the house to dinner," he told Clint. "She seemed kind of disappointed."

Clint stole a quick look at his brother. "You told 'em I had too much to do, didn't you?" he said.

"I squared it," said Andrew dryly.

"Well, it was the truth," Clint said. "I'd only had to tear away right after dinner anyway for I know you and Norman Webb had plenty of talking to do as always. I was buying things for our trip, Dick."

"I'll have to get some togs to wear up here, I guess," said Richard. "But maybe I can use my Maine outfit, or part of it."

"I've got plenty of clothes like you want," said Clint. "You're just my size an' I can fit you out. So don't worry about that part of it."

"Tell you the truth, Clint, I'm in no great hurry to start into the hills," Richard confessed. "I went up to the Rangeley Lakes district before the ice went out and it was pretty cold and bleak, with a fringe of scrub pine and white birch around the lakes, and few people. But the fishing was excellent and I got my fill of it. I'd like to wait a week or two before we hit the high spots."

"Sure." Clint nodded. "That's all right with me."

"Tell us about where you've been since we saw you last," said Andrew. He had always shown the keenest interest in his son's travels. And now Richard entertained them during the meal with descriptions of places he had been, foreign customs, and little stories of interesting happenings. "I brought back some gifts for you all," he told them as they finished eating.

The three men went out on the porch. Night had fallen and the stars were out. A light, cooling breeze was whispering in the trees. But Andrew had seen to it that there were no trees in front of the house to obstruct the view down the broad sweep of Paradise Valley. It was alive now with shadows—the graceful, downward slope of plain—and the creek was a waving ribbon of silver.

"How does it look, Richard?" Andrew said with a wide gesture.

"It looks like a mood," said his son dreamily. He was silent a few moments, then: "You know, Dad, I was going to invite a few friends out here this summer, but I wanted to wait until I learned how you and Clint felt about it. They're . . . the right kind of folks."

"Write 'em to come on out," boomed Andrew. Somehow this remark from Richard broke the spell of restraint. "It's about time we had a party here, eh, Clint?"

"Sure thing," Clint agreed, struck with the idea. "That's right, Dick . . . bring 'em out and let 'em see some real country."

"It would be a month before they could come," said Richard. "But I'm going to invite them. I guess we can entertain them and it'll be something new for them. This ranch will open their eyes."

"I haven't met any real Easterners, you might say," Andrew observed. "I'd like to look a few over at close range and see how they stack up."

"I don't think you'll be disappointed with any of my friends, Dad," Richard said, laughing. "But I want to give you fair warning that there'll be one lady who'll have questions to ask, and . . . you try to answer them."

"Yeah?" Andrew looked at him suspiciously. "A young lady?"

"Not so young," Richard replied, "except in some of her ideas. But she wants to know, Dad, and she doesn't hesitate to ask. What's more, she's worth a million that she doesn't have to ask about. She never forgets that. But you'll like her."

"*Humph,*" grunted Andrew. "Well, let's go inside."

That night Clint and Richard sat on the edge of the bed in Richard's room. Clint was staring at the carpet, listening to his brother.

"You see, Clint," Richard was saying, "that's why I want to make a long stay this time. I want to get to know you well again. We're brothers, and twins in the bargain. We ought to be just like that." He held up his right hand with the first two fingers crossed. "We've got different ways, different ideas, maybe, but underneath we are the same. We've got to run around a lot together and among other people. Let's make the towns. Confound it, I'm fed up on the East and Europe. I want some excitement. I want to do something to make Dad give me a good bawling out. Then we'll get acquainted. Do you understand, Clint?"

Clint looked at his brother with a sparkle in his eyes. "Yes, Dick, I guess I understand," he said.

But he lay in bed a long time afterward, thinking.

CHAPTER SEVEN

Next morning Richard and Clint were out at dawn for a brisk ride up the valley before breakfast. Clint had picked a thoroughbred as fast as his own for his brother and the latter lost no time in demonstrating that he could ride as well as ever. He had kept his hand in, he told his brother, mostly by playing polo. They came back hungry and cheerful, and breakfast, with Andrew French in a boisterous mood, was a pleasant affair.

After the meal Richard busied himself writing some letters and Andrew had a talk with Clint in the yard.

"Wants to make the towns, as he calls it, eh?" The stockman frowned. "Well, I suppose I can leave it to you to show 'em to him. But I want you to remember one thing, Clint . . . if you get Richard into any trouble, I'll hold you, and you alone, responsible."

"That's fair enough," said Clint with a hint of sarcasm. "I've been responsible for all the trouble in town for the last three years. But I've got a hunch that Dick can take care of himself, except maybe in a gun play. You needn't think I'm goin' to try to get him into any ruckus. What do you think I am? And what's more, if Dick knew you was the same as asking me to be his guardian, he'd be sore, I think."

"You needn't say anything to him," Andrew snapped. "I'm not asking you to be his guardian, but there are ways you can watch out for him, and you know it. Richard can't drop back into the West and be one of the crowd just by so deciding. You know the angles. And where do you figure on taking him first?"

"To Conroy, of course," Clint replied readily. "That's the hot spot. Let him have a fling down there while Blunt and his gang are not in town. Tower told me yesterday that Blunt left the same night I did. I didn't tell you about my little visit to the Stampede the night Webb was up here. I had a run-in with Rodgers that night and deliberately stepped out of a gun play. He hasn't been there since. I want Dick to visit Conroy and have it over with while it isn't too hostile down there for me."

"All right, go ahead," said his father, but his look was worried. "Anyway, Richard's got a cool head."

"And I've got a hot gun," Clint said, nettled, "which isn't such a bad combination."

His father, angry, refused to talk with him further and went into the house.

When Andrew French saw his twin sons later in the morning, he was puzzled at first to distinguish between the two. Richard was dressed in clothes belonging to Clint, from worn riding boots to the customary wide-brimmed, gray Stetson. But he wore no gun as did Clint and this was the first point that set them apart. The second was their difference in speech; for, aside from speaking better English, Richard lacked the soft, easy drawl that slipped unconsciously into Clint's speech and was more incisive. But a stranger would not have been able to tell one from the other.

"We're taking a ride out on the range," Richard told his father. "I haven't done much riding in the last few months and want to break in easy. But don't think I'm soft," he added quickly.

"Go to it." Andrew smiled, with a sweeping gesture. "You'll find plenty of room to ride in. It's purty up the valley."

The boys rode off up the wide mouth of Paradise Valley, and, as soon as they were out of sight, Andrew dispatched a man to bring Len Miller to him at once.

His manager-foreman arrived shortly before noon and Andrew told him what was on his mind. "Richard has a hankering to do the towns," he said with a troubled frown. "I can't very well stop him without goin' into a lot of tangled explaining and Clint's goin' to show him around. They're goin' to Conroy first." He looked at Miller keenly.

"Naturally." Miller nodded. "There's more doin' there than in any other town on the range north of the Missouri, I suppose."

"And more chance for trouble," Andrew pointed out. "Clint tells me he had another brush with that Blunt Rodgers down there a short spell back, but Rodgers left town as soon . . . the same night Clint did. Says he hasn't been back since. You know about it?"

"No more'n that Clint said he took quite a bit from Blunt to stop a gun play," Miller replied. "Said he couldn't afford to have any gunfightin' the way things stood."

"I'm glad he's got that much sense," growled the stockman. "But did you ever happen to think just how much those two boys look like each other? Richard put on some of Clint's clothes this morning and I had to look hard to tell 'em apart. Clint's got enemies. They might mistake Richard for him and start to work him over."

Miller's face was grave. "That's a fact," he said. "I hadn't thought about it much, but what you say is true."

"All right. Miller, I want you to send a man or two down to Conroy to keep an eye out. If Blunt heads in there, I want one of them to hustle the news to me and the other to watch him and his crowd. If you can sort out a couple who aren't so well known there, it would be all the better. I suppose you can do this."

"Yes, I can do it," said Miller quietly. "But they'll have to watch out that Clint doesn't see 'em. Clint would send them scootin' back here in short order. When are they goin' down there?"

"I don't know, Len. Richard's gettin' used to a horse again. I suppose it'll be in a day or two, though. But if Blunt should get in there before they do, I want to know it *pronto*. That's all. I'm leaving it up to you to carry out my orders and don't pick any blanks."

"I know my men," said Miller with dignity and confidence. "I'll get a cup of coffee and slope back before that pair has a chance to see me. I ain't got any password for you today, boss."

His remark puzzled Andrew but the rancher let it go unnoticed.

Richard and Clint returned late in the afternoon. They had gone up to the cave at the head of the valley, Clint told his father. "Dick picked up some Indian stuff in there that we'd missed when we was kids," he said. "Dad, we had some job finding that cave, with the brush and trees that have grown up around it and there's been a rock slide, too. It would make a fine hiding place." He halted abruptly as if struck by the thought.

"Tomorrow we're going down to Conroy in the afternoon and take a slant at some of the bad places we hear about in the East," Richard announced. "Are the bad men all killed off, Dad?"

Andrew smiled wryly. "Not all of 'em, worse luck. But they're gettin' more careful. I don't want you boys to get into any mess down there, understand. This outfit has a . . . good name." He hesitated before he spoke the last two words and Richard smiled.

"When I was living on the ranch regularly, they were supposed to live on a diet of nails and bullets," he taunted. "This doesn't look like a country where men change much. It's a long way from being tame, Dad. Let's go in and see if Hannah has done her duty."

Andrew and Clint looked at each other queerly as they went in to supper.

It was an hour past noon next day when Richard and Clint rode gaily away from the ranch house for their visit to Conroy. Richard was dressed as he had been the day before. Clint had more than once been tempted to tell his brother of his own peculiar situation on the range, of his troubles during the past year or two. But he wouldn't consider minimizing affairs and he finally had decided that what Dick didn't know wouldn't bother him any.

Already the two were fast getting back to their old familiar bantering association. They were almost brothers again, it seemed, with that invisible line between them erased. They rode fast and cheerfully to town, with Clint singing snatches of range ditties, and Richard humming the popular songs of distant cities and lands. Once he gave his college cheer and they laughed in high spirits as their horses raced across the gently, flowing plain.

As they dismounted at the livery, the barn man grinned. "I wouldn't know which was which if it wasn't for your hoss, Clint," he said. "And Dick's nag, I guess, is just as good, even if it's got a different color."

"Never mind which is which or the colors so long as you take good care of them," said Clint, tossing the man a silver dollar. "We'll be moving out late tonight."

They ventured to the main street and almost the first to greet them was Pansy Webb. She stopped before them with a puzzled look. "Who is who and which?" She laughed. "But I know you, Richard, because you're not packing a gun."

"I knew something was wrong with my outfit," Richard complained, looking at his brother in accusation. "I'm not heeled."

"Better so," murmured Clint. So Pansy called him by the name of Richard. It was the first time he had heard her do so.

"If I look so much like Clint, he maybe had better look out," Richard was saying in a teasing voice.

Clint flushed and could have shot himself for so doing.

"Clint's doing all right," said the girl with a swift look at the youth she was speaking about. "Are you coming over to the house? You didn't come over to dinner with your father the day Richard came, Clint. Won't you come to supper?"

"I've got a hunch we will," Richard replied for his brother, who evinced no desire to enter into conversation. "I've got to get acquainted again around here, Pansy . . . Miss Webb . . . and I might as well start at once. Don't worry," he added, "I'll bring Clint along."

Clint was silent as he walked with his brother along the street afterward. Richard noted this and wondered if Clint and the girl had been at odds and if he had said something he shouldn't have said. Clint was remembering the other's words to the effect that "he had better look out."

It was Richard who turned in at the entrance to the Stampede. "Might as well look this place over," he said. "It used to be the wildest in town, but maybe it has become respectable under its new coat of paint."

"Don't worry," said Clint seriously, "there's still a bad crowd hangs out here. You got much money, Dick?"

"I have enough," replied his brother. "How much do you want?"

"Oh, I don't want any," said Clint as they entered, "but this is an easy place to throw it away in. Don't hit any of the games too hard, and don't trust Red Tower. You remember him? He runs it."

"Sure I remember him," said Richard, looking down the bar as they halted at its upper end. "Here he comes now."

Tower came up to them but, unlike the others, he recognized each of them at once. "Hello, Clint . . . hello, Dick," he greeted, holding out his hand to the latter. "How does the old town look, Dick?"

"Looks newer," said Richard, taking the speaker's hand briefly. "Paint will do a lot to freshen up a place . . . even whitewash will hide a lot of . . . finger marks." He had been about to say dirt, but thought better of it in time. He realized his answer, as it was, did not sound any too cordial. But his smile made amends for his words.

"It ain't much like it used to be," said Tower. "But it's more of a business town now. You boys have a drink?"

"I'll take a beer," said Richard. "It's hot enough today."

Clint hesitated, and then: "The only chance I have to smoke a good cigar, except when I raid Dad's supply, is when Red buys me one," he said with a grin.

The smile left his face as they were being served. "Excuse me a minute," he said when he had lighted the fragrant smoke. He frowned a warning at Tower and walked down the room to where the two men Miller had sent from the ranch were playing cards at a stud table.

He signaled to one of them that he wanted to see him and the man quit the table with a scowl on his face and followed him out.

Left at the bar together, Richard and Tower toyed with their glasses. The resortkeeper appeared ill at ease and his eyes constantly roved the room. He had seen Clint and the Two-Bar hand leave by a side door.

"How long you goin' to stay Dick?" he asked rather politely.

"Till I get tired of it," Richard answered shortly. "I've got to get acquainted around here again, you know."

"Yes . . . you . . . ," Tower hesitated. "I suppose you have."

Richard looked at him quickly. "Got anything on your mind?" he asked pleasantly.

"Well, yes . . . and no," said Tower. "But I'm goin' to give you a hint, Dick, and I don't want you to say a word about it to Clint. Watch yourself. You look just like Clint, you know, and 'most anybody would mistake you two. I spotted you first off when I saw you wasn't wearin' any gun. But be careful and keep what I've said to yourself."

Richard was eying him closely. "Meaning Clint has enemies who might take me for him?" he asked in an interested voice.

"I'm not sayin' anything more," said Tower gruffly. "But what I've told you is a good thing to remember. Won't you have another drink?"

"I'll take a cigar and buy you one." Richard smiled.

At this moment the swinging doors in front banged open with a heavy impact and Blunt Rodgers came in talking loudly with some others. Red Tower made a quick signal, but, if the big bully saw it, he ignored it and strode over to confront Richard French.

"So you took my advice and left that ornament at home, eh, kid?" he said boisterously while the men with him laughed derisively.

Richard sensed instantly that he had been mistaken for his brother. He remembered Tower's warning in a flash. But he could not bring himself to inform this accoster of his error. Somehow, he felt that Clint's honor was at stake. In addition, it gave him a thrill to realize that this aggressive show on the part of the big man who stood with legs braced apart was not unwelcome. He had noted the man's swift glance at his right side and knew that by ornament a gun was meant.

"Maybe I wouldn't have forgotten it if I had known you was goin' to happen along," he said, imitating his brother's voice as well as he could. He sent a cold look along with the words.

"Wait a minute, Blunt," Tower interrupted. "You—"

"Oh, shut up!" Blunt broke in with a heavy scowl. "Hear?"

"Yes, shut up," Richard added. "And what have you got on your mind, Blunt?" He had been quick to catch the name from Tower.

"Just this much," Blunt said harshly. "It bothers me to see you around when I come in here for entertainment. Take the hint and make yourself scarce."

"Well, you're none too pleasant to look at," Richard observed lightly. "I wouldn't call you an ornament to the place. Suppose you bother me, too. Let's say we cut the cards to see which of us leaves?"

Blunt Rodger's jaw dropped, then his face darkened. "Playin' the smart aleck because you've shed your gun and think you're safe, eh? Well, you're not safe from a good lickin', kid. Ever think of that?" He took a step forward.

Richard's eyes narrowed. "Are you deliberately picking on me?" he asked in a soft voice. "If you are, shut up! No, I'm not talking to Tower, here."

"Why, you . . ." Rodgers lunged and shot out his right fist with the full power of his big frame and knotted muscles behind it. He might as well have run head-on into a wall of steel. The impact sent him staggering to his knees, groggy, as Tower yelled and every man at the tables leaped to his feet. In a moment the place was in an uproar with Tower shrieking: "No guns . . . no guns!"

Richard's right hand swooped down and sent Blunt's gun spinning across the floor. A bellow of rage came from the bully's lips.

"Give 'em room!" came the command from one of Blunt's friends, and Tower, still shouting, was thrown back into the crowd.

CHAPTER EIGHT

The six companions with Blunt Rodgers appeared in doubt as to their next move after frustrating Tower's efforts to interfere. The thing had happened with such suddenness, and Blunt's apparent knock-out had been so complete that they were left partially dazed, looking at their fallen leader groping on the floor. When Blunt regained command of his senses, he reached instinctively for his gun.

"You'll take it, or give it, as you wanted it . . . with fists!" Richard French told him sternly. "And we'll do our fighting outside in the open instead of in a dive. Come along!"

He made a move to grasp the rising bully by the coat collar but two of the man's friends leaped in. "None of that!" one cried. "Get back there and give him room!"

"For what?" exclaimed Richard. "He can have the whole street!"

Dick French hadn't been an all-around athlete for nothing; he hadn't become an expert amateur boxer and wrestler for nothing, either, and he hadn't hardened his muscles into bands of steel, quickened his footwork, improved the alertness of his eyes at football and boxing and polo without excellent results. He met the onrush of the pair with a straight left to the jaw of one, and caught the other by the waist, throwing him flat on his back as Blunt Rodgers got to his feet.

"Outside!" he ordered the bully, and didn't wait for another rush. He planted a right hook behind Blunt's ear that turned him half about. In another instant the larger man went crashing through the swinging doors to the street with the impact of Richard's shoulders against his back. As the youth leaped after him, he sent another of the man's companions to the floor with a right-hand blow carrying the force of a sledgehammer.

"Stop it!" shouted Red Tower. "That ain't Clint French . . . it's his brother!"

But the crowd had pushed forward and was jamming through the doors. Blunt's companions were mixed with the throng, struggling with the rest to get out, but one of them had recovered the bully's gun. When they got outside the doors, which were wrenched from their hinges in the process, the spectators saw a queer sight, one that was to be long remembered in the prairie town.

The dust of the street was rising in a cloud about two whirling figures. Blunt Rodgers, appearing twice the size of his opponent, was literally turning on his heels and toes in a circle, like a slow-spinning top. His eyes, sparking red, blazed from his rage-darkened face and both fists were flying in straight, vicious blows. But not a blow landed.

Dick French was turning with him, making no visible effort to keep out of range, dodging and side-stepping and turning with his adversary, and fairly raining in short, powerful punches that reached their mark almost every time. He gave Blunt no chance to lunge or to grapple and Blunt dared not attempt to swing for a knockout because Richard's footwork was too much for him and he had sense enough to realize it. But the terrific pace could not be maintained indefinitely, despite the big man's enormous powers of endurance.

He changed his tactics and endeavored to stop that spin, merely trying to ward off the blows. Richard met him at this new move by deliberately squaring off and exchanging punches with Blunt. He was going away as Blunt's blow landed with its impetus lost on his chin and he came back with a deadly right that stopped Blunt in his tracks with his hands covering his chin. But the defense was futile. Richard feinted with his right and cut under the other's guard with a left uppercut, swift as light and so powerful that it brought the youth up on his tiptoes.

Blunt's knees sagged, his hands fell, and he was wide open to be finished. But Richard merely laughed at him and shook his head. Those who watched said afterward that French appeared to be having the time of his life. The crowd was yelling, but not cheering for either of the combatants. It was applauding a good fight—the best the old cow town had seen in many a year—and one of the sort that always is popular, one in which brute strength and endurance was matched against skill and gameness.

The laugh of his younger and lighter opponent seemingly drove Rodgers mad. He rushed blindly, with a swing that, had it landed, would have put Richard in the dust for a long count and ended the contest then and there. Richard ducked the blow and Blunt stumbled to the edge of the ring of spectators.

As the bully swung about, a great shout of warning went up from the crowd. One of Blunt's friends, standing close, had slipped him his gun.

Richard caught the glint of the sunlight on the dull metal and leaped aside, expecting a shot, his face white with anger, as a third figure plunged through the throng to the center of the ring. A sudden silence came over the crowd as they recognized Clint French. Most of the spectators knew Clint and Richard were twins, but few could tell them apart, save for the fact that Clint was armed. In a moment the crowd yelled hoarsely and broke away to get out of the possible line of fire.

Blunt Rodgers, who evidently knew nothing of Clint's having a twin brother, stood staring in astonishment and indecision. At that moment, Richard dove in and struck the gun that had leaped into Clint's hand to the ground. Both stooped and groped in the dust to recover it. "Don't shoot!" Richard was crying in his brother's ear.

"He'll kill the two of us, you fool!" Clint shouted hoarsely.

This action and speech had taken a space of seconds when the gun of Blunt Rodgers split the air. Instantly a second report broke from the swirling, choking cloud of dust. Rodgers fired again, but the shot went wild as the first when he started to fall. The two brothers broke away and the gun again lay in the dust. Richard went into a clinch with his brother, and then the crowd closed in. The friends of Rodgers got to the struggling pair first, but the two men from the Two-Bar met them. The more aggressive and reckless of the onlookers piled in upon the little group and soon there was a mass of twisting bodies hidden by the dust.

The men choked and their eyes ran water. Virtually blinded, they began to crawl out of the mêlée, getting to their feet and staggering away, rubbing their eyes and cursing. Gradually the dust settled and Blunt Rodgers was seen lying on the ground, his face in the crook of an elbow.

"Here's the law!" The cry went up from scores of throats.

Half of the erstwhile spectators and participants began to crowd back into the big room of the Stampede. Clint hurried his brother by an arm into a narrow passage between two buildings. "We'll make for the hotel," he said in a voice of command.

"Like thunder!" cried his brother, pulling him to a stop. "We'll stay and face the music. This Blunt started it and he . . ."

"There'll be plenty of time to explain," Clint said angrily. "Don't forget that I'm responsible for this business, Dick."

"All right, but I won't leave town," said Richard grimly.

Clint led the way through a back street to the rear of the hotel. He called the clerk from the little lobby in front and they went upstairs to a front room without being seen. All this time he was wondering at the sudden change in his brother. Richard had always been the peaceful one of the two. Still, now that Clint thought of it, his brother, too, always had been the one who preferred to use his fists rather than resort to harsher weapons. And, under it all, Clint was proud of him. He knew, without being told, that Richard had realized he had been mistaken for him and hadn't taken the trouble to explain.

Richard closed the door after them when they had entered the room. He drew from a pocket the only silver cigarette case in that section and offered his brother a ready-made cigarette, which Clint accepted with a grin. The knuckles of the right hand that held the case were raw.

"Now," Richard said when they had lighted their smokes, "who is ... or was ... this fellow called Blunt? It looks to me as if there are a lot of things I've got to know. He landed into me firsthand-running, thinking I was you."

"And you didn't tell him any different!" Clint exclaimed.

"No, and I helped stop that Tower from shooting off his mouth." Richard nodded. "This Blunt said he was glad to see I'd left my ornament ... meaning my gun ... home, and followed it with words to the effect that, in its absence, I could take a good licking. That was what started the festivities. I didn't propose to take any licking on your account, and I didn't think it necessary to stand to look on while you had the fun of handing him one. But there's this to it, Clint ... I didn't like the gun business."

"If I hadn't happened along when I did, Blunt would have dropped you cold," said Clint convincingly. "I don't want any particular credit, Dick, but he's that kind. He's a gunman, a killer, and supposed to be an outlaw. He's called Blunt Rodgers and they say he trails with Jake Burness."

He paused and his brother looked at him questioningly "Jake Burness," Clint went on in a low, serious tone, "is the kingpin outlaw, bandit, and all-around bad man of them all. His gang has a reputation so tough that, if a few of 'em come into a town and squirt tobacco juice, they have the place to themselves. Burness is supposed to be around here somewheres, and I think Red Tower knows where he is and is scared stiff that he'll clean out Red's joint.

"I've had two run-ins with this Rodgers for little

or no reason at all, and let him get away with it both times because . . . I didn't want to tack any more black labels on my own rep. They're saying I'm bad and runnin' wild. I was going to try to keep my activities a secret, but, after what's happened today, you might as well know everything because you're bound to learn things, anyway."

"It would have been better if you had told me in the first place, Clint," Richard said with a frown. "You ought to know I'd stick with you through thick and thin. You haven't put any notches in that slick gun of yours, have you?"

"Not unless I put one in today," was the straight-forward answer. "I've tried to keep from doin' any real damage with it, but it doesn't look as if certain parties were goin' to let me keep my record clean."

"Let's get back to what happened," said Richard. "You may have killed Blunt Rodgers. That wouldn't be so good, but if it's done, it's done." He wrinkled his brow in thought. "You'll have to hide that six-gun so they can't prove it's your gun that did the shooting. And . . . we're not saying who fired the shot. Get me?"

"Don't worry about them not knowing who fired the shot," Clint said with a tightening of the lips. "Sheriff Wilson will know who fired it. There's plenty know and saw that I had to. Wilson knows you're not a gunman. He. . . ."

"Well, let them prove it!" Richard ejaculated. "There was plenty of dust. We were both grabbing for the gun. It went off and the bullet struck this Blunt. There wasn't a soul there that saw us bobbing around in that cloud of dust who could tell us apart."

Clint's eyes shone with admiration. "Something to that, Dick," he agreed. "But you don't think for a second that I'd let you take the blame for the shooting, do you? You ought to know me better."

"I started this business," said Richard firmly, "now you let me manage it. I'm getting a kick out of it, for that matter. You let me do the talking and take your cues from me as I hand them out."

Clint sat down. His eyes were troubled. "I couldn't let you get messed up in this, even if I wanted to for the sport of it, Dick," he said soberly. "I couldn't do it on account of Dad, for one thing, and on account of Pansy Webb, for another thing."

Richard leaned toward him with both hands on the table. "Well, I am messed up in it, whether you like it or not," he said sternly. "Blunt pranced into me, remember, and just because I've lived away from this range so long isn't any reason why I should take his abuse or that of anybody else. What's more, Clint, my boy, any other man who starts trouble with me is going to get a receipt for it, and nothing you or Dad or Pansy Webb, or Sheriff Wilson, can say will stop it." He frowned heavily. "Why, that wasn't even a good fight!" he exploded. "I played with that big brute and passed up chances to knock him as cold as a clam."

"But fighting with such men is done with guns," said Clint.

His tone of voice caused Richard to look at him quickly. "I suppose that's so," Richard said slowly. "I'm not very fast with a gun, Clint. Maybe I can get the knack of it, yet."

But Clint shook his head. "It's too late, Dick, and you didn't have a knack to start with. You've got to have that, you know. What's more, men like this Blunt are born gunmen . . . fast as light. It's as natural to them to draw and shoot in the wink of an eye as it is to . . . strike a match. You couldn't learn in time."

"How about yourself, Clint?" his brother asked. "It was fast work today. You must have been born with it. I remember you were always practicing, anyway. I suppose you've been up against. . . ."

"I've got it," Clint interrupted with a shrug. "Damn! That's one of the things they hold up against me. I'm not kicking."

Richard stepped to the window and looked out. "Plenty of people in the street," he observed. "Standing around in groups, and some, quite a string, heading this way."

Clint joined him quickly to look for himself. "Jumping Jupiter, here's the sheriff!" he exclaimed. "Somebody saw us, Dick, for he's comin' here sure. Wait a minute." He opened the door softly and stole out into the hall. Richard remained at the window with one eye on the door. When Clint came back into the room, Richard nodded in approval. Clint's belt and gun were missing.

"Just let 'em find out what they can," Richard warned. "We're not saying who did the shooting, remember. And anyway, Blunt was first to fire."

"We're outside or inside the law, any way you want to look at it," Clint said, nodding. "But if I don't take the blame, there might be some who'd think you did it," he added, frowning.

"Let 'em think," said Richard quickly. "Keeps 'em guessing. Listen." He cupped a hand to his ear, and then the sounds of someone mounting the stairs were plainly heard. They sat down and Richard took out his cigarette case. They were lighting their smokes when a sharp rapping was suddenly heard on the door.

"Come in," Richard invited.

Sheriff Wilson entered alone and closed the door behind him. He looked from one to the other of them keenly. "I'm not sayin' I'm sure, but I think your tan is a little deeper, Clint." He was looking at Clint as he spoke.

"Better make sure, Sheriff," Richard said cheerfully.

"Now I am sure," said the official. "I can tell by the voice, Dick. What you boys doing? Just talkin' it over?" He was a tall, raw-boned man with a leathery skin, brown mustache that drooped, a long face, and high cheekbones. His eyes were mild and gray.

"We came up here to get away from the crowd," said Richard. "We had no intention of leaving town. How is . . . how is Blunt?" He tried to put the question casually.

"He's hard hit, I reckon, but he ain't dead yet," replied the sheriff. He and Andrew French were friends of long standing. Less than two weeks ago he had taken it upon himself to read Clint a light lecture. "Someday you'll kill a man, if you keep on," he had said, "and then it won't be so good." "No gun?" He addressed the question to Clint.

"No gun, Sheriff," Clint answered pleasantly.

"But there was a gun, was there not?" Wilson asked slowly.

"Blunt had the first one and he used it first," said Richard.

"But one of you two had a gun," said the sheriff. "You didn't wear a gun into town, did you, Dick?"

"I cannot seem to remember," Richard replied, looking the official straight in the eyes.

"I see." Wilson nodded. "What happened sort of startled your memory. But you can remember, can't you, Clint?"

"Has anybody said I did . . . wear a gun, I mean?" Clint evaded.

"Well, there's a question as to which of you was

which," said the sheriff, caressing his drooping mustache. "I didn't see you myself. But one of you had a gun. It was dropped in the scuffle and it was hard to see with the dust flyin' around that way. I got there late. You'd be the most likely to do the shootin', Clint."

"I haven't forgotten how it's done," Richard said before his brother could make reply. "You know Blunt started this business, of course, Sheriff, and that he was first to shoot."

"That's what some say," drawled Wilson. "And then there's others who ain't so sure. Shootin' ain't as free and easy in this town as it used to be, Dick."

"Maybe not," said Richard. "But they haven't taken that self-defense item out of the law, have they, Sheriff?"

"I guess the three of us better go down and see Blunt," Wilson decided. "Maybe he can identify who did the shootin'. Want to come?"

"Sure," Richard said, rising, "but you know his identification wouldn't be worth a thing, one way or the other. Come on, Clint."

Clint French followed his brother and the sheriff out of the room. As the trio walked out of the hotel and up the street towards the doctor's house, where Blunt Rodgers had been taken, they appeared to be talking amicably. Out of the corner of his eye, Clint saw Norman Webb following them.

Chapter Nine

The doctor met them in the little office in the front of his house. He didn't know either Richard or Clint very well, as he had met them only at long intervals. He had not visited the French Ranch since the death of their mother, eleven years ago.

"He's just about alive," said the doctor in answer to a question put by the sheriff, and nodding curiously at the brothers. "I put him to bed here because it would be fatal to try to move him. And I cannot probe for the bullets."

"Is he conscious?" asked Sheriff Wilson. "You know I have certain duties to perform in connection with my office, Doctor, and I have to ask him if he can say which of these two shot him."

"I'll see," Dr. Crane said. "I'll have to give him a stimulant, and then you can go into the room, I guess. I don't think he has the slightest chance of pulling out of it, as I told you before."

They waited silently with their hats held nervously in their hands, in the office, as the doctor left them. Outside, a crowd had gathered in the street before the house. Rodgers's sinister reputation was known to many, while the sons of Andrew French were notable. It was the general opinion that Clint had done the shooting. But none had actually seen it, for, with the first shot, the spectators had scattered in all directions, striving to get out of range and the line of fire.

But interest was at white heat and the question that passed from mouth to mouth was whether or not the sheriff would hold the French boys. The powerful influence of Andrew French was well known and accepted generally. And the victim—who was he? No one seemed to know much about him, except that he was an undesirable.

But, as Sheriff Wilson had told Richard French, the sentiment in Conroy concerning shootings, and killings especially, had changed. Norman Webb, wealthy retired stockman, had been prominent in frowning upon "the rough stuff." This was the first killing to take place in the town in five straight years, although there had been gun battles and plenty of fist fights. Norman Webb was president of the town council and thus virtually mayor. Andrew French was his closest friend. Clint French was in love with his daughter, as all the town knew. What stand would Webb take in the matter? Gossip ran riot.

After a few minutes the doctor came to the door of the office and beckoned to them. They followed him into a room where Blunt Rodgers lay in a snow-white bed, his eyes gleaming brightly under the stimulus of the dose the doctor had administered hypodermically. He tried to rise on an elbow as they entered, but the doctor cautioned him. He kept his eyes on the two brothers, plainly astonished.

"I'm seein' things . . . again," he muttered.

"No, you're not seein' things, Blunt," said the sheriff in a soothing voice, advancing to the bedside. "This is Clint French and his brother. Can you tell me which one shot you, Blunt. Don't try unless you're sure, because you'll have to tell me why you're sure. Be careful now . . . take your time."

"Both of them shot me!" Blunt exploded with an effort.

"But they couldn't both shoot you, Blunt," said the sheriff. "There was only one gun and the man you had the fight with didn't have a gun. Can you tell which one you had the fight with?"

Richard kept his hands behind his back so Blunt could not see his bruised knuckles. His face showed no marks of the encounter. He had rearranged his clothing. Clint stared at the man in bed stolidly. He wasn't much interested for he believed Blunt was out of his head.

"I . . . guess it was Clint," muttered the wounded man. "Maybe the other. But they both shot me." The fire was dying in his eyes.

"But that couldn't be," the sheriff persisted. "If you was only shot once, how . . . ?" He ceased speaking as the doctor touched his arm.

"He was shot twice," he said in a low voice that the official and the two brothers could barely hear. "Didn't I explain that to you? I was in such a hurry, maybe I overlooked it."

"Shot twice?" said the sheriff with a look of astonishment.

The doctor nodded. "In the left arm and over the heart," he answered. "The hole in his chest will kill him," he whispered.

"Get 'em, Jake . . . there's two of 'em!"

The words rang through the house and the doctor stepped to the bed quickly. Sheriff Wilson and Clint and Richard stared.

The eyes of Blunt Rodgers seemed popping like red balls out of his head. Then the light in them changed and red froth bubbled on his lips. Before the doctor could move, the figure of the big man went suddenly limp and the diminished gleam in the eyes grew dull and glazed and staring.

The doctor hastily put his ear to the man's chest, feeling with his right fingers for his pulse. When he straightened, he motioned to the others to leave the room. "He's gone," he said simply. "There was nothing I could do for him."

If the sheriff was surprised, it was nothing as compared with the astonishment and perplexity exhibited by the two brothers. They stood in the office and stared at each other, speechless.

"Did you hear two shots?" Clint asked his brother.

"Yes," replied Richard. "But he fired one of them."

"But if he was shot twice . . ." Clint bit his lip helplessly. "And he called to Jake," he said dully. "That would be Jake Burness."

The sheriff spoke as the doctor came into the office. "Clint, I'll have to see the gun," he said.

"Why is it necessary to see the gun?" Richard asked, sparring for time. "We'll acknowledge one shot was fired at Rodgers, but . . ."

"I must see the gun," said the sheriff sternly. "Unless you show it to me at once, I'll have to lock you up in jail till it's found."

"Oh, we'll show you the gun," Clint said impatiently. "In fact, after what we just heard, you should see the gun."

"But we're not saying who used it," Richard put in firmly.

"Where is it?" the sheriff demanded, looking straight at Clint.

"It's up in the hotel." Clint frowned. "Come along

and I'll show it to you." He caught a look from Richard, hesitated, and then added: "I thought I knew more about hidin' it than Dick did."

The three of them walked rapidly back to the hotel, and this time there was no talking. The news of Blunt Rodgers's death must have spread with incredible swiftness. The groups of men made way for them and all talk was silenced as they passed. Back in the doctor's office, Norman Webb was listening to the doctor soberly.

When the trio reached the hotel, they walked quickly through the lobby and up the stairs to the room where Clint and Dick had gone after the fight and the shooting. There Clint stood at the table and spoke first to his brother.

"The sheriff wants to know if more than one shot was fired from the gun," he said. "He must know that we hurried here after the business was over. He'll be interested to see whether or not the gun has been cleaned. Isn't that so, Sheriff?"

"Where's the gun?" the official asked with a light frown.

"Oh, show it to him!" Richard ejaculated. "You put it away."

"Just a minute," Clint said, holding up his hand. "I'm not talking for exercise. Tell him, Dick . . . did we or did we not come straight to this room after it was all over? Tell him."

"Why, of course we did," Richard answered, plainly annoyed.

"That's what we did, Sheriff," Clint said, turning to Wilson. "Now, if that gun was cleaned, it was cleaned in this room and nowhere else. I haven't got a cleaning kit with me and I know Dick hasn't. If you think there's any rags or oil around, take a keen look."

The sheriff did take a look and found the room in perfect order, save for some cigarette ashes spilled on the floor. "There's the window," he drawled. "It wouldn't be hard to open that screen or hide the stuff away elsewhere. Now what else is on your mind?"

"I'll go get the gun," said Clint briefly. He went out the door and entered another room, with the sheriff following to watch. He handed his belt with the weapon in its holster to the official in the hall and the latter took it into the room where Richard waited.

Wilson took out the gun and broke it, looking at the face of the cylinder. Then he spilled five loaded cartridges and an empty shell onto the table. He held the gun barrel up to the light and looked through it. Then he replaced the weapon in its holster and pursed his lips. "Looks like only one shot was fired from it," he said slowly.

"And that's all that was fired from it," Richard said tartly. "But Blunt says we both shot him and he doesn't, or didn't, know which one of us he had been fighting with. Thought he was seeing double, perhaps. When he spoke his last words, he was suffering from severe mental shock as well as from his wounds. But he was shot twice, Sheriff . . . we cannot lose sight of that fact. Even if Clint or myself acknowledged shooting at him . . . which we will not do . . . there would be no way of proving that that shot was fatal. It looks as if someone else had occasion to take a shot at Blunt."

The sheriff looked at him mildly. "Go down and tell the clerk to come up here," he ordered. "I suppose you saw the clerk before you took this room, didn't you?"

"Sure," replied Richard. "I'll go get him."

The clerk was agitated and apprehensive. He looked from Clint to Richard until the sheriff spoke to him sternly. "Tell me when and how these boys came up here," said Wilson. The clerk looked worried and glanced quickly at Clint. "Go ahead and tell him," said Clint. "Tell him the truth and get it out."

"Why . . . why, they came right after the . . . the trouble," stammered the clerk. "They came by the back way. I was out in front and . . . and Clint called to me, and told me to give 'em a room quick. I brought 'em up here without askin' 'em to register since I knowed 'em. That's all I know, Sheriff."

"All right," said the sheriff easily. "That's all I wanted to hear. You needn't say anything to anybody else. You can go now."

The clerk left hurriedly and the official turned to the two brothers. "So far, so good," he said in a tone that hinted of relief. "I'm not goin' to ask you again now who fired that shot. But I do want to make sure who started the fight."

"Well, I can tell you that," Richard said. "The . . ."

"I don't want you to tell me anything just now," the sheriff interrupted. "Clint, buckle on that gun. You needn't worry . . . it isn't goin' to be anything against you. We've got another visit to make and it doesn't make any difference who's packing the gun."

"Then it's just as well that I packed it," said Richard.

Sheriff Wilson frowned. "I'll have to ask you boys to do as I say," he said. "I reckon you know I've been sheriff of this county for some years back and I've got a reputation for playin' square."

"Oh, let's go," said Clint, who had buckled on his gun.

They followed the sheriff downstairs and left the hotel by the rear way. The trio walked rapidly down a side street until they came to a small, square, stone building. The brothers recognized it at once and looked at each other.

"We're goin' into my office," the sheriff announced, and turned into the entrance of the county jail.

Richard signaled to his brother and they followed the sheriff inside. As they entered the office, a man leaped to his feet.

"What's the idea in havin' me over here?" a rough voice asked.

"Sit down, Tower," said the sheriff, nodding to a deputy who evidently had been guarding the resort-keeper. "Sit down, boys." He took the chair behind his desk.

Tower gave Clint and his brother a mighty black look as they sat down.

"Tower, which one of these boys came into your place first today?" the official asked. "I suppose you can tell 'em apart."

"They came in together," Tower snapped. "Yes, I can tell 'em apart. Clint was wearin' the gun and they talk different."

The sheriff nodded. "I see. Who started the fight, Red?"

"They didn't fight in my place," Tower answered surlily. "The fight was outside, in the street. Everybody knows that."

"I didn't ask where it was fought," said the sheriff quietly. "It started in your place. Now, how did it start?"

"Why not let them tell you?" Tower flared defiantly.

"Because I want you to tell me," the official said firmly.

Tower got to his feet again. "There's some kind of

a trick to this!" he shouted. "You're not goin' to make me the goat, I'll tell you that. I've never wanted trouble in my place and I've tried to keep it out. I tried to stop this thing and I guess Dick will back me up . . . if he wants to tell the truth." He glared at Richard.

"I'll back you up," said Richard. "You did try to stop it."

Sheriff Wilson was frowning. "I'm still askin' you, Tower, how it started. You were there, were you not? Answer me!"

"Sure I was there," replied Tower, cooling down. "I talked with Clint and Dick a little, and then Clint went away. He'd . . . there had been some trouble with this Blunt . . . and I never invited him to come there . . . and he happened in and pounced on Dick. I guess he thought Dick was Clint. Whatever he said, Dick wouldn't take it and they had some words. I don't know what they said. It all happened in a minute, and, the next thing I knew, one of Blunt's gang shoved me out of the way and they all squeezed outdoors. That's all I know about it." He sat down, mopping his face.

"You were there after it was over, too, were you not?"

"Naturally I would be." Tower scowled. "I have to watch my place. For all I knew, it might have been a scheme to get me and everybody else out of the place so . . . so somebody could crack it." He finished lamely, wiped his forehead. "I don't mean that it would be a scheme of the French boys," he added, "but I never liked that Blunt's looks or the looks of the men that traveled with him."

"What became of those men?" asked the sheriff.

"I don't know," Tower blurted. "I didn't see 'em again."

The sheriff shifted some papers on his desk and looked out the window. "Well, I guess that's all," he said. "Unless these boys want to ask you something." He looked at Richard and Clint, but they shook their heads. Tower appeared puzzled and uneasy. "Yes, I guess that's all, Tower," the sheriff repeated.

"It's all I know," Tower grumbled. "But I'll say this . . . Clint, here, side-stepped trouble with Blunt twice before, and . . ."

"Never mind," the official broke in. "You can go."

The deputy followed Tower out and Sheriff Wilson looked quizzically at the two youths. Both Richard and Clint were experiencing the same sensation. They suspected that the man behind the desk knew more than any of them.

"Far as I can see," said the sheriff, "this was a case of self-defense. You boys can go, but I wouldn't go home tonight, if I was you."

"Is that advice or an order?" Richard asked politely.

"You'll have to figure that out for yourself," Wilson said, frowning. "Think it over."

"That means it's an order," said Richard in a hard voice. "But we'll figure it out as advice. Come on, Clint, let's go."

Ten minutes after they had left, Norman Webb and two deputies were closeted with the sheriff in the latter's office.

CHAPTER TEN

It was Richard who suggested, when they had left the sheriff's office, that he and Clint go at once to the Webb residence and tell Pansy Webb that they would be unable to go there for dinner as promised.

"Oh, she won't be expecting us after what's happened," said Clint with a wry smile.

"That's just why we've got to go," declared his brother. "We don't want her, or her father, to think that we're staying away because this thing came up. We're not going to crawfish and we're not doing any side-stepping. We'll go over there now. And then we've got some other business to look after."

It stirred Clint to see that his brother was angry. Moreover, he had never glimpsed this stern side to Richard's character. He went along gladly, content to let Richard manage things. He was curious to see what course his brother would take. Richard—a snob, a softy, or a tenderfoot? Clint grinned with secret satisfaction.

Pansy was on the porch when they entered the gate and strode up the little walk to the steps. She rose hastily to meet them.

"Oh . . . you're early," she said, appearing slightly

flustered. "But we can visit until supper is ready, and Father ought to be here any minute." She glanced anxiously down the street, and this was not lost on the two brothers.

Richard mounted the steps with Clint following, and they took off their hats. "It's too bad, Miss Webb," Richard said, with a flashing smile, "but we've got to miss a good supper. Unexpected business has come up which requires our attention. I suppose you heard there was a misunderstanding this afternoon?" His tone was polite and he raised his brows ever so little for the proper effect.

"I heard something about it," the girl confessed. The look she directed at Clint was brimming with accusation.

"I thought so," said Richard. "A man was killed this afternoon and I expect they're blaming one or the other of us . . . Clint and me, I mean. We're not so sure we're responsible, but we're not running away from anything. What has happened makes it necessary for us to attend to certain affairs . . . on our own initiative . . . and that is why we cannot come to supper. It's just our hard luck, that's all." As he finished, he smiled again, apparently cheerful and carefree.

"Oh, Richard!" the girl exclaimed with a troubled look. "I . . ."

"Just call me Dick," he interrupted gently. "I'm discarding the formality, Pansy. That will have to go for your dad and mine, too."

Clint laughed with spontaneous delight.

Pansy looked at him quickly and her expression changed at once. "It's all your fault, Clint French!" she charged indignantly. "I suppose you think this is the way to show Richard . . . Dick, a vacation."

"Now, Pansy." Dick held up a hand. "This isn't a

vacation because I'm back on the ranch. It's the other way around. I've been taking a vacation away from the ranch ever since I finished college. I was the one who started the ball rolling today, and I got a thrill out of it."

Pansy was staring at him with a look of incredulity in her eyes. "Why . . . why, Dick French!" she sputtered. "This isn't the wide-open West any more. Father says so himself and he has been the leader in making Conroy a decent town. This will hurt him terribly."

"If that's what he wants, maybe we'll be able to help him yet." Dick smiled. He thought he had detected a change in Norman Webb during his last two visits, and now it had him thinking. "You mustn't worry about me . . . about either of us," he went on. "And now we have to be going."

"But Father will want to see you, I'm sure," she said hastily.

"We can't wait for him and we'd be more likely to meet him in town," said Dick. "And, if we miss him, please tell him to excuse us for not being able to come to supper."

"Clint, you haven't said a word," the girl accused.

"I'm taking orders, Pansy," Clint said brightly. "Dick's in full and complete charge." He grinned at her and her lips tightened.

"Something is the matter with both of you," she said stiffly. "Well, I'll tell Father you called." She flounced into the house as Clint and Dick went down the steps.

Dick called a halt in the shade of the trees down the street. "We don't want to mix around town much, Clint. I'll tell you what I had on my mind. I didn't like all that fuss on the part of the sheriff a little bit. After what Pansy said, I'm thinking Wilson made all that show for the benefit of Webb . . . for Webb's the same as running this town, you might say. The sheriff knows Blunt started the fight, and I believe he knows more than we think."

"So do I," Clint agreed quickly.

"And, what's more," Dick continued, "I think Red Tower knows more than he lets on. I want to talk with him. There's something behind all this bigger than we think. We mustn't forget that Blunt was shot twice. I know that we only fired one shot. Someone else had a mighty good reason for taking advantage of the excitement and general mix-up to take a pot shot at Blunt, and I don't believe anybody heard that third shot, or, if they did, they've reason to keep quiet. I know I didn't hear it."

"Neither did I." Clint frowned. "And that's funny, too. It might be one of his own crowd had reason to sneak a shot in. And we don't know which shot killed Blunt, for that matter."

"Which leaves our conscience clear," said Dick. "You'll remember that Blunt called for Jake when he died. There's going to be more trouble over this business and we've got to stick it out. Let's go see Red Tower first."

Clint had his doubts about the wisdom of this but he offered no objection. Dick had brains, so why not let him use them? If there should be trouble of a nature he could not handle, well, Clint, had a specialty or two. Perhaps Dick was thinking of this, too. In such subtle way was the partnership born that was to rock the Teton range, from Paradise Valley to the buttes known as The Knees.

They strode through the resort, both keenly on the outlook for any of the men who had been with Rodgers, and found Tower in his private office in the rear. The door was open and they entered unceremoniously. Dick shut the door behind them as Tower rose from the chair by his desk, his eyes narrowing.

"Haven't you fellows caused enough trouble around here without coming back so quick?" he demanded.

"Cut it and cool down," Dick commanded sharply. "It isn't up to you to get on your ear, and we don't like it."

"He's tellin' you straight," Clint put in. "And don't forget one thing, Red, this is the second time you've failed to tell me that Blunt and his crowd was around."

"I didn't know it!" Tower exploded wrathfully. "He must have just got in. I haven't seen him since that night you was here till today. And I'm not goin' to stand for you tryin' to bulldoze me in my own place, either."

"If you don't want to make a row, don't talk so loud," Dick said sternly. "And loud talk isn't going to scare us any. I'm the one who wants to see you and I merely brought Clint along. So if any bulldozing is done, I'll do it. And while you're remembering you didn't warn Clint, as he says, just remember that you didn't try to warn me until it was too late."

"You could have got out of it easy enough," barked Tower.

"Not with my self-respect, I couldn't," Dick shot back. "And I didn't feel like taking anything from that rowdy anyway. This is enough explanation for you, Tower. I came here to ask you two questions. We can make you answer them, if we want to, but . . . none of that!"

Tower had leaped for the door, but Dick caught him, whirled him about, and thrust him into his chair. At this moment Dick caught sight of a gun on the desk for the first time. He secured it in an instant, broke it, and spilled the cartridges on the desk. "You won't have a chance to use that," he said. Then he stared at the cartridges. One had been exploded!

Tower's face went white and he gritted his teeth. But it might have been because he was seized with a fit of rage.

"An empty shell," said Dick to Clint. "Target practice, eh, Tower?" He picked up the shell and dropped it into a pocket. He put a foot on a chair in front of the resortkeeper and rested his right forearm on his knee. "Where did Blunt's pals go?" he asked.

Tower's eyes flashed red with fury. "How do I know?" he answered with an oath. "I tell you I never wanted that bunch here."

"I'm inclined to believe you," Dick said with a glance at the gun. "I don't blame you. I'll put it another way, Tower. Are they still in town, or around close?"

Tower gripped the arms of his swivel chair. "Their horses are gone, and they've gone themselves. That's all I know."

"We'll let it go at that," Dick said with a side glance at Clint. "Now for the other question, Red. This is a slippery one, so be careful how you handle it." He paused to let this sink in. "Now, Red," said Dick slowly, leaning forward, "did you see the shooting?"

The fire was gone from the resortkeeper's eyes. It was some seconds before he finally answered. "No!" he exclaimed.

Dick's laugh rang in the little room, startling his brother. "You've answered my question, Red," he said with a queer smile. "And now we'll be going."

He stepped to the door and nodded to Clint. They

went out together and left by the side door. "Let's go to a café and grab something to eat," Dick suggested. "I want to buy a gun, but I don't want to buy it until dusk."

"A gun!" Clint exploded. "Great snakes, you've got a good gun at the ranch. I've kept it in good order. I didn't know you wanted it. You didn't say anything about wanting one. There's a belt, too. You don't have to buy a new one."

"But that gun is at the ranch," Dick said quietly. "It doesn't do me any good here. I want one on the ride back tonight."

Clint whistled softly. "You want to go back tonight?"

"We are going back tonight, Clint," his brother said grimly.

"There were two of the men in town from the ranch today." Clint frowned. "I didn't have a chance to find out why they were here before the ruckus started, but I'll bet Dad sent 'em in to keep an eye on us. They've probably gone back with the news."

"All the more reason why we should get back as soon as possible," Dick pointed out. "Let's eat in this Okay place."

By the time they had eaten and gone to see about their horses, twilight was drawing its soft shadows over the land. They went to a store where Dick bought a gun, holster, and cartridge belt. He was carrying them in his hand as they started back to the livery. On the side street they came suddenly upon Norman Webb.

The retired stockman's eyes widened as he saw what Dick was carrying. He looked sharply at Clint. "Why . . . ?" He paused and seemed at a loss as to what to say.

"Sorry we couldn't come over to supper, Mister

Webb," said Dick. "Guess Pansy told you she had invited us. We wanted to start back to the ranch as soon as we could make it."

"Back to the ranch, Richard?" Webb lifted his brows.

"Just make it plain Dick." Richard smiled. "We're going home, of course."

"But . . . that gun!" exclaimed Webb, pointing a finger at the holstered weapon.

"After what happened today, I thought it best to have one handy," Dick explained coolly, "so I bought one and the food to feed it."

"Don't go to packing a gun . . . er . . . Rich . . . Dick. It was a gun that got you both in bad today." He scowled at Clint, who frowned back. "But, of course, I would have seen to it that Wilson didn't put you in jail."

"We were aware that he couldn't do that." Dick's tone had become cold. "We humored him by answering a lot of questions, that's all. This town isn't ripe for any wholesale revival meetings yet, Mister Webb. I suppose the doctor told you that Blunt Rodgers was shot twice? Let the sheriff spend his time finding out who fired that other shot."

"I don't think you boys should go back tonight," said Webb.

"It was our intention to go back tonight when we came in," Dick replied. "And nothing has happened to change our plans."

"But Wilson might want to see you," Webb said, nettled.

"Then he'll know where to find us," said Dick. "But we must get started . . . and give our respects to Pansy, Mister Webb."

The former stockman stared after them, muttering to himself.

The brothers galloped out of town, leaving a seething wake of excitement behind them. The dusk had deepened into night and the early stars were out. The light breeze had freshened, the air was cool and sweet, and their horses wanted to go. They followed the main road where the going was better.

They had ridden about five miles when Clint called suddenly to his brother. "Look there!" He pointed toward the timber along the river on their left.

Dick looked quickly. "I had a notion they would try it!" he cried. "We've got to ride, Clint!"

Several horsemen were racing toward them from the shadows of the trees. Even as they let their horses out into a mad gallop, red flame spurted against the dark and guns shattered the stillness with sharp reports.

As they leaned over their horses' necks and streaked westward, Dick French was first to return the fire.

CHAPTER ELEVEN

The two cowpunchers sent to Conroy by Len Miller to keep an eye out for Blunt Rodgers and his companions, or to watch out for Dick and Clint if they got to town first, met as the fight broke up, and hurried away. In the turmoil, Dick and Clint had escaped unobserved. The first thought of the two was to find them. They separated, and, when they met at the livery half an hour later, both knew the sheriff was talking with the brothers in the room at the hotel.

The Two-Bar F foreman had picked two of his best men for this special mission, Ed Munsey and Bill Klein. Munsey was tall and raw-boned, while Klein was short, thick-set, blue-eyed. Average cowpunchers in appearance, but nimble-minded, cunning, and gunmen both.

"We'll wait until we see what his nibs, the sheriff, does about it," Klein, who was authorized to decide, said. "You hang around the hotel, Ed, and follow Clint and Dick. If they don't start back pretty quick, ride like thunder to the ranch and tell Len what's happened. I'm goin' to find out where Blunt's bunch went. Don't wait for me."

As a result of this, Ed Munsey started for the

Two-Bar F as soon as he saw Clint and Dick leave the sheriff's office and start for the Webb house. He didn't know where Bill had gone, but was not worried because of that. Klein was well able to take care of himself.

As he rode westward at a fast pace to acquaint the Two-Bar foreman with what had taken place in town, Klein was riding like the wind south across the river in pursuit of the men who had been with Blunt in town. He was keeping well in the rear in order not to be seen. He merely wanted to be sure of their destination, so he thought.

Ed Munsey rode in the lower camp on the ranch at sunset. The men still were at work, and he saw Miller riding toward him as he came in. The foreman's look showed concern, for he knew Munsey would not return unless he had news, and, since the brothers hadn't been reported back, he suspected something had happened.

"Let's have it, Ed," he said sharply as they met near the scene of the branding. "Make it short, for I can see it's important."

"Clint and Dick got in town this afternoon," said Munsey. "Bill and me were in the Stampede. Clint got me outside to find out what we was doin' there. He didn't find out, but, while we were talkin', Blunt Rodgers and some of his crowd breezed in and trouble started, inside, quicker'n a wink. Blunt mistook Dick for Clint, looks like. We . . . the two of us . . . got back inside, but everybody was tryin' to get through the front door, and we had to go back out the side and around to the front and push through the crowd there. It all happened like that." He snapped his fingers.

"Yes, yes," said Miller impatiently. "What happened?"

"Dick was fightin' with Blunt and givin' him a good lickin' when Blunt was handed a gun. Clint busted out, and Dick knocked the gun from Clint's hand. While the two of 'em scrambled for it, Blunt shot at Dick and missed. Then there was another shot and Blunt went down. Then everybody, includin' Bill and me, piled in. The dust put an end to the free-for-all, and, when we got out of it, Clint and Dick were gone, and Blunt was on the ground. They took him to the doctor's house and he died a while later. The sheriff had Clint and Dick and Red Tower in his office. Red came out first. Then Clint and Dick went off to Webb's house and I came to tell you."

"Where's Bill?" the foreman demanded.

"He went off to see where Blunt's outfit sloped to when they left town. Told me to come back here with the news as ordered."

"Who shot Blunt?" asked Miller, lowering his voice considerably.

"Why, I suppose . . . I don't actually know, for sure," Munsey replied.

Miller was looking at him closely. "That's good enough," he decided, "and be sure you tell everybody else the same thing. Do you know if Clint and Dick figure on comin' home tonight? No? Well, some of us will have to go into town. This is no ruckus . . . it's a killing! I'll go up and tell the old man. I'll pick out three of the boys and you bring 'em out to meet me on the road in half an hour. Better get something to eat first." The foreman started away, but turned back. "You're sure you haven't got anything you want to tell me sort of private?" he asked.

"Not a thing, Len. The whole business didn't take more'n five minutes, it seemed like, from the time the boys walked into the Stampede. We . . . Bill and me . . . was there because we knew it was the first place Blunt would hit if he came to town . . . and it was."

"All right," Miller said as he strode away the second time.

Andrew French was not quick-tempered and was not a profane man. He possessed the blessed faculty of being able to remain cool and keep his head in emergencies. The greater the emergency, the cooler and more calculative he became. At such times his composure was nothing short of remarkable. In trivial matters he might be quick to show disgust, impatience, or anger. His greatest asset was confidence.

He listened calmly to Miller's account of what had happened in town, as related by Ed Munsey. "And it looks to me as if there was something behind all this . . . something big," Miller concluded.

"Something bigger than you think, maybe," said the stockman. "I haven't got Jake Burness in mind, either. Burness is too wise to bother around Conroy or to get me on the warpath. It's . . . Richard."

"I wouldn't worry so much about Dick, if I was you," said Miller. "He can take care of himself, it looks like."

"Clint got him into this," said Andrew. "Left the ranch after dinner, and in trouble before sundown." The rancher swore roundly.

"From what Ed told me, Blunt mistook Dick for Clint and started something he couldn't finish," said Miller. "I'll bank on Ed Munsey."

"You know as well as I do that Clint shot Blunt," flared Andrew.

"What of it?" was Miller's rejoinder. "From what Ed says, that gun bully would have dropped Dick in his tracks. Looks to me as if Clint saved Dick's life, if you want to ask me straight."

"I'll go down there!" Andrew ejaculated. "Order the team."

"I wouldn't do that, boss," said Miller. "It would only get folks to talkin' more about the thing. And we both know Clint well enough to know that he'll insist on comin' back soon as they can. They probably went over to Webb's to see Pansy. You'd only meet 'em on the way, and I can run down with a hand or two and do that."

"You!" Andrew exclaimed. He thought for a few moments. "If you're so sure they're comin' back, why ride down . . . to meet 'em?"

"To make certain that they do get back all right," said Miller firmly. "I don't like the looks of this thing. Blunt buttin' into Dick that way, thinking he was Clint, after Clint had side-stepped him twice, shows he wanted trouble. It would be just like that bunch that travels with Blunt to try to get the two of 'em on the trip home."

Andrew looked startled. "They're not such big fools."

"Maybe they wouldn't think they were being fools," said Miller. "I think I better ride down the road . . . and ride fast. This is a time for quick ridin', and I'm the one who should go. I'm startin'." He went down the steps toward his horse.

"If there should be any trouble, use your own judgment," said Andrew. "You know what that means. Get 'em back here."

Miller failed to see the look in Andrew's eyes as he rode away. If he had seen it, it would have taken his thoughts back through the years to when the old centaur was fighting to preserve Paradise range,

building a foothold with an indomitable courage—
and bullets. It was not strange that Andrew could not
believe that the peace of the range was threatened.

With the firing of Dick's first shot, Clint threw his
gun over his left shoulder and emptied it at the oncoming riders. But all this shooting was wild. Clint,
more skilled in work such as this, realized that the
attackers had sprung their ambush a little too soon.
As he reloaded his gun, he saw that the five men
making for them were well mounted. They would
have to put their horses to the test to outdistance
them, straight ahead, or would have to cut back.
Clint now took charge.

"Stop shooting!" he shouted to Dick. "Keep with
me and do as I tell you. That gang wants to kill us,
and this isn't kid play!"

He veered off the road to the right, riding northwest on the plain. Dick saw instantly the wisdom of
this move, as it made it necessary for the attackers to
ride straight north in an effort to cut them off and
made the race a matter to be settled by superior
horseflesh. He realized, too, that here was a situation that could better be handled by Clint, who had
more range experience. Clint more than likely had
been chased before.

They urged their mounts to top speed in a dash
that soon showed the oncoming riders that further
shooting was futile until they could draw well
within range. In range they would be virtually four
to one, for none of them gave Dick credit for shooting ability. They would be able to tell the brothers
apart by the way they handled their weapons.

Clint was confident he and Dick could leave their
pursuers behind, but this confidence was shattered in

a quarter of a mile by two disturbing factors: the pursuers were better mounted than Clint had any reason to expect, and Dick's horse was slowing its pace.

Clint pulled up a bit. "Can't that horse of yours make it?" he called. He couldn't understand Dick's dropping behind, because he was an excellent rider and had been given one of the fastest horses on the ranch.

"This is the best he'll do!" Dick called back. "I think he's going lame." They were running side-by-side now, and Clint saw that Dick's mount was doing its best. He looked quickly at the other riders. The distance between remained unchanged, but, if Dick's horse was giving out already, their pursuers would certainly overtake them before they could reach the ranch.

Clint's mind snapped to instant decision. "We'll have to turn back!" he shouted. "I don't think your horse can make it."

With this, he swung around and headed back toward town with Dick following. This maneuver widened the breach between them and the hostile riders. Shouts and the reports of a volley of wild shots came to them on the wind. They had barely straightened out for town when a new message came on the wind that caused them to twist in their saddles for a good view behind.

The air was vibrating with the sharp staccato of gunfire. They saw a number of swift-moving shadows sweeping from the west, and pinpoints of red winked in the night about them.

"They're from the ranch!" yelled Clint jubilantly. "The boys in town must have took word back. Come on, Dick . . . we'll cut 'em off!"

He swung his horse again and saw that their pursuers had turned back for the river, riding like mad.

The riders from the west were thundering down upon them, guns blazing. Clint dashed in pursuit, cutting southwest directly toward the fleeing horsemen. He left Dick behind, but he got into range just as the men from the ranch closed in.

"Let 'em have it for keeps!"

Len Miller's voice came clearly distinct in a lull in the firing. Clint's heart leaped. His own gun spat its message. Then a hot flame seared his right shoulder, high up; the air shivered with a fusillade of shots, horses went down, flinging their riders, men slid out of their saddles, yells of pain and anger mingled with the snorting of horses and the crunching of hoofs. Clint's shoulder burned, but he emptied his gun. Dick came, but Miller was again roaring an order. "That's enough!"

Three men were on the ground. Two of them lay motionlessly. The third was standing, hatless, his wizened face white in the moonlight, his gun missing. A fourth rider had broken through and was disappearing in the shadows along the river. The fifth evidently had made his getaway first of all.

Len Miller was off his horse and looking over the captive who was standing. "Hello, Lowell," he said in a drawling voice. "Planned a little surprise party, did you? I. . . ."

The foreman was interrupted by Ed Munsey. "Bill should be comin' in," the cowpuncher said. "He was supposed to follow 'em. Ask him if he saw Bill."

Clint surmised that Bill Klein had been the fifth man, but realized at once that this couldn't be possible. Perhaps he had been watching from the river. But why hadn't he ridden out when the chase started, if he had been where he could see it begin?

"What're you goin' to do?" asked the captive. "Of course, we planned a surprise party. We wanted to ask that pair a few questions. I suppose you know Clint French bumped a friend of ours. Are these fellows dead?" He looked about, hawklike, and his eyes were beads of darting black.

"I reckon so," drawled Miller. "The old man told me to use my own judgment, and that ain't so hard to do when I'm dealin' with your kind. Have you seen any other Two-Bar men . . . one, in particular?"

"No," snarled the prisoner. "You had to shoot my horse to get me, I notice. You ought to be proud of that. I'm not answering questions. You've killed three of us here, and. . . ."

"I'm right glad we didn't hurt you, Lowell," Miller interrupted sternly. "You'll answer questions any day . . . any minute of the day or night before you'd swing. I know your breed like the printin' on a rodeo poster. You stepped on hot ground when you got five miles out of town toward Paradise. Now we'll just take you the rest of the distance to where we've got plenty of nice, big cottonwoods, with smooth limbs sticking out all made to order to hold your kind with their feet off the ground. You'll talk plenty, but you'll shut up now or I'll knock your tongue down your throat!"

The captive's eyes were sparking fire and his right hand was shaking with the itch for a gun, but he made no reply to Miller.

"You boys all right?" asked the foreman, looking up at Clint and Dick seated in their saddles.

"Sure thing," said Clint cheerfully. "Dick's horse showed bad or we would have led this outfit back to the ranch."

"All right," Miller said sharply. "Some of you boys look after these men on the ground. Catch up a horse for this bad one. We'll drift back to the Two-Bar."

CHAPTER TWELVE

Andrew heard the story in the living room of the Two-Bar F ranch house. He sat in a huge easy chair with the light from the shaded lamp on his big hands that gripped the arms of the chair. He listened first to Len Miller, glancing frequently from his foreman to Dick or Clint, who were there. His face was set and stern and a bit gray. He interrupted the speaker only once or twice, for Miller was gifted in the art of elucidation, and he explained what had happened and the causes leading up to the events of the night clearly and tersely.

"You say you've got Lowell tied up down at the camp?" he asked, when Miller indicated that he had finished.

"Yes. We can keep an eye on him better down there."

"Very good." Andrew nodded with a grim smile. "I'll be down first thing in the morning for a look at him. If any of the others of that crowd come along to try and get him loose, shoot him first. You better go back, Miller. Wait a minute," he added as the foreman started to rise. Andrew turned to Clint. There was no frown or look of accusation in his eyes. "You were tellin' me, Clint, that you had trouble a while back with Blunt Rodgers. Twice, you say?"

"The first time was about a month ago," Clint replied. "It was in a card game when he chose me for no reason but to pick trouble. I called him, but Tower butted in and quieted things down."

"And the second time?" prompted Andrew.

"Was just the day before you told me Dick was comin' back. He jumped me again, and that time Tower didn't butt in and failed to warn me that Blunt was in the place in the bargain. I walked away from Blunt to avoid trouble. When he went after Dick, he thought it was me again, I reckon. He might have killed Dick if . . . if . . ." He clamped his jaw shut with a swift look at Miller.

"If what?" Andrew demanded in a commanding voice.

"If he hadn't been shot himself," Dick supplied. "We're not saying who killed him, Dad, because we don't know. There were two shots fired at him instead of one."

"Two!" cried Andrew, looking from one to the other of his sons. "Did you both shoot him? I've noticed you're wearing a gun, Richard."

"I didn't wrap that on until afterward," said Dick. "I'll explain exactly what took place in town." He proceeded to give his father and Len Miller an exact and clear account of the whole affair as it was enacted in Conroy.

When he had finished, it was Miller who put the first question, and he put it to Clint. "Did Bill Klein and Ed Munsey follow you into the center of the crowd where the fight was?" he asked.

"I don't know," replied Clint. "It happened . . . too much of it . . . in too short a space of time for me to see what was goin' on around me. Everybody piled in, it seemed, after the shooting."

"We only fired one shot," said Dick firmly.

"Then Bill or Ed must have fired the other!" Miller exclaimed.

"I don't think so," Dick said, "but I'm not saying anything. I think the less we say, Clint and me, the better off we'll be."

Andrew growled. "There's a lot in that. Wilson wouldn't have dared to jail either of you. And Webb's gone to seed since he's been in town. Since Klein didn't come back, you can bet he's on some kind of a trail. If Burness is mixed up in this, Bill will find out. By gad! If Burness tries to mess up this range . . ." He turned wrathfully to Miller. "The sheriff's authority ends at our east boundary!" he thundered. "Remember that, Miller."

"I guessed that," Miller said calmly. "Only I stretched the boundary to within five miles of town when I saw those riders chasin' Clint and Dick. You say there were six of 'em with Blunt, Dick?"

"I'm pretty sure there were six," Dick answered. "I ought to be, because I was counting the odds against me."

His father's eyes sparkled momentarily.

"There were only five after you down there," Miller pointed out. "Looks like Bill Klein either met up with the sixth or followed him alone."

"Klein will turn up with what he knows in due time," said Andrew. "I guess you can go back, Miller." He rose with the foreman. The two men looked squarely at each other. Both were tall and straight, with Andrew the heavier of the two and about fifteen years older. Capable-looking men, these two, and they understood each other.

"If Burness is mixed up in this business, Len," said Andrew in a hard voice, "I'll blot him out. Look!" A white miller had alighted on the green tablecloth. "Like that!" Andrew cried hoarsely, obliterating the miller with his thumb.

"Maybe Blunt was on his own," said the foreman. "He never had much sense. I haven't even heard anything about Burness bein' around these parts. But he don't usually advertise himself till the time comes . . . and then he comes and goes fast, I believe."

"If he comes this time. . . ." Andrew checked the hot words that were on his tongue. "After I've seen Lowell in the mornin', I'll want you to move the cattle out of the lower range, Miller. You can graze 'em along up the valley. How many head you missing?"

"About thirty, maybe more," Miller answered. "I mean cows."

"Send a bunch out to look for 'em at daybreak," Andrew ordered.

When Miller had gone, Andrew remained standing, looking thoughtfully at his sons who were seated by the table. "I don't see that I can blame you, Clint," he said finally, "so we'll forget that part of it . . . but I want to speak with Richard alone."

"Sure," said Clint, rising. Then his face flushed. "Say anything you want to say to him," he said angrily to Dick, "and if you can tell him anything more than I've already told him, it will be one on me, and something I've forgotten."

"Dad, if it's anything about Clint, I'd rather have him here," said Dick. "What's more, if it is anything about him, I'd rather not hear it at all. We're in this thing together. That's as it should be. I don't care a whoop about anything that has gone before, except as it affects our trouble today. We're sticking together. We told the sheriff that, and I guess I made Norman Webb understand it, too. And please call me Dick, and we'll toss aside the formality."

Andrew was staring at him. Dick was actually reading him a lecture. And it had been his intention to make excuses for Clint. Suddenly he smiled. "Well, Dick, if that's the way you feel about it, all right. I was goin' to say something about Clint, but it wouldn't have been so bad. I'm sorry your vacation has had such a start, though, and that's a fact."

"This isn't a vacation, Dad . . . I'm home." Dick laughed. "I've been having a vacation away from home. I told Pansy that, but I guess it went over her head. And before we do anything else, we've got to look after Clint, here. He has a bullet scratch on the shoulder."

"You hit?" asked Andrew in astonishment, addressing Clint.

"Just touched," Clint answered. "Dick fixed it up down below, and I reckon it just needs washing and a better bandage."

"Come out in the kitchen," ordered Andrew. "Susan . . . Susan!"

The housekeeper and Dick soon had Clint's slight wound on the shoulder cleansed thoroughly and properly bandaged. The bullet had merely grazed him, but Andrew sobered to the degree of grimness when he looked at the wound. The sight of the blood was enough.

Clint went to bed, and Dick sat in the living room with his father. Andrew was studying him surreptitiously. Although he would not come right out and say as much, he was secretly proud of the fact that Dick had licked Rodgers before the bully could get hold of a gun. Suppose Blunt had shot the youth to death. Andrew stirred uneasily in his chair.

"I wasn't going to say much about Clint," he said, clearing his throat. "After all, I'm not so much worried about him. Not now, anyway."

"I hope you're not beginning to worry about me," said Dick.

"Well . . . this may be serious," Andrew evaded. "You might have been killed today, Rich . . . Dick. Why don't you want me to call you Richard?"

"It seems out of place," replied his son. "It has a tendency to set me . . . well, apart. The men all call me Dick, and so does Clint. I corrected Webb and Pansy this afternoon. The way Webb acts"—Dick frowned and paused—"you'd think I needed a guard."

"Webb's changed a lot," growled Andrew. "He's got soft and law-abiding since he quit ranching. Not that I don't believe in law, Dick, but . . . this is still too tough a country to reform in a minute. It's a whole lot tougher than you might think, Dick. You must remember you've been away most of the time since you were a kid, and you've been living in peaceful parts."

"Is this Burness as bad as he's painted," Dick asked casually.

"He's worse," Andrew declared. "He's a born killer at heart."

"What would he be doing in this locality?" Dick queried.

Andrew shrugged. "Burness is an outlaw. When he hits a place, it's for one of two reasons. Either he is not working, so to say, and is givin' his men a chance to blow off steam in a spending and drinking spree, or he has a job in view. If he's around here planning a job, he isn't goin' about it as he usually does. When he works, he works fast, like Miller said. I've never seen him, and I only know about him by what I've heard. But he's dynamite."

"Do you know this man they captured?" asked Dick.

"Lowell? Why, yes," Andrew answered reluctantly.

"What about him, Dad?" Dick persisted.

"You'll find out about him in the morning," said Andrew with a grim smile. "I'm goin' to take you boys down with me so you can get a look at him in daylight. But I don't want you to call each other by name or do anything that would make it possible for him to tell you apart. And now I guess we'd better get to bed, Dick. We must be up at dawn, and that isn't far away."

After Dick had gone upstairs, Andrew sat in his big chair and thought. His rugged features were stern, his eyes half closed. Susan Enfield, the housekeeper, came softly into the room.

"What! Are you still up, Susan?" Andrew asked, frowning.

"Yes, naturally." Mrs. Enfield, a widow, had been Andrew French's wife's housekeeper and confidante for some time before Mrs. French had died. Now she was—and by right, seemingly—Andrew's confidante. And she was almost another mother to his sons. "Is this serious, Andrew?" she asked.

"I don't know," he confessed, and suddenly he looked tired. "But I'm goin' to find out without delay. If there is goin' to be any more trouble on this range, it's goin' to be the last."

"But . . . Richard," she warned. "You must be very careful."

Andrew's eyes brightened and he smiled. "Rich . . . Dick took care of himself today," he said. "That is, until it came to guns. Then Clint took a hand." His face became grave again. "I've tried to make it clear to Dick that this is serious. And, by the way, Susan, Dick says he doesn't want to be called Richard any more." The smile had returned.

But Susan didn't smile. "I've always told you, Andrew, when I sensed trouble coming," she said soberly. "I sense it now. And I know you well enough to see that you sense it, too. I . . . you know Clint might have been killed."

"I know." The stockman nodded. "And Dick might have been killed. That's why I won't take as much as a whispering chance. Now you go to bed. We men folks want breakfast before sunup."

"Hannah will have it ready," Susan promised. "Good night."

The sun was a burning ball of red in a sea of gold on the eastern horizon's rim when Andrew French rode away from the ranch house with Dick and Clint. The air was cool, the sky crystal-clear, and meadowlarks were fluting their morning song in a world of depth and beauty.

Clint's shoulder was not bothering him much. Dick was wearing his old cartridge belt, holster, and gun. Andrew looked at them slyly from time to time, well aware of their similarity in both form and feature. These were not boys, he realized, but grown men—strong men. Andrew felt pride swell within him and at the same time he frowned fiercely at the prospect of meeting the man who had been captured the night before. He had been careful to give his sons instructions as to how to act and had forbidden them to say anything.

Len Miller met them before they reached the chuck wagon. "I've got a bunch out lookin' for the strays," he told Andrew, "and we'll start movin' the herd later on. Lowell's actin' pretty sore."

"Where is he?" Andrew demanded, looking about with a scowl.

"I've got him over here out of earshot of the men, with Ed Munsey standing guard over him," Miller said with a faint grin. "He's in bad humor because he was tied up the rest of the night. Come on and take a look at him, boss."

They rode with the foreman to the edge of the timber along the creek. There they found the captive, his wrinkled, hawklike face screwed into a look of menace, squatting on the ground. The tall cowpuncher stood a few paces away.

"Did he act up any, Ed?" Miller asked Munsey.

"No," replied the cowpuncher. "Won't even talk. Seems mad, or something. Maybe his breakfast didn't agree with him." Munsey's drawl fell deliciously on the ears of his listeners. The captive's beady black eyes snapped fire. But he held his tongue. He looked closely at Dick and Clint, as if striving to discover some mark by which he would be able to distinguish them apart if such need should come. He looked at Andrew French last.

"Didn't make a move, eh?" Miller was saying. "I was half hopin' he would give you a chance to ventilate his gizzard, Ed." He turned toward Andrew. "If he doesn't want to talk to you, boss, just go away and leave him to us. Just go away and you won't know anything about . . . anything."

Andrew got off his horse as did the others. The prisoner rose to his feet. He had looks for no one now save the stockman.

"So it's old Limpy Lowell," Andrew said, looking the man up and down. "The same spindle, bowlegged, snake-eyed, sneaky-faced Limpy. For an all-around horse thief, rustler, stage robber, and gun-fighter, it's a wonder to me to see that your long, scrawny neck hasn't been stretched an inch since last time I saw you."

If the look Lowell shot between his narrowed lids could have killed, Andrew would have died before he had uttered more than half a dozen words. The diminutive gunman closed his teeth over his upper lip to hold back the torrent that was on his tongue.

"Who're you travelin' with now? Andrew asked sternly.

"I'm travelin' alone," came the hissing reply.

"A natural-born liar as usual," declared Andrew. "How come you were ridin' with four other skunks last night?" The rancher's face had darkened, and both Clint and Dick were seeing this phase of their father's rugged character for the first time. They looked at each other and at Miller, whose face also was coldly grim.

"Blunt Rodgers was a friend of mine, and that pair shot him down like a dawg," Lowell answered in a vicious voice, jerking a finger toward Clint and Dick.

"Another lie like that and I'll turn you over to Miller, regardless!" thundered Andrew. "You seem to think you're in a soft spot, Limpy, but you're not. You're just as low as a horse is high from a rope. Figure it out . . . just the distance from the ground to the back of a horse, and there are plenty of trees handy. Now, can you remember what I asked you?"

Lowell's eyes had shifted away from Andrew's burning gaze. "I'd just come to town," he said. "I didn't know there was two of 'em. Neither did Blunt, or he wouldn't have got plugged."

"I'll take that for an answer," said Andrew. "I've only got one real question to ask you, Limpy, and your answer will decide whether you ride off this ranch or stay. And if you stay, Limpy, you stay for good." Andrew waited just long enough to let his threat sink in. "I reckon you know I'm a man of my word, and I never meant anything more in my life than what I just said," he finished.

"I'll say you'll stay for good," Miller put in, and none there doubted for an instant that he, too, meant exactly what he said.

"What do you want to know?" asked Lowell, seeking to bolster his falling spirits with an air of bravado.

"Are you runnin' with Burness?" asked Andrew, stepping closer.

"Why, I don't even know where he is," replied Limpy with a blank look.

But Andrew and Miller both read the true answer to the question in the gunman's eyes.

"All right," said Andrew in a voice of finality. "That's all." He turned toward his horse with a nod to Miller. Ed Munsey stepped quickly to Lowell's side.

"Wait a minute!" croaked Lowell. "What you goin' to do?"

"Nothing," Andrew said, taking up his reins. "I'm leaving."

"Not yet!" cried the gunman in a shrill voice. "You ain't told Miller to let me go. I answered your question." His tone became a whine, and Dick's lips curled as he gazed at the man.

"Sure you answered it," Andrew said grimly. "But you lied."

Lowell leaped forward on his good leg, but Ed Munsey caught him and whirled him about. "Not so fast," said the cowpuncher. "You ain't goin' any-where, Limpy. You're stayin' right here."

"Listen, French . . . come here!" shrieked the gunman.

"I gave you a chance," Andrew said sternly. "Now I know what I wanted to know without you tellin' me in so many words. Burness is up this way somewhere, and you've been trailin' with him. So was Rodgers. Why, it's spread all over your rat face."

"But, listen. You goin' to let 'em . . . ?" He couldn't get the dreaded words out of his mouth. They gurgled in his throat.

"Why not?" Andrew asked sharply, walking back to him. "No one would ask much about you . . . unless Burness should get curious. And he'd get the same thing. You won't even be missed, and, if you are, there'll be a dozen sheriff's glad of it."

Lowell's face was pale now. "I been runnin' with Burness," he blurted. "So was Blunt. Burness was in the Snowies, but I don't know if he's left the hills or not. So help me. . . ." He stopped and the rage surged into his face. All five men listening knew he had spoken the truth.

Andrew's lip was curling in contempt. "You're as low as a man can possibly be made, Limpy. You'd double-cross your best friend, if you could have a friend. You're scum. I'm goin' to let you sneak back and tell your story to Burness. Just tell him I'm waiting for him, if he wants to come, you rat."

"I'll tell him, you . . . ."

The vile epithet had barely passed Lowell's lips when Andrew's right fist shot out, landing fully in the gunman's right eye. Lowell was knocked sprawling on the grass, his right hand clutching futilely for the gun that was missing from its holster.

"Take that black eye back with you, Limpy," Andrew said scornfully. "Show it to Burness. Tell him it's my card, understand? Tell him we'll be lookin'

for him any time he's ready to come. As for you"—
Andrew turned to Miller—"put him on a horse and
send along two men to see that he gets on his way.
Send him without a gun. Give him six hours' start,
and then order every Two-Bar F man to be on the
lookout for him, and to shoot him on sight."

CHAPTER THIRTEEN

When Bill Klein cautiously emerged from the trees across the river south of town, after riding in swift pursuit of Blunt Rodgers's companions, he checked his horse and looked quickly up and down the river and across the plain that stretched southward. Instead of six riders, only one was in sight.

Klein pursed his lips and whistled softly. The lone rider was riding fast, leaving a trailing swirl of dust. In a short time he would be out of sight. As it was, the horseman was rapidly becoming a mere dot on the sweep of prairie. He was heading toward the southeast, and Klein knew the town of Muddy Flat was down there—a questionable town with a small population, mostly composed of shady characters. It was a halfway stopping place between the north and south ranges.

It didn't take Klein long to make up his mind. His best bet, he reasoned, was to follow the one rider in sight and not waste time, with dusk coming on, trying to find the others. He would find out who this rider was and where he was going. It might be—yes, there was a chance he was making for Burness's headquarters. Len Miller had told him a thing or two, and had given him free rein as to his movements. In any event, Ed Munsey was on his way to the ranch, or would be shortly, and there was a possibility that Clint and Dick would go on home. Klein hesitated no longer. He struck out after the distant rider. The man had a good start and a good horse, and Klein didn't expect—nor wish—to catch up with him. But he did want to ascertain his destination before night fell.

If the rider became aware that he was being followed, he gave no evidence of it. He continued on his course into the southeast at a stiff lope while the sun went down and twilight shaded the land. When night came, Klein was convinced that the town of Muddy Flat was the rider's objective. The prairie was bunching now into slight ridges, coulees, and miniature ravines. Soon the black shadow of timber loomed, and Klein knew he was approaching town. He swung off to the east and crossed a creek before he turned straight south in the direction of the town. He never had been in Muddy Flat, and had no reason to think there would be anyone there to recognize him, although he had worked for the Two-Bar F for more than ten years straight.

The going became rougher, tall cottonwoods grew along the creek, there were clumps of scrub fir and buckbrush. It had been dark little more than two hours when Klein saw the yellow lights blinking through the interlaced branches of the trees. He came into town about the time the clash between the Two-Bar riders and Limpy Lowell and the others ended.

Muddy Flat was well named. It was perched on the edge of a great flat of gumbo that stretched southward, with the rugged country at its back. It would be unapproachable from the south in wet weather. Although it took its name from the flat, it was its appearance that justified the name. Its one short street was without sidewalks. The few buildings were unpainted and weather-beaten, the houses little more than shacks. There were three resorts in the place, all similar in appearance except that one was larger than the others. The legend, HO-TEL, was painted on the one building that boasted a porch. At one side of it, set back some distance from the street, was the livery barn. Klein rode to the barn first to put up his horse.

The liveryman was a stoop-shouldered, thin man of uncertain age with a shifty gaze. He peered at Klein, made certain he didn't know him, and seemed satisfied. "Come far?" he croaked with a smirk. "Ain't many ridin' these days."

The cowpuncher knew at once what he meant, just as he sensed the class of trade that this man thrived on. Also he saw his opportunity. "Not so far," he said casually, pressing a gold piece into the man's right palm which was handy. "Expected a . . . a friend to ride in ahead of me," he continued, with a wink. "Anybody just in?"

"Somebody come a bit ahead of you," said the liveryman. "Don't know who he was. Tall, sandy mustache, diamond ring." He looked at Klein swiftly as he mentioned the ring, for that would be a distinguishing mark on any man.

"Isn't him, I reckon," said Klein. "He ain't got money enough to sport a diamond ring any more'n I have . . . right now." He winked again, and the other favored him with a knowing grin.

"It's the off season," said the liveryman. "Here all night?"

"I suppose so," said Klein carelessly. "Maybe my

man's gone on to Conroy. Take sweet care of that hoss."

He went out pleased with the information he had obtained. He would be able to spot the lone rider almost the moment he saw him. Anyway, it was a relief to know he had come to Muddy Flat.

Bill Klein believed in luck, and, when he entered a small, drab-appearing café to get his supper, he knew luck was with him. On the next stool but one, at the counter where he sat down, a man was eating. He had sandy mustaches, and on the middle finger of his left hand he wore a diamond ring. Here was the rider he had followed. He couldn't remember having seen the man in Conroy, and so assumed he had gone there with Blunt Rodgers and had fled with the others after the fight and the shooting. Regardless of where the others had gone, Klein could not bring himself to believe that this man had just fled the scene and stopped in this town by chance. The cowpuncher ordered a piece of pie and coffee so he would be through in time to follow his man when he was through. There was a chance that this man had just happened along, but to Klein such a coincidence would be too farfetched. He finished his pie and coffee, and rolled a cigarette while the other was finishing his meal.

Klein paid his score, and went out just behind his man. The other crossed the street and entered a resort that happened to be the largest one in town. Klein waited a few moments, looking up and down the deserted street with its yellow beams of lamplight streaming from windows and doors, then crossed the street leisurely and entered the place of gaming and refreshment.

The man with the diamond already was at the bar

as Klein noted with a swift glance about the room. No Stampede, this, but a dirty, smoke-begrimed room with a battered bar, plain tables, and sawdust on the floor. The light in the place was dim, for the lamp chimneys needed cleaning. Not more than twenty men were in the place.

Klein stepped quickly to the bar, apparently noticing no one. He signaled the bartender and ordered a drink. This gave him an opportunity to observe his man through the medium of the spotted, dusty mirror over the backbar. He was talking with another man who was the center of a group that comprised most of those present. Klein caught one word: "Blunt." It was spoken in a loud, startled voice by the man in the center.

The others spoke to each other in asides, and then there was a general medley of voices, and Klein made out that the conversation was about Blunt Rodgers. It was the man in the center of the group who interested Klein most. He was a tall man and superbly proportioned for his height and weight. His face was dark and full, his eyes black, his lips thick. He wore a black mustache, neatly trimmed and, by his features, Klein placed him as a quarter-breed Indian or possibly part Mexican. He smiled once, and his teeth were white and even and flashing. In a way, the man was handsome.

The bartender pushed back Klein's money. "Party down there is buyin'," he explained. "Stranger? 'Puncher, maybe?"

Klein realized instantly that explanations of a sort were in order when a newcomer entered the place. "Yes," he answered. "And I reckon I'm a 'puncher, too. So you've hit it off right at the start. Who'd you say was buyin'?"

"Burn-'Em-Up," said the bartender with a wink, and withdrew.

Klein had heard of the nickname—Burn-'Em-Up Burness. He offered a silent prayer of thanks to the goddess of luck and raised his glass. He put it down suddenly as a hand touched his left arm.

"Wait for the rest of us," said a deep voice.

He turned to the speaker and found a rough-looking man with a stubble of beard, thick-set, with a pair of sharp gray eyes. There was nothing particularly aggressive in the man's look or manner, but Klein resented the intrusion.

"Who's the rest?" he demanded,

"Everybody on the rail," was the swift rejoinder. "Or . . . are you drinkin' alone?" The man was looking at him keenly.

Klein changed his tactics. "No," he replied in a more friendly tone. "But nobody was payin' any attention to me, and I don't know which one is buyin' the drink, and I can't afford to buy one back."

"That's all right. I'll drink with you." The speaker picked up a glass from the bar, nodded to Klein, and the two drank.

"Just get in?" the man asked, signaling the bartender.

"Had time to eat before I drifted in this place," replied Klein. He had caught Burness looking at him in the mirror twice, and now he suspected that the outlaw had told the man who had accosted him to find out what he could. He was on his guard, but he welcomed an opportunity to get acquainted with one of the bandit's followers.

" 'Puncher, ain't you?" asked the other as they were served again.

"Mostly," Klein confessed, "but I'm not workin' just now."

"This is supposed to be a tough town," said the man, "but I reckon you know it better'n I do."

"Never been here before in my life," said Klein. "Doesn't look to me as if there was enough of it to make it very tough."

The other laughed and flashed a look over Klein's shoulder. Klein was certain it was a signal, but could only guess as to what it meant. Perhaps the man was telling his chief that he, Klein, was harmless. The cowpuncher strove to make that impression.

"Been workin' up north?" asked his companion.

"Out east," said Klein with a frown. "Where you from?"

"South. My name is Warren. I do odd jobs at the tables."

"My name's Bill," said Klein, looking the other squarely in the eye. "Was it that big fellow down there who bought the drink?"

"Don't you know him?" Warren appeared surprised. "Yes, he set 'em up. He's a spender. This is a good town to spend in."

"No town is a good town for me to spend in," grumbled Klein. "I'm flat . . . almost. But I won't be that way long if I have to . . ." He cut his words short with a sharp glance at Warren.

"Sure." The man nodded. "I know. I've been there myself."

"Let's take this drink," Klein suggested with another frown. "Is that big fellow buyin' again?"

"No, I bought this," Warren replied, taking up his glass. "It won't hurt us any, and I'm doin' a little spendin' myself."

At this moment there came an interruption. The

bar shivered under the impact of a heavy fist. "Blunt was a fool, and Limpy's worse!" The words seemed to crash in the room.

Klein looked, and saw the face of Burness black with anger. There was a short silence. Then several spoke to the outlaw at once.

"The big fellow seems mad about something," Klein observed.

"He's had a few," said Warren evasively. "Good man to let alone when he's that way." His glance at Klein was cold as ice.

"Tough, eh? Maybe he's the one who runs this town," said Klein.

"That's about it," the other assured him. "When he wants to."

"Who's he talkin' about?" Klein asked with a scowl.

"Oh, they're probably havin' some kind of an argument."

"Shut up!" The words cut through the rising voices, and Klein looked to see Burness glaring about him. It was the outlaw who had given the command, and the talking ceased abruptly.

"Since when has anybody been givin' me advice?" Burness demanded, banging the top of the bar again. "And tonight's your last night at this stuff, understand?" He jerked a thumb at the bottle on the bar. "I'm still givin' the orders . . . don't let that get out of your heads."

In the silence that followed, the door suddenly burst open. A man came in with a rush, a man as large as Burness, if not larger. He stopped halfway the length of the room, almost opposite to Burness and the men with him.

"Who wants it first?" he shouted, closing his fists

and peering out from under black, bushy brows that matched his mustachios. "I'm the bull from the Musselshell, I am."

"And this'll help you on your way back there!"

Burness swept several men aside with his left arm, and leaped. His right caught the wild celebrant fully on the jaw, knocked him over a chair to the floor. But Burness was not through. He grasped the fallen man by the collar and dragged him to the door. There he jerked him to his feet and hit him again, knocking him through the door. The outlaw's eyes were burning with red murder as he whirled on the others. "I'm still givin' orders," he roared, "and carryin' 'em out if I have to!"

He stepped back toward the little group just as a gun cracked outside and six bullets splintered the door and embedded themselves in the wall.

But Burness had leaped again. His right hand held a gun. The draw had been so fast that Klein realized he hadn't seen it. The door burst open and the big form of the newcomer loomed again. A short report rocked the room, and the man went to his knees with blood trickling from his forehead, just between the eyes. Then he plunged forward on his face.

Burness looked over the man's body at the group at the bar. "Any more?" he shot between his teeth.

None spoke.

"Then we'll drink to another playmate for them below," said the outlaw, starting for the bar. "The Bull and Blunt ought to make a team!"

CHAPTER FOURTEEN

Klein had stood motionlessly with his back to the bar while these kaleidoscopic events had taken place with incredible swiftness. Now, he watched Burness step lightly back to his place and smile. The men with him broke their silence timidly. Two others dragged the lifeless body away, leaving a wide, bloody trail in the sawdust. Klein's face was white, and his eyes narrowed when he looked at his companion.

"Nice amiable sort of gent, isn't he?" was his comment.

"Can't blame him," said Warren with a shrug. "Bull was drunk. He shot through the door, and then busted in to get it. He usually carries two guns. He might have known better. He would have known better if he had been in his right mind."

"Oh, you know him, then," said Klein. "Bad actor, eh?"

"Not bad enough to fool with Burness." Warren uttered the name in a sibilant tone, drawing out the last letters in a hiss. He looked at Klein sharply.

"So that's the big fellow's name, eh?" Klein saw no reason why he shouldn't profess ignorance, just as he saw no reason why he shouldn't plead he was broke. He didn't want to get into any game because he didn't wish to stay in town more than overnight. It was his intention to be on his way at daylight so he could report what he had learned to Andrew French. He felt sure that Burness was behind Blunt's activities in Conroy. And he knew now that Burness's reputation for being a killer—inexorable, tricky, and dangerous—was well founded. The dispatching of the man called Bull was nothing short of deliberate murder. And such speed with a gun! Klein was not slow to realize that he himself was in a dangerous spot. If Burness knew he was a Two-Bar F man. . . .

"Better down your drink and don't let what you've just seen worry you," Warren advised. His glance and the nod that went with it were significant and were not lost on Klein.

"It's none of my business," Klein said with a shrug, taking the drink. He had to play safe. He could take no risk of not getting away from town next morning, unharmed.

"Want to play a few cards?" Warren asked. "You might win a small stake if you've got enough to come in for a little stud."

Klein shook his head. "Nothin' doin'," he said. "And no more likker. I got a long ride ahead of me tomorrow. I'm tired and I'm goin' to bed. Suppose there's a bed at the hotel?"

"Reckon so," said Warren. He was again looking over Klein's shoulder. "I know the proprietor up there, and I'll walk up with you. I haven't got anything else to do, and it looks like this bunch was in to make a night of it."

He led the way out the door and they walked in the dust of the street to the hotel. Inside the small lobby, Warren spoke to the sleepy-eyed clerk. "Fix this man up," he ordered. "He's a friend."

"Sure," yawned the clerk, pushing a stub of pencil out on the desk. "Put your name on the book, mister."

Klein wrote in a jagged scrawl something which looked like Bill Smith, with Warren peering over his shoulder. He rummaged in a pocket and brought forth a ragged $5 bill. "Reckon that'll more'n pay it," he said in a grumbling voice.

"Just right," said the clerk, his eyes brightening up momentarily. "First door on your right at the head of the stairs." He handed Klein a key attached to a piece of wood.

"Well, you're all fixed," said Warren. "I'll say good night."

"Good night," said Klein. "I'm much obliged to you."

Klein went upstairs, entered the first room on the right, and, leaving the door open, struck a match with his left hand. His right was on the butt of his gun. There was a lamp on a small table in the center of the room and he lighted it. There was a bed, a bureau with broken mirror, two straight-back chairs, and a washstand. He closed the door and turned the key in the lock. He knew full well that Warren had accompanied him to the hotel to ascertain his quarters, and to make certain he was staying for the night. There was no question in the cowpuncher's mind that Warren was a member of the Burness gang.

He put his hat on the bureau, took off his coat and boots. A glance at the window showed a green shade tacked above so that it reached halfway down the upper pane. The window was half open.

Klein unbuckled his gun belt and put it on the bureau. The gun he dropped at the head of the bed. Then he blew out the light in the lamp, and noiselessly moved a chair to the window.

He sat down and looked out. The open space in front of the livery barn was just below. He could see the lantern hanging in the barn. The moon and starlight shone coldly down. No one was in sight. It was nearing midnight, and for a moment Klein considered changing his mind about waiting until morning to leave. Why not steal down and leave at once? He decided immediately, however, that this wouldn't do. If anyone associated with Burness was to see him go, it would excite suspicion and he might have a chase on his hands. Burness was not one to be poorly mounted, and Klein was not familiar with the country in this section. It would be the better part of wisdom to wait until day broke. By that time, the outlaw leader and his men would doubtless be through with their carnival and asleep.

They had no reason to suspect him of anything, and it seemed but natural that Burness would wish to keep an eye on any stranger in town, especially after the killing of Rodgers. The bandit had made it all too plain that losing Rodgers had angered him. Klein was trying to remember the name Burness had connected with that of Rodgers, but couldn't.

After an hour at the window, Klein lay down on the bed. He dozed and woke when he heard footfalls on the stairs. Someone was going to a room and having trouble negotiating the steps. Finally a door slammed and all again was still.

Klein was a light sleeper, and it was the pound of a horse's hoofs in the dust of the street that woke him the second time. He sat up in bed and heard the rider turn into the livery. In a moment he was up and at the window. A man was dismounting near the door of the barn, and Klein saw the night man shuffling out of the little front office.

"Take care of this horse," came the gruff command on the still air of the night. "I had to ride pretty hard."

Now another man came walking swiftly around the front of the hotel from the street. The rider had left the livery, and the two men met almost directly beneath the window of Klein's room.

"Where are the others?" asked the man from the street.

"Dead or grabbed," was the sharp answer. "Did Moore get in?"

"Just after dark. Said you fellows rode up the river to head off the French pair. You seem excited. Did you . . . ?"

The speaker was interrupted by a volley of oaths from the rider who had just arrived. Klein sensed that by Moore, the man meant the rider Klein had followed to Muddy Flat—the man with the diamond. The cowpuncher now knew at least two of Burness's followers by name, Warren and Moore.

"A bunch from the Two-Bar F mixed in on the play," the rider was saying. "Rode in on us from behind before we knew they were within miles of us. I was lucky enough to get away. They got three of us, and the last I saw of Limpy, he was turning a somersault over his horse's head. Come on. I want a drink and Burn-'Em-Up will want an earful. Well, I've got enough to fill both his ears."

They walked around to the street, out of earshot. But Klein had heard enough to enable him to size up the situation. He again lay down on the bed. Limpy? The name was vaguely familiar, but he could not recall anyone who it fitted, could not even remember when or where he had heard it. But the fact that

Blunt's companions had tried to ambush Clint and Dick was enough. His duty was to get back to the ranch as fast as possible. He slept when he had decided this was all he had to worry about.

Brilliant sunshine was streaming into the room when Klein next awakened. He sat up with an exclamation of chagrin, rubbing his eyes. Accustomed as he was, at this time of the year, to going to sleep after dark and turning out in the hour before dawn, it seemed ridiculous that he should oversleep. "Must have been the likker," he muttered to himself as he pulled on his boots. "Wasn't very good stuff, at that." He looked at his watch and found it was seven o'clock.

Donning his gun belt, with his weapon snugly in its holster, he put on his hat and coat and went downstairs. There had been no water in the pitcher on the washstand so he went to the barn to perform his ablutions. The cold water roused him thoroughly. The man in charge at the barn was not the man who had taken his horse the night before and Klein noted that the few stalls were occupied. But he did not find his horse.

"Where's my horse?" he asked the barn man. "Bay gelding with two white forefeet and . . ." He bit his lip as he suddenly remembered that his mount wore the Two-Bar F brand.

"See him here?" asked the barn man languidly.

"No . . . is he outside?" Klein demanded.

"Dunno," was the listless reply. "I wasn't here when you rode in, was I? There's some hosses in the corral out back. Might look there."

Klein knew, as he strode to the rear of the barn, that he would not find his horse. This was a move to keep him in town, of course. His face darkened with a scowl. But he could blame no one but himself. Why hadn't he left his horse outside of town? And then have to explain why, perhaps? That would have looked more suspicious than to have ridden right in boldly, as he had done. After all, there were plenty of horses on the north range bearing the Two-Bar F iron that were not the property of the French hands or of the ranch.

Klein grew angry. He walked back to the barn man. "Hey, you . . . you, I'm talkin' to!" He grasped the man by the arm and jerked him forward. "Wake up and tell me where my horse is. If you don't snap out of it, I'll hand you a crack on the jaw that'll bring you to!"

The man pulled himself away, his eyes narrowing. "I don't know anything about your hoss," he said in a loud, shrill voice. "If you get gay around here, you'll stop something hot."

"Yeah? From you, huh? You're a yellow liar!"

"Here, here, here!"

The voice came from behind him, and Klein recognized it instantly. He whirled to confront Warren. "You know I rode in last night, don't you?" he demanded. "I put my horse up here, and this yap says he don't know where it's at. The other man put it in a stall. Just told me I'd stop something hot if I didn't . . ."

"Beat it!" cried Warren in interruption. But he was addressing the barn man, who immediately walked away and entered the barn office. "Had breakfast?" he asked Klein coolly.

"No, and I don't eat till I know where my horse is," Klein raged. "If somebody has stole my horse, I'll get him if I have to chase him across the line or down to the border!"

"I don't expect anybody has stole your horse," said Warren. "Just take it easy and come have a bite of breakfast with me."

"Say," Klein said, wrinkling his brows, "are you travelin' with that big fellow who did the shootin' last night?"

"What difference does it make who I travel with?" Warren cleverly avoided.

Klein realized that it made no difference whatsoever, insofar as what he could say was concerned. "Well," he said in a less antagonistic voice, "I thought maybe some of that crowd was drinkin' and might have made off with my horse by mistake."

"Don't worry about your horse," Warren said sharply. "C'mon and have some coffee and maybe I'll tell you something."

Whatever the intrigue might be, Klein was now determined to see it through. He accompanied Warren to the little café where he had eaten the night before. He remembered that the man who had ridden in during the early morning had referred to a man as Moore, and it had been Moore who had raced from town to tell Burness of Blunt Rodgers's killing.

They both ordered ham and eggs.

"I'm a cowpuncher myself, now and then, when I've got to do a dog's work to get by," Warren confided when they had given their order. "I know what it is . . . eighteen hours a day on hard leather, eatin' dust and soakin' up rain and gettin' ready to die off young. A man don't have to be very smart to be a cowpuncher."

"It's bein' a whole lot smarter than gettin' in jail or goin' hungry or ridin' the line," growled Klein. He believed he knew what his companion was getting at and wondered if he was to be invited to join the Burness band. The prospect thrilled him. In any event, his horse had been taken to prevent him from leaving unobserved.

Warren was looking at him keenly. "What makes you say that?"

"Because you act as if you had something on me because you're not punchin' cows," Klein retorted. "I don't know what you're doin', and I don't care, but you've got something up your sleeve or you wouldn't buckle up to me the way you do and talk that way."

"You could do worse than listen to a thing or two I might be able to tell you," said Warren crossly. "You're not so dumb."

"What makes you think so?" asked Klein.

"I can tell a man who's been around the minute I lay eyes on him," was the rejoinder. "You ain't punched cows all your life, either."

"No? Well, then, you know more about it than I do."

"And if you have, it's nothin' to brag about," Warren said with a sneer.

"There's no use in two strangers quarreling over nothing," Klein observed. "If you can steer me to something easy, I'm willin' to listen. But I wouldn't be ready to promise anything."

"Don't worry," said Warren. "I'm not tryin' to steer you. But Burness said he might like to talk with you before you moved on, if that means anything to you."

"Oh! So he had my horse put away so I couldn't leave, eh?"

His companion said nothing, but the cowpuncher realized he had hit the nail on the head. Doubtless, Warren had been delegated to ride herd on him all night, and see that he didn't leave town. And now, for the first time, Klein wondered if the outlaw had an inkling of his identity as a Two-Bar F rider. The brand on his horse.

The waiter brought their breakfasts at this juncture and they fell to eating. Warren ate silently without once looking at Klein, and the latter did the same. Klein decided he would let Warren take the lead in any conversation. He wondered if the others were asleep.

When they left the café, Warren suggested that they drop in at the resort where they had met the night before and see "what's doin'."

"I'm losing time," Klein grumbled. "If this Burness wanted to see me, it's a wonder he couldn't have said so last night when I was handy. Suppose he told you to keep an eye on me . . . is that, it?"

"Maybe he did," replied Warren to Klein's surprise. "But if he did, you ought to feel flattered, boy, instead of makin' out you're mad. Burness don't take up with every stray 'puncher that comes along. If you look good to him, it might be something in your pocket to act polite. But I'm goin' to get one thing off my chest. Burness wants to see you, and you're goin' to meet up with him before you leave town, whether you like it or not. That'll save us a lot of talkin'."

"It's sensible of you to tell me," said Klein. "What's . . . what line is this Burness in? Or maybe I'm not supposed to ask questions."

"Now you're beginnin' to get wise." Warren nodded. "Questions won't do you no good unless you ask 'em of the right party . . . and I ain't that party."

Klein smiled. "You know how to say things between words," he observed. "It isn't hard for me to figure out that, if I've got anything to ask, it's up to me to ask Burness. Well, if I'm stuck here till he sees me, I hope it won't be long. I haven't got any prospects in this town as far as I can see."

"Maybe you're not lookin' in the right direction," Warren hinted. "Let's drop in here."

They entered the resort. Klein saw two men at the bar and half a dozen others playing stud poker at a table in front. They merely glanced at the new arrivals.

"You want a drink?" Warren asked Klein.

"It's one thing I don't want," snorted Klein. "And if I did want one, I'd ask him where he keeps the good stuff."

Warren laughed, and the bartender shot the cowpuncher a sharp look. "Burn-'Em-Up been around this mornin', Mac?" asked Warren.

"You know better'n that," the bartender replied. "If he shows up at noon, it'll be about right. But I look for him 'bout 'leven."

"That's fair enough," said Warren. "We'll have to stick around," he told Klein. "Don't get sore, because there ain't anything else to do. Maybe I'd like to be hittin' the hay myself. I ain't had much sleep. Got enough to play a little low-stake high jack?"

"Just about," said Klein.

They sat down at a table to play cards until Burness arrived.

When they started to play, Warren brought forth a huge roll of bills—yellowbacks, every one—and deliberately winked at Klein. "It's yours if you can win it," he said with a grin. "And I didn't make it punching cattle, either."

"That doesn't mean a thing to me," Klein said calmly. But his eyes gleamed feverishly at sight of the money, nevertheless. He had about $100 on his person—an amount that he always carried—but this didn't mean that this sum was all he possessed in the world. He brought out a lone $10 note. "That's my table stake," he announced. "You might say we're playin' to pass the time."

"Sure." Warren nodded. "I don't want your money, and I wouldn't play a good stake against a thin bank roll, either. Go ahead and deal. And listen, Bill, when you do meet Burness, handle him careful. It'll pay to listen to what he has to say, and then . . . if you're not interested . . . it'll pay you to forget it." His look was significant.

"There's just one thing you can tell me, if you want to," said Klein in a low tone. "Was that fellow you called Bull, who got shot last night, travelin' with Burness?"

Warren frowned. "Why . . . yes," he hesitated. "Oh, there's been bad blood between those two for some time, and Bull had it comin'. You needn't worry about that affair. That was private. Burn-'Em-Up is a square shooter. Bull thought he was goin' to catch him in front of that door when he sent those six bullets through it. He was never so drunk he couldn't shoot, and that was one trouble with him, see?"

"I see," Klein said. "It happened mighty sudden, that's all."

Warren made no further comment. As they played a leisurely game, with Klein a small but steady winner, more men entered the place and the bar gradually was lined. There was no loud talking this morning, no cursing or singing or quarreling, and, although none of the men apparently paid any attention to him, Klein intercepted many surreptitious glances directed at him, and knew he was being sized up by the men. That they all were in the same band was evidenced by the fact that they knew each other and there was a friendly atmosphere of familiarity and comradeship about their intercourse. There were more in the place before noon than had been there the night before. Burness doubtless had his whole gang in this isolated rendezvous, and Klein estimated the outlaw's outfit's strength as forty to fifty men. This could mean but one thing, in his opinion: Burness had a big job coming up.

It was exactly noon when Burness came in. He was alone, and his keen eyes swept the place twice as he went to the bar. A place was made for him at once. Klein was surprised at the deference shown this outlaw leader. It amounted to polite respect. Perhaps the brutal killing of Bull the night before had something to do with it. But it was also quite apparent that his men treated him in an altogether different manner when all were cold sober. Klein sensed that the drinking bout the band had been enjoying was over, and evidently over by command of Burness. The Two-Bar F cowpuncher suspected that Burness had issued an ultimatum that every man must be on his feet with a clear head by noon.

"Gimme a double snort," he told the bartender briskly. "The bunch been behavin' this morning?"

"Gettin' their bearings in good shape." The servitor smiled.

"Quit grinning!" snapped Burness. "I can see for myself."

CHAPTER FIFTEEN

Burness gulped his drink and followed it with a glass of cold water. The man with the diamond, as Klein knew him, was first to receive a nod from the chief. This man, Moore, joined Burness at the bar and the two talked in an undertone. Klein saw Warren stealing furtive glances at the pair. Somehow, Klein felt Burness's personality to a marked degree in the bright light of day. It did not take him long to realize that the chief did not hold his band loyally together by mere gun skill or harsh tactics alone. The man was a natural leader in his nefarious business just as much as other men were able in directing an industry or legitimate enterprises.

The talking had died down when Burness entered and it remained subdued until Burness issued a sharp order. "Spread 'em all around, and listen, you men! This is the last easy one. It'll be poison by night."

It was in this way that the chief subtly gave the order to stop indulging to any length and to quit entirely by night. Klein was conscious of a vague uneasiness. What, after all, did Burness wish to see him about, and, if matters were not to his liking, what would he see fit to do with him?

The men had hardly downed their potations of the fiery liquor when a grotesque figure burst in the door and paused, momentarily blinded by the gloomy interior of the room after coming in from the blazing sun. It was Limpy Lowell. His clothes bore a fine film of dust, indicating to the practiced eye that he had just finished a long, hard ride across open prairie. He had, in fact, just arrived in town after riding from the Two-Bar F Ranch. His holster was empty.

"Come here!" Burness roared the command in an angry tone.

As Lowell's eyes were now accustomed to the light in the place, he recognized Burness first as the result of the outlaw's loud order. He apparently had not seen Klein, who had recognized him after short search of his memory. He knew him only as Limpy, but the identification sufficed. About ten years before, in fact the very year that Klein had first gone to work for the Two-Bar outfit, this Limpy had been involved in a petty rustling game, on the north range, that had failed. There had been no rustling to any extent since. This was partly why Limpy Lowell's features and his limp stood out in his memory. But at that time, long since passed, Limpy had been associated with no such outfit as Burness boasted. Burness constituted a genuine menace to the peace of the range.

Klein was greatly concerned because of the advent of Limpy, although he was by no means sure that Lowell had been with the men in town. If the little gunman should recognize him. . . . Klein smiled, and Warren thought it was because he had drawn good cards. But he smiled, as he remembered that, while Limpy looked much the same, Klein was older and now wore a mustache. He believed himself to be safe from identification with the Two-Bar F.

"Have you made a fool of yourself, too?" Burness was asking.

"A fine mess!" Limpy exploded, with an oath. "Gimme a beer, barkeep, so's I can wash the dust out of my throat."

"I wish there was something you could wash your brains out with," Burness snorted as Lowell drank the beer and signaled for more.

"Listen!" Limpy's red-rimmed eyes flashed angrily as he addressed Burness. "Blunt was runnin' that business in Conroy, and you know it. This was the first time I'd been in. I didn't know French had two kids and that they looked just the same. If Blunt didn't know it, he should've knowed it for he's been in town often enough. He tackled the one of them, and in the fight the other one bored him. How was I to know that . . . about the other one, who's just got back, I mean? They're twins, I guess. You can't tell 'em apart!"

"I'm not askin' you what happened in town!" roared Burness, slamming the bar with a thick palm. "Maybe I know more about that than you do, you runt. Mebbe you don't even know how many shots were fired. But what you been mixed up in since? You blow in here with a black eye. And where's your gun?" he asked with a sneer.

A hot retort was between Limpy's teeth before he thought better of it and bit it off. "Old French sent that black eye with his compliments to you," he said, nodding in a leer, "and he said he was ready and waitin' for you any time you wanted trouble. They took my gun and I had sense enough to ride straight here, instead of blowin' back to Conroy for a new one."

"Oh, uhn-huh," Burness said, scornfully. "You let 'em grab you, eh? What was you carryin' a gun for in the first place? You told where you was from and let 'em plaster you and then make a messenger boy out of you, eh? I allers thought you was yellow and I reckon I've known you just ten years . . . too long."

Limpy caught the menace in Burness's tone and caught himself for a second time on the point of bringing the business to an end—for him. "The rest of us followed the French brothers out of town," he explained hurriedly, "after Moore started for here to tell you that Blunt was bored for keeps. We sprung an ambush on the French boys and had 'em gathered in when the whole Two-Bar outfit swung in on us unawares from upriver. I don't know if anybody got away or not, but my hoss stepped in a hole and threw me, knockin' the gun out of my hand. That's how they got me and I know enough to talk straight with you."

"If you do, it's the only sensible thing you do know," said Burness grimly. "It's lucky for you that I happen to know you've talked straight so far, 'cause one of the boys did get away. Let's hear what you've got to say 'bout what happened after the French outfit got you sewed up. I reckon somebody poked you in the eye and you got off by spillin' the beans all over that range. And then sneaked back here. If I find out that's how it was, I won't even bother to shoot you. I'll tell off two or three of the boys to hang you."

"No!" Limpy Lowell choked on the word. "I didn't tell 'em a thing about you!" he fairly shrieked. "I told 'em I was runnin' with Blunt and that he'd been shot down in the fist fight. They threatened to hang me, too, but didn't go through with it. I wasn't armed, and old French gave me this eye when I talked back to him. They let me go, told me to beat it in any direction I wanted, and go as far as I could think of. Then they shot at me as I was ridin' away. I made sure that nobody followed me, just the same. But old French does think you're around and he thinks Blunt and me was ridin' with you. When he told me to tell you what I said, I sneered in his face. That's what brought on the trouble 'tween him and me. He thinks I'm small fry." Limpy swore and downed his second glass of beer, shaking his head when the bartender looked at him inquiringly.

Burness frowned. There was just enough logic in what Limpy said to make his explanation appear plausible. And Lowell's last squeal, that French thought he was "small fry," convinced him that Limpy was, indeed, telling the truth.

"What'd they do . . . take you up to the ranch house?" he asked. "Remember, I'm not sayin' I believe what you say. But if you lie to me, I'll find out soon enough. You can lay to that, you sap."

"They took me to the camp where they're brandin' on the lower range," Limpy replied in a tone of relief, "and tied me up for the rest of the night. Old French and his two brats rode down in the mornin'. I couldn't tell 'em apart. But one of 'em can shoot and the other can't. I know that much."

"Sure," Burness remarked dryly, "you know that much. Now the thing for you to do is find 'em and draw down on 'em, and the one that drills you will be the one that can shoot. That's easy enough."

There was a general laugh at this, to Limpy's discomfiture, but Burness silenced the merriment with a single look at the semicircle of faces. "If another man laughs, I'll just naturally shove it down his throat with two fingers," he threatened in a slow, soft voice. He turned again to Lowell. "You know that country up there?" he asked.

"Knowed it for years," Limpy boasted.

"But you know it better now?" the outlaw suggested.

"Yes, I suppose I do," Limpy acknowledged.

"Lay off the hard stuff," Burness warned with a scowl. "Go throw something to eat under your ribs and catch some sleep. Then maybe I'll be willin' to give you orders again. Slope along."

After Limpy had gone out, Burness turned to Moore. Another man joined them at a signal from the chief, and Klein surmised that this might have been the man who had ridden in early in the morning after escaping from the Two-Bar F riders who captured Limpy Lowell. They talked quietly for some minutes, and then Moore and the other went out.

Burness drank a long glass of water. Others were filing out of the place and this seemed a source of satisfaction to their leader. "Grub and coffee . . . that's the ticket now," Klein heard him tell a pair that looked very well washed out. As the Two-Bar man heard this and saw the looks Burness cast about, he decided, whatever job Burness had in mind, it now was getting time for the first move. Not once, since he had first moved to the bar, had Burness looked in Klein's direction. But now he turned and walked to the table.

"Let's go in the back room a minute," he suggested to Warren.

"Sure," said Warren. "Won't take us but a second to settle up here."

"Bring him along," Burness said, jerking a thumb at Klein.

"Right with you," promised Warren as Burness moved to the rear.

"Looks like he maybe wants to take you on," whispered Warren as they settled up the game. "But watch your step, 'puncher."

When Warren and Klein entered the single room in the rear of the resort, they found Burness seated at a green-topped card table, lighting a cigar. "Sit down," said the outlaw, without looking up. Having lighted his weed satisfactorily, he looked keenly at Klein. "What're you doin' here?" he demanded.

The cowpuncher knew he had to think fast and make the proper replies. "I'm waitin' for my horse," he answered without hesitation. "When I tried to get him or get word of him, Warren here suggested maybe you might want to see me. So I waited."

"You needn't have waited," said the outlaw. "Your horse is in the livery and has been there all mornin' so far's I know."

Klein believed Burness was lying, but he hardly knew what reply to make to this bold statement that the outlaw made with apparent unconcern. The outlaw was cool and collected, but Klein knew there was something behind it all, but just what this was . . .

"Where'd you come from?" Burness asked, his voice hardening.

"I don't know who you are, 'cept by what I've been told," was Klein's cool answer. "Just why should I answer your questions?"

Burness did not flare up at this. He appeared, rather, to relish it. "Because if you don't answer 'em," he said, playing with the words, "I'll have to beat the answers out of you, that's all. You sneaked in on my range last night and I want to know why."

"It was on my way," Klein returned. "I couldn't miss it."

"Yeah? From where, and to where?"

Klein bristled. He was keeping an eye on Warren as well as on Burness. At the first slight indication of hostilities, he meant to go for his gun. He was not slow with his weapon. He believed he could beat Warren to the draw, but he would have to draw on the outlaw leader first, beat him to it, and fire before he could deal with Warren. It was a ticklish situation, but in the face of danger the cowpuncher cooled. "I was on my way from that first town up north," he said evenly. "Conroy, they call it. And beating it to the south range. I've never been through here before."

"Then, how did you know the town was here?" Burness inquired craftily.

"I stumbled on it," Klein retorted with a scowl.

"You wasn't sure you'd hit any town last night, eh?" The outlaw's eyes had narrowed. "How come you pushed into this place?"

"I expected to find a town somewheres along the creek down here. I came into this place after eating, for an hour or so, and picked it out because it was the biggest joint in town."

"You mean to tell me that you would start on a long ride like that without a speck of grub in your slicker pack?" Burness demanded sternly.

"It wasn't takin' such a big chance. I could expect to find a ranch down here. And I've gone more'n one night without grub. The fact that I'm travelin' light is due to my low funds, maybe. Or maybe. . . ." He was losing his bearings and ceased talking.

"Maybe is right," Burness said with a sneer. "You had money enough to slip something to the livery-man. Isn't that so?"

"What of it?" countered Klein, his face reddening a bit. "I've got to pay for the keep of my horse in town, haven't I? And if I'd hit a ranch, I wouldn't have had to pay for my horse or for grub for myself."

"But you didn't hit any ranch and I reckon you didn't expect to hit any ranch. You could have bought enough rough grub to last you quite a while with just what you gave the liveryman. Now, then, what was your idea in followin' a man, one of my men, from Conroy down here? Answer that!"

"I didn't know the rider I saw was one of your men, and I don't know it yet," Klein replied harshly. "I saw a rider ahead late yesterday afternoon and took after him fast as I could, expecting he was headed for a ranch. When dark came, I lost him. I kept on and then saw the lights through the trees. I didn't know if it was a town or a ranch."

By this time the cowpuncher knew Burness was smart. "Well, your not makin' any bones about following this man is on your side." Burness frowned. "Where was you goin' in the south?"

"Lewistown, first, then maybe Miles City," replied Klein.

"If I was you, I'd drop that word, maybe," said Burness. "It won't get you anywhere, one way or the other. If you left Conroy yesterday, then you saw the gun play up there."

Instantly Klein shrewdly decided not to deny this. "I saw it, of course. Everybody was in the street watchin' it. It was one reason why I quit town so sudden. I was a stranger there and they'd be sure to ask me questions I might not want to answer."

Burness laughed a short, sneering laugh. "How come you've got the Two-Bar F iron on your horse?" he asked in a grim voice.

"It was on there when I bought it and I ain't never

changed a brand on a horse yet," Klein replied boldly.

"Got a bill of sale, I suppose," Burness suggested meaningfully.

"No, but the sale's all right." He simulated concern. "That's a big outfit up there somewheres and there's any number of horses wearin' that brand that can be bought. Buyin' a new horse, and a better one, was what near broke me. If anybody can prove I didn't come by the horse square, he can have the horse and me, too. And I can't afford to lose him."

Burness burst into a guffaw, but he sobered instantly and his eyes hardened. "There's no reason why I should fool around with you any longer," he snapped out. "You're workin' for the Two-Bar outfit. Think I'd be fool enough not to know that? I'd know it even if the man you followed hadn't seen you in town with another Two-Bar skunk the day before the trouble. Why, you ain't even a good liar and that old fool of a French ought to have taught you that."

Klein's eyes were narrowed to slits. So it was going to be a shooting. He felt certain it would do him no good to pretend longer. He would not have pretended in the first place if he hadn't thought it was his duty to get back to the ranch and report as quickly as possible. And Warren had been faking all the time. He flashed a look at Warren, but the man's face was expressionless.

"Know that fellow who came in with the hard luck story a little while ago?" Burness asked rather casually.

"I know him for a sneakin' little rat who tried to get away with some horses and cows up north some years back and didn't have the nerve or the brains to get away with it!" Klein flashed.

"Sure you do." Burness nodded. "And you heard what he told me, too."

"Couldn't help but hear it the way he bawled it out to you."

"You needn't think you're the only one who knows he's brainless and yellow," said Burness sharply. He looked at Klein with a quizzical expression. "You know, of course, that that fool Blunt fired a shot . . . one shot. But there were three shots fired. Guess you know who fired one of the other two shots. Do you know who fired the third?"

"No," Klein answered without an instant of hesitation.

"I don't believe you do," said the outlaw. "But I do. Get up!" He leaped from his chair as Klein dove for the floor, jerking out his gun in a trick draw.

The room rocked with the crashing report of the outlaw's gun and Burness laughed as Klein's weapon was knocked from his hand. The cowpuncher sat on the floor, holding his numbed right fingers in his left hand. They were dripping blood.

"Go on and finish it," Klein gasped out. "I'm not puttin' it past you."

"I wouldn't shoot you on a bet!" cried Burness. "Go back to the Two-Bar and show those fingers to that old fool French. You needn't be ashamed to tell him you tried to draw with me. Tell him I let you go home with a crippled gun hand rather than kill you. And tell him that's my answer to the message he sent by Limpy Lowell."

He turned to Warren, standing near. "Tie up his hand and put him on his horse and start him home. Ride far enough with him to see he don't make for Conroy. He's tricky and, if he don't mind what you say, give it to him for keeps. If they find him in the grass, it'll be just as good. His horse would carry back the news."

Then Burness stamped out of the place, slipping Klein's gun in a pocket of his coat.

Something seemed to snap in Klein's brain and blackness closed in, shutting out the entire world about him.

CHAPTER SIXTEEN

When Bill Klein regained consciousness, he was lying on the floor of the back room in the Muddy Flat resort. Warren was there with him alone. A pail of cold water was on the chair nearby, and the cowpuncher's face and hair still were wet from the drenching he had received to bring him to. Warren was bandaging Klein's right hand.

"Didn't think you'd pass out entirely," Warren said when he saw Klein's eyes open and clear. "You wasn't hit bad. There isn't any doctor here and we don't need one. I'm fixin' you up all right. But you'll have to watch it when you get back to the ranch."

Klein strove to sit up, but Warren put a hand on his chest and pushed him down. "Wait'll I get this hand done up," he ordered. "Then you can get up and take a drink and get started. You surely were a fool to try to draw on Burn-'Em-Up."

"What was he doin'?" Klein asked belligerently. "He was goin' for his, wasn't he?"

"Never made a move to get his gun out till you made that trick fall," replied Warren calmly. "Now you can tell 'em how fast he is. You wouldn't have had a ghost of a chance, anyway, with me here in the bargain."

"Reckon not," Klein said angrily. "You knew what was up all along, you . . ."

"Don't get heated up," Warren commanded sternly. "Burness ain't in the habit of tellin' what's on his mind ahead of time. I didn't know any more'n you did, except I had orders to see that you didn't leave town, and I thought Burn-'Em-Up was goin' to ask you to join up with us. I didn't know you was a spy and I'm not blaming you for lyin' your fool head off when I did find it out. You're mighty lucky in two ways, 'puncher, if you only knew it."

"I'm lucky I'm alive for one thing," snorted Klein. "Burness would have killed me in a second if he hadn't wanted me to go back to the ranch with some kind of a story about what a terrible man he's supposed to be. He's wadin' in the syrup if he thinks he can throw a scare into Andy French or the Two-Bar outfit."

"I wouldn't talk too heavy if I was you," Warren warned him, deftly continuing with his first-aid work. "Burness wouldn't have killed you . . . he wouldn't even have wounded you if you hadn't made that break. In fact, I guess the chief enjoyed trappin' you in your story. He intended to send you back . . . I'd bet my roll on it. But you was lucky in that fast gun play that he didn't hit where he didn't intend to, see? You was wormin' like a snake and in a second you'd have shot."

"What of it?" Klein spat out viciously.

"I wouldn't shoot off my mind too swift," said Warren. "He might change his mind. If Burn-'Em-Up hadn't been such a swift and sure shot, he wouldn't have took a chance on knocking your gun out of your hand. What's more, he's treatin' you better than you think. Your fingers'll heal all right, and, after they get limbered up again, your gun hand will be as good as ever, I'm thinkin' . . . although I'd be a bit more careful with it, if I was you."

"Thanks," said Klein dryly. "How else was I so lucky?"

"You're dog-gone lucky in havin' me to look after you," replied Warren with a sober nod. "Burn-'Em-Up practically left it to me to take you out near the ranch and leave you with your face in the grass for them to find you. I ain't that kind, it happens, and the chief knows it. He trusts me, if I do say it myself, understand? I'm one of the boys who don't drink much, for one thing, and he picked me for an important job in watching you."

Klein considered this thoughtfully. For some reason, he had been inclined to believe this man from the start. "So you don't intend to plug me in the back at all, then?" he asked curiously.

"Nope," Warren replied, working fast. "But I'm tellin' you, 'puncher, that it won't be healthy for you to try any tricks. I'm depending on you havin' enough sense to do as you're told and be quiet."

"I could make a lot of trouble, couldn't I?" Klein said with biting sarcasm. "Here I am with my hand tied up and my gun gone. Who got my gun?"

"Burness took your gun," answered Warren. "He gave it to the barkeep to raffle off among the boys as a joke. It won't pay to get mad at that, either. It won't pay you to do anything but mind. And you needn't try any faintin' stunts with me, either. Sit up, I'm through. How does it feel?"

Klein got up and sat in the chair. "Feels all right," he said. "Gimme a big glass of that water, will you?

I've been hit worse than this and didn't faint, as you call it. I reckon I passed out because I was so all-fired mad . . . and helpless. But you can bet your roll I wasn't scared none. Much obliged for this job on my hand."

"Here's the water," said Warren. "Don't you want a good shot of hot likker? Wouldn't hurt you any."

"No, thanks," Klein said, drinking the water gratefully. "It wouldn't be good for me with a man's-size ride ahead in the hot sun."

"Well, let's get started," said Warren. "Feel able?"

For answer Klein stepped briskly to the door. He had not seen fit to tell Warren that the fainting spell was due to a heart affliction to which he had been subject for years. Even Andy French and Len Miller at the Two-Bar were unaware of this. It was dangerous for him to become overexcited. Only his close pal, Ed Munsey, knew he was taking a big chance in working cattle. But Klein wouldn't be at home in any other kind of work and consequently carried on. However, the knowledge that the tension he was undergoing might prove fatal at any moment had nothing to do with Klein's drawing his gun on Burness. The man was fearless. Even now, he regretted he had lied to the outlaw in the first place and yearned to tell him so right to his face.

They went out a rear door and proceeded to the livery barn. Klein was disappointed when he saw that the man who had originally taken his horse and his money was not there. He had wanted to say a few words to that fellow.

"Get the Two-Bar horse," Warren ordered the man on duty crisply, "and remember everything's paid. I'll get my own horse."

Warren tied a small slicker pack behind his saddle and mounted with Klein. They rode out of town, apparently unobserved, by a different way from that by which the cowpuncher had entered the night before. The trail took them out of the tumbled country in a short time and they turned true northwest, with the three blue pyramids of the Sweetgrass Hills to guide them. Klein had ridden ahead, following directions given him by his conductor, in the wild section about Muddy Flat, but now they rode side-by-side and the Two-Bar man was soon aware that his outlaw companion knew the country.

The sun was beginning its long dip into the west. Warren set a moderate pace, which Klein estimated would put him on the Two-Bar range by sunset and seven o'clock. Reasonably sure that he would not be shot down in cold blood, he began to worry about his range partner, Ed Munsey. But Limpy Lowell had said nothing about any of the Two-Bar men being hurt. Klein suspected that Burness had reserved further questioning of Limpy until Klein had left. Then, too, there was the likely possibility that Munsey had started for the ranch ahead of the French brothers.

"Hey, Warren!" he called suddenly. "Did Limpy or any of 'em say anything about anybody from the ranch bein' hurt in the fracas?"

"Not that I know of," Warren answered. "You'll find out when you get there. I'm goin' to leave you when we hit the river, above here, and ride back down along the river, although I don't think you'd be fool enough to try to ride clear back to town."

"Don't worry about that." Klein scowled. "And you want to edge in toward the river so the boys can't take after you if they should see us comin'. I asked about anybody bein' hurt because I've got a runnin' pardner with the outfit I think a lot of ... that's all."

Warren nodded. For some reason a bond seemed to have sprung up between these two men—one a cowpuncher, earning an honest wage, and the other an outlaw. Ordinarily there should be a gulf between them.

The afternoon wore on with the sun slanting low in the west. Warren now changed their course so that they rode due north for the river. When they reached the edge of its timbered banks, he slowly reined in.

"Here's where we part," he announced. "Your best bet is to ride straight west along the river till you reach your range. Don't worry about me. If a bunch from your outfit tries to chase me, they'll run into something worse than a bunch of hornets' nests. So long."

"So long," said Klein, "and I don't know exactly why I should, but I feel pretty much obliged to you. Too bad you ain't in a better business."

"I'm satisfied," said Warren coldly. "Now I've got a few drops in a bottle along if you think you might need 'em before you get home." He seemed actually anxious that Klein take the drink.

"Nope." Klein grinned. "Anyway, my drinkin' hand is out of commission." He held up his bandaged right hand.

Warren made no comment. He whirled his horse and set off at a stiff pace down the river. Klein rode slowly westward, twisted in the saddle to watch Warren out of sight. If the latter should decide to take a few pot shots at him, he could jump his horse into the trees. But Warren apparently had no such intention and only looked back over his shoulder two or three times.

Klein increased his pace. He felt tired already from the long, hot ride. He thought he knew just about how clever Burness was. He would tell Len Miller everything, and then would probably have to repeat his story to Andrew French himself. What had happened since he had been gone? He knew the story of the fight on the range.

Just what moves had Miller and French made after they had released Limpy that morning? He didn't doubt for a moment that French and Miller had wrung the truth from Limpy and had actually sent him to the noted outlaw with the message of defiance. And his being away all night and all day would not necessarily worry Miller. The foreman would assume he had run across a clue and was following it.

Taking it all in all, not forgetting what he had seen in Muddy Flat, especially the killing of the outlaw called Bull, Bill Klein considered he had been lucky. Burness could easily have killed him and none would have been the wiser for days. Perhaps the outlaw had a double motive in permitting him to go back to the ranch. It might be that Burness hadn't drawn until Klein had dived to the floor and had gone for his gun. It was possible that Burness was sending him back to the ranch to lead the Two-Bar F outfit to expect an attack in that quarter while he attacked in another quarter. Klein was struck with the idea. And suppose they had actually gone through his pockets. What would have been the outcome in that event?

Klein was favoring his right hand, and riding with the reins in his left as usual. Now he bethought himself of something and secured the reins to the saddle horn temporarily. He reached into his left hip pocket with his left hand to make sure his roll of bills was there. He swore suddenly, the horse lunged ahead, and he quickly regained the reins with his left hand. *Easy*, he was saying to himself, *easy, Bill. Don't get excited. Just keep as calm as you can.*

The bills were gone. Klein never kept his roll in any other pocket. The money he had spent in Muddy Flat had been loose in one of his trousers pockets. Someone had stolen his roll. In a flash he fixed the blame. Warren had done it while Klein was unconscious in the rear room of the resort back there.

Warren! An outlaw Klein almost had come to like was just another mean, sneaky outlaw. "They're all alike," he said bitterly aloud. Then he pulled up his horse as he saw a rider ahead, coming toward him. In a few moments he recognized the well-known form of Ed Munsey in the saddle, and breathed a deep sigh in relief.

Munsey reined in his horse with a wave of greeting. "Just startin' out to look for you, Bill," he said. "They. . ." He stopped, his face showing plainly his grave concern. "You've been hurt, Bill!" he exclaimed. "Your right hand is tied up and your gun's gone! Who'd you meet up with, Bill? And with that tricky heart of yours. Bill, I'll kill whoever did this."

Klein held up his left hand in a gesture that stopped the flow of talk. "Never mind about the hand and the gun being gone, Ed. You'll hear all about it quick enough. Not so bad as you think. As for the heart, Ed, I believe it's a lot better than I thought. Let's beat it to the ranch *pronto*."

CHAPTER SEVENTEEN

After the frantic departure of Limpy Lowell in the early morning from the lower camp on the Two-Bar F range, Andrew French and Len Miller, his manager foreman, went into consultation, with Dick and Clint French and Ed Munsey, trusted cowpuncher, in attendance.

"So Burness was, and is, at the bottom of it," Andrew said with a deep frown. "But what I can't understand is why he should want to get Clint, here, or Dick. Maybe he didn't know I had two boys. But Blunt certainly was out to get Clint. Anybody could see that. And I believe Limpy told the truth when he said that both he and Blunt had been runnin' with Burness. Blunt isn't runnin' with anybody now, but Limpy is, and he's on his way to report to Burness."

"I reckon you've got it straight, boss," said Miller. "That's the way I figure it out, although I go further than you do."

"Eh? What do you mean by saying you go further, Miller?"

"We'll get right down to brass tacks," said Miller. "There are cattle missin' down here, boss, whether you like it or believe it, or not. We're short, goin' on a hundred head, or . . . wait a minute. We're short goin' on fifty good cows and, if they all had calves trailin', we'd be short goin' on a hundred head. I've had men out lookin' for those strays . . . we'll call 'em that . . . for several days, but not one animal has been spotted. They're gone, boss, and they were sneaked off easy in pairs or some such fashion."

"Are you sure of this?" French asked his foreman.

"Well, you know I'm not the kind to talk out of the side of my mouth," Miller said with a trace of indignation. "I've been hintin' right along that I thought something was wrong, but you wouldn't listen."

"I had Dick's coming on my mind," Andrew said, dismissing with a wave of his hand the implication that he hadn't been interested in his stock. "Seems funny that Burness would come up here and sneak off with a few head like that. He's supposed to travel with a big bunch at his back and to be out for big game and nothing else."

"That's just the point," drawled Miller. "I don't believe Burness knew a thing about these cattle bein' stole. He ain't the sort to stop halfway of a complete and profitable job. This is the same kind of a trick Limpy Lowell tried up here ten years or so ago. You heard what Limpy said. He said him and Blunt Rodgers had been trailin' together. All right. Blunt's nerve and brains were better than any Limpy ever had. Limpy could talk him into this thing and maybe show him how easy it would be, since we ain't been watching our stock so hard of late years. And Blunt could engineer the rustling and make a go of it. I figure that this stealin' up here was done by Blunt and Limpy, with some others helpin' 'em without Burness knowin' a thing about it. You might say, it was sort of a sideline."

"By golly, there's something in it!" Andrew exploded, smiting the palm of one hand with the fist of another. "But the trouble with Clint in Conroy." He looked at Clint keenly. "You say he started it, Clint. Talk straight turkey, boy.

"He didn't have to make much of a fuss to have me call him," said Clint dryly. "But there's no getting around it, he did start it."

"There you are, Miller. You can see that Clint is telling the truth. In fact, Clint never has deliberately lied to me yet."

Dick smiled at Clint at this and the two youths winked at each other. Neither of them ever had deliberately lied to Andrew French about anything to which importance could be rightfully attached.

"I know Clint wouldn't lie about it," said Miller, "but I don't know why Blunt should pick on him. It may just be that, when Blunt found he couldn't bully Clint, he made it a personal matter. It sure couldn't have been Burness's orders because what good would it do that bandit? Burness don't usually advertise himself when he's in a section with a job in view. And, if he had a job in view here, the last thing he would want would be trouble with any of our outfit . . . especially with one of the heirs of the ranch, for that would be noted quick."

"Dad, can I say something?" Dick French asked.

Andrew brightened. "Sure," he said in a pleased voice. "Go ahead. You've got brains." Andrew seemed to want to impress the rest.

"Oh, I wouldn't want you to tell that around, Dad," Dick said, laughing. "But it looks to me as if it were a personal grudge on Blunt's part, as Miller says. What's more, from the way that Red Tower, who runs the Stampede in town, talked last evening, I'm convinced he really didn't want Blunt hanging around his place. He was afraid of

Burness . . . that is the whole secret. I mean Tower is afraid of Burness. He didn't dare say anything to warn Clint because he was afraid Blunt would get wise. There's something else I believe. We talked with Tower after we had seen the sheriff. I picked up the gun on his desk because he was pretty sore at us. This annoyed him and made him nervous. When I broke the gun and spilled out the cartridges to find one empty shell, he turned pale for a spell. I believe Tower saw a chance to shoot Blunt during the fight and what followed, and not be blamed for it. Consequently I think it was Red Tower who fired that third shot."

Silence that lasted several seconds followed Dick's speech. Even Clint stared at him, impressed, and Ed Munsey's jaw dropped in astonishment. Andrew and Miller looked at each other, and Miller nodded.

"Might be," said the foreman. "It sounds like Red's style."

"It wouldn't surprise me a bit!" Andrew blurted out. "Did you say anything much to him, Dick?"

"I asked him if he had been doing a little target practice," replied Dick, "and he didn't answer. I surmised enough by the look in his eyes and the way he acted to convince me that he fired the third shot. I didn't accuse him of it because I thought it would be better to let him think I wasn't too suspicious of him."

"And a sensible thing to do," Andrew said heartily. "But there's this much to it, Miller. If Burness didn't have any idea of coming up here, he will have when Limpy gets back and tells him a few things. Limpy'll make it look as black for me as he can. The first thing to do is get the cattle down here up into the valley."

"And there's another thing," Ed Munsey broke in. "Bill Klein ain't back yet and I'm worried. I think I ought to set out to look for him, and I don't think I ought to lose any time gettin' started."

"No!" Andrew thundered. "Bill isn't back because he's hit on something and he's followin' it down. Bill can take care of himself. Miller, don't you let a man leave this ranch. Those are my orders and I expect them to be carried out, understand?"

Miller nodded. "I get you. I need all the men here anyway." He turned to Munsey. "I don't think we need to worry about Bill," he said. "I think like the boss that he's on a trail, or maybe he's off somewhere where he can't leave in daylight. If he isn't back tonight, there's still plenty of time to start lookin' for him . . . and spoilin' his play, maybe."

"But I know something about Bill," Munsey began—and stopped his talk. He had promised Klein never to speak of his infirmity. Klein had exacted his promise and he had to remain loyal.

"Yes," Miller prompted. "But just what do you know about him, Ed?"

"He's . . . he is liable to take too big chances," Munsey stuttered, holding true to his trust.

"You think that because you are his sidekick." Miller smiled.

Munsey reddened, but he had no reply to make to this.

"Not a man off the ranch, Miller," Andrew repeated. "I want this herd close in by night. Dick and Clint, come on . . . we'll go back up to the house." He caught up his bridle reins.

"Why not let us stay and help with the cattle?" Dick suggested. "Looks to me like Clint and me ought to be doing something in a time like this.

Clint knows cows and I can do something, that's sure."

Andrew looked bewildered. It was as if thought of Dick's working on the ranch had never once occurred to him. He looked at Miller with appeal in his eyes.

"Wouldn't be a bad idea," said the foreman, catching a meaningful look from Clint. "I can use 'em both."

"Well," said Andrew in indecision. "Well . . . all right. But they're not to go lookin' for strays, understand that. And if you get tired of it, Dick, come up to the ranch house where you belong."

He swung into the saddle and rode off. After all, he did feel as if he wanted to be alone. Perhaps he had an idea in the back of his head that this was one of those rare occasions when he should seek the counsel of Susan Enfield. For the first time in many years, Andrew French was not sure of himself this day. He was worried, although he wouldn't have acknowledged it for worlds. But Burn-'Em-Up was no mean enemy. Perhaps he had made a mistake, after all, in letting Limpy Lowell go back to the outlaw leader. What was this? Was he getting old; was he doubting the worth of his own judgment? Norman Webb might have gone to seed in town, but Andrew would have welcomed his company this day. He confessed so to himself.

Ed Munsey, whose worry showed plainly in his eyes, tackled Len Miller as soon as Andrew French had gone. "Listen, Len," he pleaded. "Let me work on the strays so I can sneak out of the timber once in a while to look and see if Bill is in sight comin' back. I've got a reason to worry and I just can't tell you why, because . . . I promised Bill. And I'm a good hand at findin' strays if there's any around, or dry tracks for that matter."

Something in his manner caused Miller to grant his request. "But don't ride off the ranch," he said sharply. "Those are orders."

"I won't," Ed promised. "I've been tending your orders a long time, Len . . . and so has Bill." He rode away contented.

Clint and Dick worked through the long, hot day and were about to knock off at sunset and ride to the ranch house that was close by when a shout from one of the men startled them and Miller. They looked and saw Bill Klein and Ed Munsey riding up from the creek. Klein's bandaged hand showed plainly in the failing light.

"Here comes news!" cried Miller, and spurred his horse toward the approaching riders. Dick and Clint followed him quickly.

"What happened?" Miller demanded of Klein when they met. He was surprised to see Munsey signaling him to be cautious. Then Munsey put a hand on his heart and nodded significantly while the trio, which had ridden to meet them, stared in surprise.

Klein's face was rather white. "It's quite a story," said Klein. "But I saw and talked with Burness and he gave me this and said to show it to the old man as an answer to the message he had sent to Burness."

"You saw him and talked with him?" Miller gasped. "But. . . ."

"I've had a long ride from Muddy Flat," Klein said with a frown. "I suppose I'll have to tell what I know to the old man, as well as you, Miller. Suppose we go to the house so I can tell you both at once.

I . . . don't feel any too well. I had to drink some rotten whiskey while doin' this job and it must have got me."

Andrew French, his two sons, and Miller listened to Klein's story in the living room of the ranch house while the sun sank behind the western hills and the twilight gathered its purples, blues, and golds. Once Klein asked for a "snort of good likker" and got it immediately. When he had finished, Andrew asked a few questions to fix certain details in his mind. Then he looked at the circle of faces about him. His own face was stern; his eyes gleamed.

"Burness is starting something tonight," he said finally. "He isn't coming here . . . yet. I think he had Blunt in Conroy looking over the lay for a bank robbery, or maybe Tower's place. But he'll be comin' here next, sooner or later, we can count on that." He rose. "Susan!" he called. When the housekeeper appeared, he pointed to Klein. "Look after him, Susan, he's hurt," he directed. As the housekeeper led the wounded cowpuncher away, Andrew turned to the others.

"Get half a dozen men to the chuck wagon for supper quick and pick 'em careful," he ordered Miller. "Clint and Dick will eat here with me, and then we're startin' for town."

An hour later, Andrew, with his sons beside him, and Miller, with six picked men behind, were riding swiftly eastward toward town. Dick and Clint had insisted on going and Andrew had not held out against it. Munsey had stayed behind to nurse his wounded and exhausted friend. The balance of the Two-Bar F outfit was stationed below the ranch house.

Night had fallen. And with the first outcropping

of stars more than two score riders had moved across the shadowy plain south of Conroy. It would take Andrew French and his outfit three hours to reach town.

CHAPTER EIGHTEEN

Tower had worried and fidgeted in his little private office in the Stampede in Conroy for more than an hour after Dick and Clint had left. He picked up his gun and reloaded it, taking a cartridge from the top left drawer of his desk to replace the empty shell that Dick French had appropriated. Then he had spilled out the loads and had carefully cleaned and oiled the weapon. With its cylinder again full, he had put the gun in the top left drawer of his desk where he ordinarily kept it.

He was nervous, muttered to himself, and paced the small room with a scowl on his face. When an employee—the bartender who was also his bodyguard—reported that the men who had been with Blunt Rodgers had left town, he breathed a sigh of relief. "I want you to keep a sharp eye on me," he told the man with a knowing look. "And here's an extra fifty so you won't forget." He gave the man a bill. "I want you to keep a sharp line on who comes into the place, too."

These instructions given, Tower went out to the bar and took a stiff bracer. The rest of the afternoon and early evening, he kept aloof from his customers.

His bodyguard reported the departure of the French boys, and of Bill Klein and Ed Munsey. None of Blunt's companions had been seen since the fight and shooting.

Gradually Tower's spirits returned. He spent the night jovially, even joking with Sheriff Wilson when the latter dropped in twice before midnight, which was unusual. He went home to his cabin at one in the morning, and no word was brought to him of the fight on the range west of town. Neither did he receive any word the day following, since both the Burness men had returned to Muddy Flat, and Andrew French kept his knowledge to himself. Even the sheriff was unaware of the new trouble.

Just what the sheriff would do about the killing of Blunt Rodgers wasn't known, but the opinion was freely voiced about town that nothing would be done to Clint French, who was generally considered as being responsible for Blunt's death. "Andy French is too big a man," they told each other with wise nods, despite the fact that both Norman Webb and the sheriff himself had boasted there would be no fatal shootings in Conroy without swift action on the part of the authorities. But it was pointed out that Webb was a close friend of Andy French and that Pansy Webb and Clint French were going together in "steady company." The citizens wisely avoided questioning Wilson or Webb personally.

But the sheriff did not remain idle the day following the trouble in town. He buried the body of Blunt Rodgers and made some discreet queries in certain directions that brought slight information. Among other things, he learned from Dr. Crane, who had known nothing of how the fight had been waged, that the bullet that had killed Blunt had been fired from the left side. Both Clint and Dick were directly in front of the victim when he had fired the first shot. In the early evening, at almost the hour when Bill Klein had been making his report to Andrew French, Wilson had been in close conference with Webb.

"Why don't you go up there yourself?" Wilson had demanded.

"Because . . . well, Andy French and me are too good friends," Webb had evaded. "Besides, I nosed in about us . . . Andy and me . . . maybe doing something to cool young Clint down a few days back, and I don't think he liked it. He would probably resent seeing me coming up there, but it would be natural for him to expect you to come, Sheriff."

"If I had my way about it, I'd let things stand just where they are," the sheriff had snapped. "Blunt Rodgers was no good."

"But what has he been hanging around here for?" Webb had asked.

"Oh, I'll go up," the sheriff had decided savagely. "But that's all I'll do in that direction. I'm sheriff of this county and this business falls in the course of my duty. But I'm goin' to make my own investigation in my own way, and act when the time comes."

That very evening he started west at about the time Andrew French and the others left the Two-Bar. When they met, there was bound to be a conference, after which all might go into town, or French and his men might return to the ranch, leaving Wilson to go back to town alone.

It is not to be supposed that Burness didn't have an agent in town. Anyway, within an hour of the time of the sheriff's departure, a numerous band of riders swept into the timber along the river from the south. The town was built in a bend of the river with the trees close on two sides.

Red Tower looked up from his desk with an exclamation of annoyance as the door of his private office opened and a man stepped in without the formality of knocking. But the exclamation died in his throat and his jaw dropped as he recognized the intruder at first glance.

"That's it," said Burn-'Em-Up Burness as he pushed back his hat so Tower could see him clearly. "Don't do any loud talkin' and don't yelp. Don't worry. I won't shoot you if you act hostile. I'll just tie you up and gag you. I've got about twenty able men inside this joint who know their business, and I've got thirty more outside. And I'm in command personally, you understand? I haven't forgot how to run things since the last time we met, Red. But it was foolish of you to beat it with a thousand or so. Why didn't you take plenty while you were at it? You couldn't even have got away with fifty . . . forever." The bandit's voice was low and cool, and carried easily to Tower's ears. At the mention of a former association between the two, the resortkeeper's face went white.

"I didn't have a thing to do with it, Burn-'Em-Up," he protested earnestly. "Honestly, I didn't and I can prove it." The gun—out of reach in that upper left drawer—and, even if he had it in his lap, it would be foolhardy to attempt to touch it.

"I have plenty of time for what I intend to do," said Burness. "Even the sheriff has left town. Gone up to chew the rag with old French, I reckon. And Webb will have a couple of visitors from his front yard if he tries to leave the house again. But I haven't got time to listen to you lie. I even know, and can prove, to the fraction of a cent what you took out of the kitty when you beat it long before you'd ever heard of this place. Why, you've been expectin' me, haven't you? You knew I'd come sooner or later, didn't you? Honest, now."

Tower gulped and inclined his head slightly. "I mean I didn't have a thing to do with this fight and killin' here," he croaked. "I thought Blunt was run-nin' with you and as much as asked him to tell you I wanted to see you . . . that I'd even go to where you was."

"Sure." The outlaw nodded. "Blunt told me. But I had made up my mind to come and see you when I was ready. Meanwhile, I had Blunt investigating a few things. I happen to know that you're afraid of banks, for some reason. Practically everything you have is in that big safe there, or hidden somewhere around close. If you don't dig it up, that'll be just your own hard luck. We'll let the other go. I'm col-lecting my principal with the interest, and that last item comes high, Red . . . with me, it does."

"You're . . . you're goin' to . . . rob me!" Tower gasped out.

"Be careful of your language," Burness warned in a stern voice. "I'm goin' to collect, Red . . . make it that way . . . goin' to collect."

"But you'd know naturally I'd be a fool to keep much. . . ."

"Cut the lying!" Burness interrupted savagely. "I've warned you!"

Tower looked into the cold, hard eyes of the out-law and saw something in their depths besides rob-bery, something. . . . "Since you don't go in for small jobs, I'd think you'd take the bank, while you're at it," he mumbled, perspiration breaking out on his forehead. He reached to a hip pocket for his hand-kerchief and saw Burness's right hand fall lightly on the butt of his gun. "Just . . . a handkerchief," he stammered, growing red in the face.

"It wouldn't make any difference, Red," Burness said easily as the resortkeeper mopped his brow and face. "I'm figurin' that you haven't got any idea of committin' suicide, though. Now, suppose you open the safe."

Tower's face went white again and he seemed frozen in his chair with his hands gripping its arms. Burness stepped to the door and tapped twice upon it. It opened instantly and two men entered. The victim in the chair needed no second look to apprise him of the fact that these men were members of the Burness band.

"Just want you to keep an eye out here, boys," said Burness. "If Tower, here, gets excited or anything, grab him, gag him, and tie him up. If any shootin' has to be done, leave it to me." His last words carried the metallic ring of grimness. He stood over Tower. "Now, Red, is this goin' to be orderly, or am I goin' to have to put you through the works? I haven't got as much time as I had when I drifted in. Now I mean business." He pointed to the safe.

Tower rose on legs that seemed made of lead and dragged himself in front of the safe. Burness was at his side and now the outlaw's gun was in his hand. Tower spun the dial of the combination disk and soon the big, heavy door swung open. There was a second door that Tower opened hastily as Burness's gun tapped him on the shoulder. Perhaps Burness would kill him after all. Tower went cold.

When the second door opened, a number of locked compartments were revealed as well as two drawers and spaces for books on either side. Burness grunted with satisfaction. "I'll give you credit for having a good safe, Red," he said, almost in a genial tone. "It would take a first-class man, such as several I carry, a few minutes to crack this box thoroughly. Unlock the strong boxes, Red, and, if you're goin' to fumble with the keys, I might as well take 'em and do it myself. If there ever was a time to hold your nerve, it's now."

Nevertheless, Tower's hands shook as he sorted out the keys on the ring he carried and opened the locks. He had hardly done this when he was grabbed unexpectedly from behind by Burness's companions and quickly tied and gagged and thrust into a chair. One of the men covered him with his gun. Burness nodded approvingly.

The outlaw chief now took a saddlebag from one of the men and opened the drawers and compartments one by one. He took out thick packages of yellow-backed bills of big denominations from the compartments, three small sacks of gold, and packages of bills from the drawers with a large amount of silver. All but the silver, he placed in the leather saddlebag. The bag of silver he gave to one of the men to carry. Then he ordered the gag removed from Tower's mouth.

The gun was in the bandit's hand again. His eyes were cool and alert. "Call your head bartender," he instructed Tower. "Call him in such a way that he'll come pronto without suspectin' what's goin' on. I've got men out there at the proper points and, if you try to give a warning outside this room, they'll promptly shoot your men at the bar and tables and take what they have. You haven't got a chance, Red, and I hope for your own sake that you realize it by now. I'm doin' a clean-out job here, if I ever did one in my life."

Burness opened the little door leading to the rear of the bar and Tower called: "Jim! Come in here a minute." After all, it would be better to have his head bartender, who was also supposed to be his bodyguard, handy in this dire emergency.

When the man stepped into the office, he was confronted by the outlaw's gun as Burness quickly closed the door behind him. "Take it easy," the bandit warned. "This is a stick-up . . . a real hold-up bein' carried out in a quiet businesslike way. If you'd rather have it the other way, just make a false move and we'll start the rough stuff . . . start with you and Red first."

Tower was shaking his head in warning to his employee. "Is it all right to tell him who you are?" he asked Burness. "It'll make him all the more careful, maybe. We don't want any rough stuff, Jim."

"Oh, I know," said the man in a low voice. "I'm just workin' here for a livin', Mister Burness"

"Then you must be livin' pretty high," the bandit said in disgust. "Just drop the mister and carry out my orders and you can keep on livin', whether it's fat or lean livin'." He turned to the man who had been covering Tower. "Call Warren," he ordered.

When Warren entered, Burness issued his instructions carefully. He spoke directly to the head bartender. "You'll go to every man in the slot at every table and collect his surplus in bills. Move quietly and manage to smile so as not to disturb the players or make 'em suspicious. If the surplus isn't large enough, I'll let you know when you get back. Be careful, understand?"

"I understand," said the man as Tower nodded energetically.

Burness turned to Warren. "Trail this man at a distance, and at the first sign of a signal or other trouble, drop him. Take what he has. The other boys will know what to do when they hear the shot."

The bandit motioned the man called Jim out the door and was obeyed. Warren followed. Burness told the man in charge of the bag of silver to stand where he could see outside without being seen himself. Then Burness sat in a chair opposite Tower, with his gun across his knee. "I've improved a bit in my methods, don't you think so, Red?"

"I want to see you get it over with," replied Tower. "You're takin' all I've got."

"It won't take you long to get another stake together," Burness said casually. "You had more'n I thought in here."

Tower's spirits rose and his face glowed dimly. Then Burness really had no idea of shooting him after all. He would be satisfied if the outlaw allowed him his life.

There was no further talking, and, in a shorter space than he had expected, Tower saw his man enter with Warren following him. Warren closed the door. Burness took the packets of bills that the man disgorged from his pockets. These he stuffed into the saddlebag and buckled it.

"I'm goin' to leave you what's behind the bar to operate on," he told the man, Jim. "You can give the alarm any time after we've gone. I'm leaving two men here and either one of 'em can hit you with a bullet as easy as hittin' a barn door. Tower, here. . . ." He paused suddenly and everyone in the little room was alert. From somewhere outside came a dull detonation like a distant peal of thunder.

Warren and another man made a leap for Tower. In a second his thongs were cut. "Not a word out of you," Burness snapped. "Take him along." He turned to the bartender. "You stay here and tell the sheriff it was a neat job. That was the bank you just heard blow up." With a harsh laugh he hurried after his men and Tower, and they left by the rear door before anyone knew what was up.

CHAPTER NINETEEN

Outside the resort, Tower found himself hustled toward the trees with one of the outlaws on either side of him, pulling him forward by his arms. The resortkeeper now realized that the bank had been attacked. Why was Burness taking him away? A great fear surged within him. He shrieked in terror. One of the men dropped his arm and the next instant he went down and out from a powerful blow to the jaw. He was to regain consciousness finding himself held on a horse with a rider behind him.

Burness, with the saddlebag suspended from his shoulder by a strap, had sped swiftly for the rear of the bank. There, Limpy Lowell was emerging, white-faced. "I cracked it for keeps," he told Burness.

"What're you runnin' away for?" roared Burness, drawing his gun.

"They're bringin' the stuff!" cried Limpy. "My job was to blow the box. All they've got to do is pick up the money. I was goin' to join the guard out here."

Other men had closed in. "Keep an eye on him," Burness ordered. Then the outlaw chief entered the bank.

The explosion in the bank had attracted attention.

Already men were in the street asking each other what it was that they had heard. In the Stampede, Tower's bodyguard walked along behind the bar. He wasn't sure there were any of the outlaws in the place, but he was taking no chances. He took a drink and looked around casually. He saw men looking at him, but there was as yet no excitement in the resort.

"What was that noise?" a customer at the bar asked him.

The man was a stranger and the head bartender scowled at him. "What noise?" he demanded. "I didn't hear anything." He already had made up his mind to protect Burness as far as possible. Wasn't Tower gone—taken away by the outlaws? That would mean that he, in charge of the employees, would have to make up the cash, and he intended taking every cent he could lay his hands on and leaving as fast as a good horse could take him.

The man who had asked the question said nothing further.

Norman Webb, not so long returned from his conference with the sheriff, heard the muffled sound of the explosion, also. He hurried out on his front porch, with a paper he had been reading in his hand.

Two men mounted the steps swiftly. He caught the glint of the starlight on their drawn weapons. Bandannas were drawn about the lower parts of their faces. "Go back inside and go quick!" he was ordered.

Webb had sense enough to know that these men were outlaws and his mind leaped to the decision that Burness had raided the bank. He turned back into the house and the two armed men followed him. Pansy was in the living room, reading. She rose, but her father motioned to her to sit down. He turned to the outlaws.

"I suppose you know this is pretty serious business?" he said.

"We're hoping that you know the same," was the answer. "You and the girl sit down and take it easy till we go. If you let a yelp out of you, we'll turn loose the cannons."

"Just as you say," Webb said, sitting down and staring at them from head to foot. "When you see Burness again, if you do, tell him for me that he can't get away with this." He nodded soberly.

"Oh, shut up, you old, dried-up chair setter!" exclaimed one of the men in a jeering voice. "You might've been range stock once, but now you're a quilt-maker so far's we're concerned."

Webb's eyes flashed red fire. "Even if I was in your rotten business, I'd have nerve enough to do my dirty work without hiding behind a mask!" he cried.

One of the outlaws took a step toward him.

"If you want trouble with me, put aside your gun," Webb commanded sternly.

"Father!" Pansy exclaimed. Then she rose and turned on the two outlaws. "I suppose you think you're brave men to attempt to. . . ."

"Silence!" her father thundered. "Pansy, sit down!" He turned his hard gaze on the outlaws. "There's enough range stock left in me so that I'm ready to shoot it out with either of you," he declared. "If I'd have had a gun in my hand, instead of a newspaper when I went out on the porch a minute ago, at least one of you wouldn't be here."

"We wouldn't think of shootin' it out with you, you old foot warmer," said one of the pair. "We'd take your gun away from you and spill the loads down your neck to tickle your fat hide. You made a lot of show talk about this bein' a law-tight town, didn't you? Well, we're takin' your town for everything that's worth takin'. If you was able to ride a hoss, you could find pieces of your tin-can bank scattered for five miles around in the morning." The outlaws laughed at this and Webb clenched the arms of his chair until his knuckles went white.

At this moment six shots rang on the night air. Instantly the pair whirled and leaped out the door. Norman Webb hurried to the desk in the room and took a six-gun from a drawer. He took a handful of cartridges and spilled them into the right-side pocket of his coat. Then he made for his hat with Pansy flinging herself upon him, pleading with him not to go out. "You've got me to think of, Daddy!" she cried.

He pushed her aside. "I've got more than that to think of," he said grimly. "With the sheriff gone, I'm the authority here." He speedily vanished down the street, as the housekeeper came running down the stairs to gather the girl in her arms and prevent her from going out, too.

The street before the bank was filling. Men were running in all directions. None seemed to know just what had happened or where the six shots had been fired. They didn't know, of course, that the shots had been the signal for the Burness men to take to their horses and leave town.

"The bank's been robbed!"

"The Stampede's been cleaned out!"

"They've raided every joint in the town!"

Such cries as these and many others went up from the gathering throng. Two deputy sheriffs were soon on the scene. One sped to the bank, where, with a dozen cautious men at his back, he went around to the rear. The forced door there told the story as plainly as the shattered vault and scattered papers.

Another deputy ran to the Stampede, which now was in an uproar.

"There wasn't a gun flashed in this place," announced Jim Hagen, head bartender and Tower's bodyguard. "There's been no hold-up here, unless Red held his own place up himself."

Customers were hurrying outside and it was easy for the deputy to verify Hagen's statement to the effect that there had been no hold-up—no visible robbery, anyway.

"Where is Red Tower?" the deputy demanded.

"That's it," countered Hagen. "I don't know. And I'm not goin' to do any guessing. There wasn't any shooting in here, mister. Tower had a couple of men in his office and seemed to be makin' some kind of a deal. He sent me to get the surplus cash from the tables and went out with his friends, or whoever they were. That's all I know."

"Yeah?" The deputy seemed suspicious. "Suppose you don't know the safe in the office is open."

"Wouldn't surprise me a bit," Hagen said calmly. "Tower had the keys and knew the combination. Any man in the place can tell you I couldn't get in that safe. I've carried money home more'n once, when he wasn't here to take care of it, and give it to him later."

Just then a man burst in with the information that the bank had been robbed. "Looks like a double job," the deputy said as he hurried out.

By this time, Norman Webb was in the bank office, holding a conference. "As president of the bank I can say that a lot of cash is gone, but the institution is insured and in healthy condition and this robbery won't affect it a bit. It was the Burness gang that operated here tonight and the six shots you all heard was the signal to the band to beat it."

An awed silence fell over his listeners as he said this and it was an opportune time for the deputy to burst in with information that Red Tower was gone and the Stampede's money, or most of it, had gone with him. He explained what Jim Hagen had said.

"That's Burness's own personal work," Webb snapped out. "He held Tower in his office at the point of a gun, made him do as ordered, and then kidnapped him to keep him from talking or maybe to kill him later." He paused, his eyes narrowed. Then: "One of you deputies start for the Two-Bar as fast as you can," he ordered. "Sheriff Wilson rode out there tonight to see . . . on business. Bring him back. Tell him I'm temporarily in charge. He will have to form and take full charge of the posses. Burness isn't goin' to get away with this." He banged a desk with his fist, and none there could remember ever having seen him so angry. His present rôle was not that of a smug, retired stockman.

Meanwhile, Hagen was acting on his own initiative at the Stampede. There were only a few in the place and he announced that all games were off for the night. He took the banks of the dealers and practically all the money in the cash boxes behind the bar. He snapped out orders to his assistants, put on his hat, and went out, announcing that he was "goin' to see what was doin' at the bank."

Instead, he went directly for his horse, and, after a short stop at the cabin where he lived with Tower to get some personal belongings and such money as was there, he rode swiftly out of town unobserved.

Hagen decided to ride directly east. After such a big haul, Burness was certain to ride north to the Canadian line, he reasoned. Burness might even ride west to the mountains; he might split his band. But he could hardly be expected to ride east in a direction where there were towns and many ranches.

Hagen had been in the saddle exactly an hour

when he swept through some light timber and willows along a small stream and rode straight into a group of eight or ten riders. He could hardly check his horse when a rope whistled high, settled over his shoulders, and pinned his arms to his sides. He was relieved of his gun in a twinkling and heard a man laughing harshly.

"Look who's here, Red," said a voice he recognized at once as belonging to Burness. "It's Jim, your head man, come to rescue you."

Then Hagen made out Red Tower on a horse with another man. He could see Burness, too. He'd have known them in the dark. The others were members of the Burness band, of course.

"You were a fool to come out here," Tower said angrily. Why had Hagen come alone? If he had been so sure Burness would ride east, why hadn't he at least tried to bring some men with him?

"What was your idea in coming?" Hagen asked with a sneer.

"Oh, no, he isn't any fool to come out here, Red," Burness said contemptuously. "He was on his way to points east and beyond. He didn't intend to rescue you, either . . . if you had to be rescued. He was thinkin' this was the one direction I . . . we . . . wouldn't take, eh, Jim?" He laughed again.

"Just take his roll off him, boys," the bandit directed. "He must have some in that little pack on his saddle, too. Just look him over careful. You know, Red, I figured this was a sure way to get what remained. I knew this hombre would keep his mouth shut and try to make off with what was left. And here he's brought it right to me. I didn't even hardly have to outguess him."

"You was in on all this," Hagen snarled at Tower. "You crook!"

"Listen who he's callin' a crook," said Burness. "Ain't that awful, boys. Maybe Red thought he was in on it, Jim, but he ain't packin' any of the proceeds. Now, we'll see what you had."

Hagen swore but refused to talk any further while Burness was investigating the sum he had carried.

"Not so bad," Burness said when he had finished and told one of the men to take charge of the money. "He had enough on him to get a start somewhere, Red . . . somewhere east."

"Callin' me a crook!" Tower exclaimed foolishly.

"That's what I say," Burness said in an injured tone. "First thing we know, he'll be callin' me a crook. He's an old slick tongue. Keep his gun, boys. Now, just put Red up on the horse with him . . . put Red behind." The bandit chuckled to himself as his orders were carried out.

"Now, listen, you two," he said, sobering when Hagen and Tower were both on Hagen's horse, "I'm sendin' you back to town. You can frame up a story on the way there, see? Tell 'em I took everything. Say Hagen rode out and found you, Red, wandering in a daze on the lone prairie after I'd taken you off and ditched you out of pure cussedness. The sheriff's fool enough to believe that . . . maybe. Or you, Hagen, can tell the sheriff the truth . . . that you found Red making off with me after bein' in on the night's activities, and I let you both go rather than shoot you. You know what happened in Red's office. You'd probably get a medal and part of the reward for catchin' me . . . when I'm caught. Or you, Red, can sneak a chance to slip a slug of hot lead between Jim's shoulder blades just like you shot Blunt in the side in that fracas. That would shut Jim up, and you could say he was in with me or anything you wanted to. There's a lot of ways you boys can get out of this, besides goin' back and tellin' 'em that I went east. They'd know better than that and probably jam you both into a cell. But, whatever you do, get goin'. Show 'em off, boys."

Hagen's horse was jerked around and a quirt applied. The pair rode off, westward, as fast as their mount could carry them with Burness's laugh roaring in their ears.

At almost this precise moment, Sheriff Wilson and Andrew French and the others were galloping into Conroy.

CHAPTER TWENTY

The sheriff rode with Andrew French, Clint and Dick French, Len Miller, and the deputy they had met on the way to town, directly to the bank where Norman Webb still was holding forth, impressing his listeners with the fact that the bank still was sound and promising that Burn-'Em-Up Burness would not get away with the daring robbery.

"What's the idea in hangin' out here?" demanded the sheriff after a swift look about at the disorder and the blown vault. "Why not have a couple of the clerks put things in order, Webb? I'll leave two deputies here on guard, although I hardly believe Burness will come back. Looks as if he had done a complete job."

"Oh, you here, Sheriff? Good! And you, too, Andy. That's better still." Webb directed a questioning glance at the two French boys and Miller. "Yes, he made a good job of it in here and took the Stampede for good measure. The. . . ." Webb swore for the first time in months.

"We'll make our headquarters in my office," Sheriff Wilson announced, giving Webb a queer look. "Suppose we go over there now."

"Whatever we do, we'll have to be gettin' busy pretty quick," Webb snapped. "That bandit isn't goin' to get away with all this."

"No? Well, you've been preaching the law for some years now and we better move careful," drawled Wilson with a side glance at Andrew.

"There's only one brand of law in this case," Webb declared with heat, "and that's range law, pure and simple. I'm for stringing this Burness up as soon as we lay hands on him!"

"That wouldn't be accordin' to law," said Wilson dryly. "Anyway, we'll go over to my office and conduct our investigation from there."

In his private office at the jail, Sheriff Wilson, with a deputy at his left, heard the accounts of the bank robbery and the supposed looting of the Stampede. He turned to the deputy. "Go over and get that top bartender, Hagen, and bring him here," he ordered.

"I don't think we have to bother so much with the Stampede as with the bank," Webb said crossly. "It was the people's money they got at the bank. What do you think, Andrew? You're a director and a big stockholder in the bank and your advice counts at such a time."

"Well, I think we better let Wilson go at it his own way," said Andrew French slowly. "You don't want to forget that Tower is gone."

"I wouldn't put it past him to have had something to do with it." Webb scowled. "Really don't look to me like he'd let 'em get away so easy.

"Something in that." The sheriff nodded. "Still, Burness might have handled that end of it personal. I reckon Tower would do just about what he was told to do with Burness pettin' his six-gun. Looks to me like Burness had run him off to stop him from talkin' or maybe to kill him. Wouldn't surprise me a bit if he'd kill him."

"I don't care what he does with him!" cried Webb angrily. The sheriff's coolness was maddening. "The thing we want to do is get a bunch together and get right out after this outlaw. I'll go myself . . . Andy, here, will furnish a bunch of men and we can get some in town."

"Not so fast," said the sheriff with a frown. "Maybe I've had more experience chasing bad ones than you've had. Anyway, we're not goin' to fly off at the handle . . . not when we're dealin' with Burness. Oh . . . this looks like some news."

The deputy had entered accompanied by two employees of the resort. "Hagen's gone!" he announced in excitement. "Closed the games, took what money there was in the place, and beat it right after the robbery."

"Then Hagen was in with 'em, too!" exclaimed Norman Webb.

"Keep still, Webb," the sheriff ordered sharply. "I'll do the examining here. Was you on shift?" He spoke to one of the men with the deputy.

"I was behind the bar durin' the whole thing," said the man. "And Joe, here, was dealin' stud at a table near the office door." He pointed to the one who was standing by his side.

"All right," said Wilson. "Let me talk to the dealer. What did you see?" he asked the second man.

"I saw two men and then another go into Tower's private office. One of 'em was stout enough to be Burness, but I don't know Burness and never saw him. After a while another, shorter, man went in the office, and then Jim came out and took half the surplus of our banks. The short man came out and kept

near him, watchin'. They went back to the office and
Jim stayed with 'em a minute or so when we heard
the explosion. Tower came out with the men and
they seemed to be leadin' him, I thought . . . I'm not
sure. Jim came out behind the bar like everything
was all right. Later on, when we heard for sure the
bank had been robbed, Jim closed the games, took
most of the cash in the place, and disappeared.
That's all I know about it, Sheriff."

"And what about you, bartender?" Wilson ask the
other man.

"I haven't much more'n Joe had to say. Tower
called Jim into the office, and then Jim went out and
collected at the tables like Joe said. Then Jim came
out behind the bar and took a drink, and I couldn't
see that he was excited about anything. After the
news was brought in about the bank, he made up
the cash, not leaving us much to work on, put me in
charge, and said he was goin' out to see what all the
noise was about. He usually . . . always . . . takes the
cash when Red ain't on hand. He ain't been back
since and I found out he took his horse."

"That's all we need to know," said Wilson. "You're
still in charge, of course? I see. And my man is over
there on guard? All right. When we get through
here, I'll be over for a look around. You can both go."
He turned to the deputy. "You better go over, too.
The man you left there is all right, but I may need a
fast rider for a messenger and that's his long suit.
Send him back here."

"There you are," Webb said in a tone almost of triumph. "The two of 'em are gone over there. First,
Tower goes with Burness when the gang fired the
signal to leave, then this Hagen sneaks out with the
rest of the cash later, and . . ."

"What signal you talkin' about?" Wilson demanded.

"The six shots," explained Webb in some excitement. "I heard the explosion and went out on the porch and two masked ruffians. . . ." He bit his lip and paused. He hadn't intended to bring out that about the two outlaws forcing him back into the house, or being there at all.

"Yes?" Wilson prompted sternly. "Two of 'em tried to hold you up, too? What did they get, Webb?"

Webb exploded. "Not a cent! I wouldn't have handed 'em so much as a two-cent stamp! They both had their guns out and I backed into the house where they kept me and Pansy covered. It was the sensible thing for me to do, what with Pansy there . . . no, I didn't think so much about Pansy at the time. But it made me fightin' mad and I told 'em Burness couldn't get away with this and a few other things. I told 'em plenty!" The former stockman's eyes flashed red fire.

"And they took it without talkin' back?" the sheriff drawled.

"No!" Webb cried, losing control of his anger. "They called me a chair setter and said I might've been of range stock once, but now I was a lot of other things, and none of 'em complimentary. I offered to shoot it out with 'em. . . ."

"Which would have been suicide," the sheriff observed.

Webb glared at him because of the interruption. "Just then six shots broke and they ran out the door and to wherever their horses were, and the whole bunch was gone when I did get down here," he finished.

"Don't get mixed up with that gang," Andrew warned him soberly.

"Well," said the sheriff, frowning, "I don't believe that Red Tower was in with the outlaws. I think, as I thought from the first, that Burness ran him off. I'll tell you why later. And I think that this Jim Hagen was just a cheap thief and ran off with what was left after they took Tower away."

"Why would Burness want to run off with Red?" asked Andrew.

"Because . . . maybe you don't know it . . . but Blunt Rodgers was shot twice and he fired wild at the boys. I'm guessin' that it was nobody but Red who fired that other shot and hit Blunt in the left side. It was that shot that killed him. Goodness knows how Burness could find this out for sure, but some of his men might have seen it. You told me Limpy was sent back after that fight west of here. Another got away up there and Klein followed a man from here. Any of 'em could have seen it. But they couldn't do anything about it. Their move was to get out of town as fast as they could."

"That's just what Dick said!" exclaimed Andrew, looking at his son in surprise. "Dick said he thought Red shot Blunt."

"What made you think that?" Wilson demanded of Dick French.

"Because of the way he acted when Clint and I saw him after the fight," said Dick. "There was a gun on his desk when we went in his office. He didn't seem pleased to see us and he didn't like it at all when I picked up the gun. I spilled the shells out and there was one blank. He went white at that."

"Why didn't you come and tell me about that and about what you thought?" Wilson asked in a tone of great annoyance.

"Because I wasn't at all sure of what I thought and didn't want to confuse you in any line you were working on," replied Dick. "Besides, for some reason, I thought it best to keep what I suspected to myself. Also, we wanted to get started back to the ranch as soon as possible."

"You had time to go buy a gun," said the nettled official.

"And maybe you'll tell us where you're getting with all this talk," Andrew put in sharply.

"I wanted to make sure that Burness did this job," the sheriff said evenly. "I feel sure he did. I wanted to find out about Red Tower and I believe I know all I need to know on that end of it. Now, maybe you'll tell me how to go about catching Burness and his gang."

"Not being the sheriff of this county, I don't propose to assume such a responsibility," Andrew said testily. He didn't like what the official had said to Dick.

"Well, I'll make a suggestion," Norman Webb volunteered. "We won't catch him sittin' here in this office talkin' about it. You've got to raise the biggest posse that ever went on a manhunt on this range. You can pick up some men in town, get others from the ranches hereabouts, and I'm sure Andy, here, will send his outfit and they're good enough to clean out that Burness band of outlaws alone."

"On the contrary, I won't send a man," Andrew French announced coolly. "I won't go myself, I shall ask Dick and Clint not to go, and I'll refuse to let a man leave my ranch, unless he takes his time and quits."

Webb leaped to his feet. "You won't help?" he cried. "Why, you're a director in the bank and one of our first citizens."

"That may all be," was Andrew's calm retort, "but I'm not protecting this town with my outfit. There's nothing personal in this, Webb, but you've been preachin' law and order, and tellin' the world what a tough place Conroy would be for gunmen or outlaws, and runnin' things down here in general. Now you can keep on runnin' 'em. I guess you've been out of the stock business just long enough to forget that I have a ranch and cattle to protect, and this Burness outfit made a crack to get Clint, here, in the bargain. I'm not goin' to send my outfit out on any wild-goose chases and leave my ranch unprotected."

"But you don't have to send all of 'em," Webb pointed out.

"I'm not goin' to send any of 'em," Andrew announced firmly. "But that doesn't mean I haven't got anything more to say or anything to suggest." He turned in his chair. "Miller, suppose you and the boys go out and keep the men handy for an early start back. I want to talk with Webb and the sheriff a few minutes."

When the three had gone, he pulled his chair closer to the sheriff's desk and his expression became more serious. "I want you two to listen to what I have to say for a minute," he said. "Now, then. . . ."

He told them briefly of the fight on the prairie, the slight wounding of Clint, and the capture of Limpy Lowell. He told what he had got out of Limpy and how he had sent him back with a defy to his boss, Burness. He told what Klein had seen and heard and the manner of his return to the Two-Bar F.

"And what's more," he finished, "we've lost some cattle. Miller thinks Blunt and Limpy stole 'em on the side. He doesn't think Burness knew a thing about it. But Burness won't pass up my challenge, and he's figurin' right this minute, if he hasn't already made his plans, as to how he's goin' to even things up with me. He had this town job laid out for some time or he couldn't have struck so fast and sure. His next move will be made against me. And that's the move that is goin' to trip him up."

Both Webb and the sheriff listened with interest to what the stockman had to say. They respected his judgment, especially when dealing with an outlaw as tricky and dangerous as Burness. And they knew that in a general move against the notorious bandit, French would make a better leader than either of them.

"All right," said Sheriff Wilson, "let's hear the rest of it, Andy."

"Go ahead." Webb nodded, smiling, although he was annoyed as the reins of authority slipped from his hands.

For half an hour the trio remained in conference behind the closed and locked door of the sheriff's office.

Meanwhile, two tense dramas were being enacted—one in town, and the other on the shadowy, flowing plain to eastward.

CHAPTER TWENTY-ONE

Red and his former bodyguard, Jim Hagen, sped westward under the star spangles after leaving Burness and his men. In the heart of the former was a consuming rage. At first he raged inwardly at Burness, who had robbed him of nearly all the money he possessed. True, he was not broke by any means, for he had a good stake in the bank in Great Falls—and he still had his place in Conroy, but gradually his anger centered on Hagen. The low, common thief. He had trusted the man, he told himself bitterly, and this was his reward. Hagen had been fleeing with what was left in the resort—a grubstake.

As Tower thought more and more about this, he forgot Burness altogether. Finally, after they had ridden about two miles, his anger kinkled into a fury that blazed forth in frenzy. His grasp about Hagen's waist loosened and he struck for the throat of the man riding with him. But, quick as he was, Tower was not too quick for Hagen. Hagen struck back with his right elbow, putting all his strength into the blow that struck Tower fair in the chest. Tower missed his hold on Hagen's throat and clutched at his shoulders as the horse leaped under the spurs.

Tower went off, thrown upon his back on the plain. He was just able to get to his feet as Hagen whirled his mount and flung himself from the saddle.

"I knew you'd try it," said Hagen. "I was ready for it. After Burness double-crossed you so pretty, you thought you'd take it out on me, eh? Left me alone, didn't you, to face the music? Wouldn't I have been a fool not to take what I could and beat it?"

"Nobody double-crossed me except you," hissed Tower. "You knew who Burness was and you knew what he was there for. You knew he was holdin' up the place, and, after he ran me off, you kept quiet so's you could make off with what was left there. Well, all I've got wasn't left there, you fool. You're nothin' more'n a sneak thief."

"Yeah?" Hagen put his hands on his hips. "I suppose you don't know that the bank was robbed. I don't suppose you was givin' that Blunt Rodgers information every time he came in. I don't suppose you was in on the play, eh? When Blunt got his, Burness had to act quicker'n you expected. You didn't have time to send your stake away and you didn't dare go without it any more than you dared to let that outlaw get away with the bank money before you'd had your cut. Think I don't know anything? Who's the fool, now?"

Tower fumed. "You . . . you are simply dumb!" he exploded. "Do you think for a minute that I'd be fool enough to go off with Burness alone, with all, or most, of my stake? Trust myself with that money on me with him?"

"Do I think you would?" Hagen said with a sneer. "Of course, I think so. Your brain isn't big . . . it ain't any bigger'n your watch charm. All you could think of was keepin' what you had already and gettin' your bit from the bank loot. You was probably figurin' on traveling with Burness steady. You've acted queer lately. How long do you think you'd have lasted with that cut-throat? As it is, you got away quicker'n was planned, through me, at that . . . and you got away with a whole skin."

Tower swore and called Hagen a foul name. "Only a marblehead like you could imagine such rot," he finally got out. "I'm not goin' to argue with you because I don't have to. I . . ."

"Oh, yes, you have to," Hagen interrupted. "You're not goin' to call me a sneak thief and a marblehead and this and that and get away with it. You're dumb and yellow in the bargain."

This was too much for Tower and he leaped in with a blow that grazed Hagen's left cheek. He took one on the left ear from Hagen in return that staggered him. Then the fight was on. If either of the two had had a weapon, the struggle would have been of short duration. But they were unarmed and neither had ever carried a knife.

In choosing a man for his bodyguard, the resort-keeper had picked Hagen because of his record, which led him to think he had the man under his thumb, and because he was large, strong, and a good fighter. Hagen had always been the official bouncer in the Stampede. In size they were to all appearances evenly matched, and Tower, in his day, had been an excellent fighter. But Tower had not had occasion to do any fighting for a long time. He lacked his former light footwork, although this was not of prime importance because of the uneven prairie on which they now fought. The placing of his blows was not accurate, but he could take an enormous amount of punishment, and his blows, when they did land, did damage.

Three times Hagen went down, but got up before

Tower could fling himself upon him. Tower went down but once. The resortkeeper began to tire rapidly as they fought on in the semidarkness under the star-lit sky. His burning rage more than offset his opponent's superior skill and condition. Tower decided it would not be wise to attempt to wrestle with Hagen. He tried to look about for a weapon—a stone or anything he might be able to use to put his adversary out cold. Then he would kill him. And what next? What would come after? How would he explain?

His teeth ground together in disregard of future consequences as he caught the pale glint of the stars on a stone in the grass. He drew back from a blow, taking but a fraction of its force, but dropped full length on the ground, his right hand closing over the oval-shaped missile. He twisted on his side and leaped to his feet to whirl just as Hagen made a flying tackle and brought him down. His head hit the stone in falling and the sky blurred and blended into a dark shadow with Hagen sitting on his chest.

"There's nothin' . . . about this fight . . . I'm proud of," Hagen panted. "You're either goin' to get . . . your senses or I'm . . . goin' to knock you out . . . for good."

The words came to Tower's ears as if from a distance. "Let me up," he managed to say. "It's foolish for us to. . . ."

Hagen slapped him on either side of his jaw with jarring force. "Snap out of it!" he commanded. "Try and act like you had a brain, and get ready to listen. Hear me?"

Tower tried to sit up. "What is it?" he asked, ceasing to struggle. "I lost my wind, that's all."

"With a rock in your hand!" Hagen said, jeering. "Now I've got the rock, see? I can smash your head in and would do it in a second if I thought it would get me anything. But I know something better than that. We'll go back to Conroy, hear? We'll go back! I'll tell 'em I took out after the outlaws lookin' for you . . . thinkin' I might be able to help you, understand? I'll tell 'em I didn't want to say anything about the hold-up in the place for fear they'd get me mixed up in it or something. I'll fix that part of it. We'll say they robbed you and took you out of town so's you couldn't say anything quick, see? You can say they took what you had and set you loose in the brakes and you had to find your way back and we met up with each other. For all they know, I've still got what little money I took. What do you think of that?"

"Let me up so we can talk easy," Tower said gruffly. "You win."

"I'm goin' to win in more ways than you think," Hagen said grimly as he got up and permitted Tower to rise. "We can clear ourselves easy enough. I can clear myself easier than you could talk yourself out of it. The sheriff don't like you none too well, at that. I could tell 'em you was in with Burness and even mix myself up in it, and they'd believe me and let me go. Ever think of that?"

"Don't be a fool," was all Tower could think of to say then.

"I don't intend to be a fool," Hagen said. "I'm not sure yet that there wasn't some two-way double-crossin' and that my happening along didn't break up the play. But you're not so bad off, and maybe we're both lucky we didn't stop lead. You've still got your joint and it can be run at a profit same as ever, except"—his tone hardened—"from now on you and me are pardners."

"What's that?" Tower asked sharply, hardly able

to believe his ears. "Pardners? How do you mean, we're pardners?"

"Just what I said," Hagen said sternly. "We go fifty-fifty on the joint. You can keep what you've got hid away and take back what you'll have to put in to start runnin' again. But we'll be pardners in the Stampede from now on. We understand each other pretty well. You can watch me, and I'll watch you. But when this thing is all settled, we'll get over that. There's no reason why we shouldn't get along. Whether you believe it or whether you don't, I would have got you away from Burness if I could. Just how does it all sound to you anyway?"

Tower had been listening intently and thinking rapidly. He wanted peace with Hagen for the time being, and Hagen's word, combined with his, would prevent the sheriff from thinking something that wasn't true. After all, he had to keep his place running now. Later, he would find a way to get Hagen.

"Maybe we can work things out," he said craftily. "But we've got to frame our story before we get back to town or before they can find us by accident. The first thing we ought to do is get down by the brakes."

"Now you're showin' some sense," Hagen said in a satisfied tone. "We'll ride over toward the river, like you say. But this time you'll ride in front, Red. And if you try another trick. . . ."

"Let's get goin'," said Tower impatiently as he started for the horse some little distance away.

When Miller, Clint, and Dick left the sheriff's office at Andrew's request, Miller suggested that they go to the Stampede. The Two-Bar men were close at hand and he walked toward them. Dick told his brother that he was going up to the hotel and not mix around town at present. In reality, he wanted to be on hand to see his father alone, if possible, when he came out from the conference with Webb and the sheriff.

"That's a good idea," said Clint. "You stay in the background a while, Dick, till I get a good line on things. I'll see you later."

Instead of going to the hotel, Dick turned down a side street into the shadows under the trees where he could see the front of the jail and the lighted window of the sheriff's office. He was thinking of several things and merely idled along, back and forth, on the dim street. It was a matter of a few minutes when a slight form came around a corner, a hand took his arm, and a girl spoke to him in a low, excited voice.

"Do tell me what it is all about, Clint."

Dick recognized Pansy Webb's voice at once. "You shouldn't be out like this at this time of the night," he told the girl.

Pansy knew him by his voice at once. "Oh, I thought it was Clint," she said, releasing her hold on his arm. "But, Dick, you'll do just as well. I've got to know what has happened. I had to slip out of the house by strategy. I'm so worried . . . about Father."

"Your father is all right," Dick said, taking her hand and patting it to reassure her. "He's with my dad and the sheriff in the sheriff's office. Everything is quiet now and I'll take you home."

"But what . . . what did they do?" the girl insisted. "Two masked men were at our house and threw their guns on us. They talked dreadfully to Father and something was said about that outlaw, Burness, and the bank. I won't go home till I'm sure. . . ."

"Wait a minute," Dick interrupted. "You can't help things by getting all worked up, Pansy. Burness and his gang raided the town and took some money from the bank and the Stampede. Nobody was hurt. It was well carried out and your father and Dad and the sheriff are making plans to capture the outlaws. That's all you need to know now. You must go home. Your father will tell you all the details later. There's nothing to conceal, Pansy. The whole town knows, or will know, by morning."

"Did they take much from the bank, Dick?" Pansy asked quickly. "You know that will hurt Father. It might hurt your father, too."

"I don't know what they got," said Dick. "But your father isn't worried about the bank and neither is mine. The bank is sound and nobody will lose a dollar. The fact that Burness had the nerve to come in here and pull this is what has them riled. Now you must let me take you home. Anyway, we can talk on the way to your house. Don't you think you can trust me?"

"Oh, yes," faltered the worried girl.

Anything further she had intended to say was stopped as another figure swung into the street and strode quickly to where they were standing. Both had recognized the newcomer at once and Dick wondered if his last words had been overheard. Later, it struck him as peculiar that he should have shown this concern.

"Hello," Clint said in a queer voice. "Didn't expect to find you two here. This isn't on the way to the hotel, Dick."

"I was waiting to see Dad when he came out," Dick said, nettled at his brother's tone of suspicion. "Pansy came along to find out if her father was all right and we happened to meet here."

"Of course," Clint said with just a trace of sarcasm. "You told her, of course?"

"Clint, don't be silly!" the girl exclaimed irritably. "I thought Dick was you and came to him, naturally. I couldn't tell you boys apart in the dark any more than a lot of people could tell you apart in bright day. And you've no business to talk in such a voice."

"I guess you're right," said Clint.

"I came here by accident, too. I went over to your house and found you'd left, so I started to look for you. Seein' that you're in safe hands, I'll beat it."

He turned to go and Dick realized he still was holding Pansy's hand. He dropped it and grasped his brother by the arm. "You'll do nothing of the sort," he said sternly. "You'll take Pansy home. Good night, Miss Webb."

He was walking rapidly away before he could be stopped, and Clint and the girl were left staring at each other in the shadow of the trees.

CHAPTER TWENTY-TWO

Clint didn't say anything as Dick disappeared down the street. Pansy stood still, looking at him with a queer smile playing on her lips. Clint hadn't shown much tact in displaying his annoyance in finding his brother and Pansy together. The girl hadn't suspected that a jealous trait could so easily be aroused.

"Don't you think you've been very foolish, Clint?" she asked in a slow, low voice. "A little hasty, too, perhaps?"

"I don't like this business on Dick's part of sayin' he's goin' one place, and then finding him in another," was Clint's cross retort.

"Suppose he had said he was coming to my house," said the girl.

"That was probably where he was goin'," Clint said angrily. "But there's no use of you and me havin' words over this business."

"Oh, yes, there is," said Pansy haughtily. "You and me are the ones to have the words, and not you and Dick. You ought to be able to see that. Maybe you've forgotten that, if Dick, or any other man, wants to see me and talk to me, that's his business and my business, and not yours. You had no reason to speak to Dick in the tone you used, and you've no right to talk to me as you're doing. You're acting like a schoolboy."

"Yeah?" Clint was mad and it made him more angry to realize that what Pansy told him was true. "Maybe you're right. But . . . oh, let it go. Come on and I'll walk home with you."

"I think you'd better tell me that you're sorry," the girl said firmly. "And you'd better make the best of it with Dick, and . . ."

"You seem to be quite interested in Dick," Clint flared.

"Oh, it's no use. I'll go on and walk home with Father," Pansy said with a shrug. "You probably have something to do."

"You can't do that," Clint said quickly, stepping in front of her as she started to go. "Your father and mine and the sheriff are talkin' things over in the sheriff's office. No tellin' when they'll be through or what they'll have to do when they're finished with the confab. You can't do anything downtown, Pansy, and the sensible place for you to be is home."

"That's just what Dick was telling me when you came along like a charging bull," said Pansy. "I came out to find if Father was all right, and Dick told me just what you've told me. He said . . . but no matter. I'm going home, but I'll go alone. Those outlaws have left town, and, anyway, I don't believe they would bother me. Good night."

"I'm sorry this happened," Clint confessed, keeping at her side as she started for home. "It'll . . . look better, if I go home with you. We mustn't quarrel over such nonsense, Pansy."

"Our quarrel, if we had any, is over, Clint." Pansy's tone was cool and her words carried a note of finality that was not lost on the young man at her side. He suddenly felt a surge of resentment. After all, Dick was as good as himself, and he had no wild record, not on the range, at least, or anywhere else that Clint knew of. It was possible that a certain glamour that naturally attached itself to Dick might appeal to the girl—impress her.

It seemed strange to Clint that he should be jealous of his brother, but he began now to realize just how much he thought of Pansy. Why, he was heart and soul in love with her! He wouldn't lose her without a titanic struggle. He would warn Dick, and then the best man could win. And he would win if he had to go out and bring Burness in or kill him by himself. Such was the dramatic trend of his thoughts as he walked home with Pansy Webb. Meanwhile, Dick was waiting patiently until the conference in the sheriff's office should break up.

As they walked along with the starlight breaking through the dark leaf clusters of the trees, the silence became maddening to Clint. He took Pansy's arm, slowed her brisk walk. They were almost at the house. "Have I put myself in bad?" he asked, but without the slightest suspicion of concern in his voice.

"You've just acted foolish," she said with an impatient toss of her head. "You've simply been silly, and there was no excuse for it."

"There doesn't seem to be much excuse for anything I do," Clint observed rather lightly. "And I wasn't brought up to do silly things, either. That's the most foolish part of it. Suppose I do something that isn't foolish . . . or silly."

"I don't care what you do," Pansy declared frigidly.

"Well, that gives me a little leeway," Clint said mockingly. "Here's your house, Pansy." He opened the gate for her. "So long."

"Good night," she said as she hurried up the walk and steps to the front door. There she turned to say something more, but Clint was walking rapidly down the street. She slammed the door with force.

Clint heard the door slam, and he stopped in his tracks. He scowled at the closed front door of the Webb house, and then again swung on his heel and passed out of sight of the house quickly. Pansy was right. He was acting like a school kid. It would be a good thing to leave her alone for a while. Let her wise up to herself.

But Dick must keep away, too—and there was the rub. He couldn't very well dictate to his brother any more than he could tell Pansy what she must do. His humor did not improve as he reached the main street and turned toward the jail. Why was Dick anxious to see their father alone? Clint had always— perhaps unknowingly—been of a suspicious as well as a shrewd nature. He now was obsessed with the idea that something was going on behind his back, and he was determined to investigate.

He ran into Dick so suddenly and unexpectedly that the meeting he anticipated disconcerted him. They faced each other in the dim street and finally Clint was the first to speak, but not before his brother had shown that he had no intention of starting the conversation.

"Waiting for Dad?" Clint asked coldly.

"I am that," Dick replied with a shrug.

"What're you waitin' for him for?" Clint demanded, scowling.

"I was going to suggest that he sanction a little expedition with you and me as the members," Dick said stiffly, "provided, of course, that you felt like going. I thought it might be better if I talked with him about it alone."

"What kind of an expedition?" Clint asked in a curious voice.

"To trail this Burness. I've a hunch that the best bet is to follow the last man out of town. The last man to leave was Hagen from the Stampede. Somehow I cannot get it out of my head that he knows what he's doing. I'm not so experienced at such things, but I have a hunch that he rode east, which would be the last direction Dad or the sheriff would expect Burness and his band to take."

"Swell chance we two would have with that bunch," Clint snorted. "You heard Dad say he wouldn't let a man leave the ranch to join a posse, didn't you? Fat chance that he'd be willing for us to go."

"I thought I might be able to talk him into it," said Dick. "And, by the way, Clint, I'm going to speak to you about something before you have a chance to bring it up yourself, if you have any such intention. I guess you realize by this time that you acted the fool a while back."

Clint's rage returned. The same thing Pansy had told him now was coming from the lips of his brother. "Maybe you better explain," he snapped, "and then I'll see if I'm interested. Shoot."

"I mean when you met Pansy and me," Dick said gravely.

"I'm not goin' to have you or Pansy or anybody else tellin' me I'm a fool," said Clint belligerently. "You told me you were goin' to the hotel and. . . ."

"We can leave that out of it entirely," Dick interrupted. "I'm entitled to change my mind if I see fit, Clint. My point has to do with the manner you assumed when you found Pansy talking with me. You acted sore and you talked pretty sharp. Now I don't know how matters stand between you and Pansy, but I do know how I stand with the two of you . . . I'm your brother and her friend. The quicker and the harder you get that in your head, the better, if you value your own peace of mind. I'm not going into any lengthy explanations of my conduct, when it doesn't concern your well-being. I'm for you, and you ought to know it. And I won't be rode . . . to use a common expression out here . . . any more than I'll be worried in the slightest by your flying off the handle without good and sufficient reason as I see it."

Dick was telling him straight, which made Clint mad—and telling him right, which made him madder. "See it your own way, Dick," he said hoarsely, "but lay off the girl."

Dick held back a hot reply that was on his tongue, and remained silent until he could control his temper. "You'll think better of what you've just said," he got out at last, "and I'm going to overlook it. I can make you mad enough to fight by telling you one or two truths, and I'm not afraid to fight you, but I'm going to let it ride."

His speech sobered Clint, for the latter realized that they were coming to blows if the talk continued. "All right," he ground out, "but I'm not taking back anything I said, nor sayin' any more about it."

"Meanwhile, I don't think there is any reason for my talking to Dad," Dick decided. "I guess it will be just as well to let the older heads run this business."

"For that matter, I might take it into my head to go after Burness alone," said Clint. "And I wouldn't ask Dad's permission, either."

"Which is exactly why I'm going to stick with you and not let you out of my sight for a minute, old top," Dick said in a flash.

"Old top, eh?" Clint's tone came near conveying a sneer.

"I get you," said Dick grimly. "Eastern stuff, but it can mean just as much as a lot of expressions and names that are used out here."

"It won't get us anything to stand here talkin'," Clint said in a voice again angry. "Let's go over to the joint where the rest are."

Dick caught hold of him as he started for the resort on the other side of the street. "It isn't time for us to go over there or to join the bunch . . . not yet, it isn't." He nodded grimly.

"Oh, you want to go through with it, eh?" Clint fairly yelled. "Well, I'll tell you not to butt in where you're not wanted except to my face. I know something's bein' pulled behind my back by you, if not by some others."

"Whatever you're thinking, kid, it isn't hurting your brain to think it," replied Dick. "You're thinking in the wrong direction, anyway. I'm a little bit sore, and you're hotter than is healthy for you. But we can't be breaking with everybody knowing it, as they will, for it wouldn't be fair for others besides ourselves. If you're bound to make a mountain out of a grain of sand, and want trouble, you'll get it . . . and, if we're going to have trouble, we might as well have it now."

Clint's eyes flashed fire. Neither of them saw the jail door open and two men emerge. Clint, always the hotheaded of the two, lost control of his passion. "It looks like it was up to me to start it!" he hissed, and struck with his right.

The blow landed fairly, and Dick dropped on his side. He was whirling on an elbow, hand, and knee to his feet, when two figures loomed in the dim light of the street.

"What is this?" Andrew French thundered. "Tell me at once!"

"Just a misunderstanding," Dick said suavely. "Clint, here, acted quicker than I expected, but I want him to know that I appreciate his compliment and here's one in return."

Dick leaped, struck Clint's defense aside, and rocked him with a left to the jaw that planted him in the street.

"Stop it!" shouted Andrew, clutching Dick's arms.

But Norman Webb grasped Andrew in turn, so that Dick freed himself speedily. "Give him a chance," said Webb. "Don't hold him to be hit by the other fellow."

By this time the affray had been noticed by others, and they were running toward the scene of the disturbance. Clint had got up and had squared off. He was ready to fight on, although groggy, but he said to his brother: "We'd better postpone this and not set the whole town talkin' . . . just as you say."

"That's something sensible you've said tonight," Dick returned.

They were laughing and Andrew Webb closed in, realizing the situation. "No, I never knew that one," Clint chuckled at Dick as some men came up. "But you save that trick for Burness, if we ever meet up with him. It's better'n a gun any time."

"I'll show you how it's done," said Dick. "It's just a trick. . . ."

"Now, you boys come along with me," Andrew said in a growl. "Do your scufflin' on the ranch, if you've got to practice that jujitsu, and you needn't pay too much attention to it for there ain't been a Jap in this country ten years that I know of."

Webb was puzzled. He knew the two brothers meant the blows. But why? "Let's go over to my house and have a bite to eat," he suggested eagerly. He might learn what it was all about.

Clint shook his head at his father. "Dick and me better stick with the boys," he said significantly, as Dick nodded to Andrew.

"I guess that's best," Andrew told Webb. "We're not goin' back to the ranch before mornin', it looks like, and if we're here then, we'll sure drop around for breakfast."

"I suppose so," Webb said thoughtfully. "If you don't come to breakfast, I'll be powerful mad. And if anything turns up, let me know . . . quick. Don't forget, Andy, that I can still ride a horse and handle a gun, and I want to be in on whatever is done."

"I'm remembering," Andrew said cheerily. "So long."

Andrew French and his two sons walked a short distance down the street and halted in the deep shadows. "Let's have it," said Andrew. "What was you two fussing about?"

Dick pressed his brother's arm. "I'll speak for both of us," he said earnestly. "It was a bit of tom-foolery and we both were a little excited . . . on edge, I mean. That's all we have to say about it, but in due time you may find out."

"You mean to say you won't tell your own father," Andrew blustered. "Why . . . what do you say, Clint? Speak up!"

"Dick has said all there is to say," Clint drawled.

"Look!" Dick exclaimed suddenly. "Two riders at the side of the Stampede. They're tying their horse and . . ."

All three looked and recognized Red Tower and Jim Hagen as they walked around the corner and entered the resort.

"I was going to tell Dad I expected something of the sort," Dick said slowly.

"Can I trust you two to wait here while I look in

over there?" Andrew asked nervously. "Some of the boys will be there."

"Go ahead and we'll wait," urged Clint.

"Sure," said Dick.

Andrew hurried across the street and entered the resort.

CHAPTER TWENTY-THREE

"Something fishy about this," Clint grunted as they moved up the street. "That pair had only one horse. Can you see it?"

"I didn't notice it at first, but I see it now. But they both went away on horses. Tower left before Hagen, and he must have been on a horse, and Hagen didn't walk away."

"'Course not." Clint grinned. "But Tower went away with the Burness gang, and he was probably on a horse with one of the gang. He left his horse in the barn, so as not to cause any suspicion. Then Hagen jumped out with what was left on his horse and made no bones about it 'cause he knew he'd be the last man they'd look for."

"I had an idea he'd be the first man they would look for," Dick said. "I was going to tell Dad that, for a fact. I didn't want to tell him in your presence or with any one else around, for I thought you, or they, would think I was weak mentally. As it is, my hunch was right."

Clint laughed softly. "Why didn't you tell me right off the bat?" he asked. "I'd have backed you up. But what do you think of the two of 'em comin' in together on one horse, probably Hagen's horse?"

"Dog-gone! I'm no prairie detective!" Dick complained.

"Nor me, either," said Clint. "But it looks to me that Red was to get away out there some way and that Hagen was to pick him up. Smells like a lot of double-crossin' or a mighty queer play."

"Listen!" Dick exclaimed softly. "Maybe Hagen did try to get away, and came across Tower out there somewhere, and Tower made him bring him back. Burness might have ridden off with him, and then set him down afoot for Hagen to run into. What do you think?"

"Oh, I've quit thinkin'," drawled Clint. "When Father won't let the outfit go out on the chase, what're we to think? We can think he doesn't want to lose any men, or we can think what they'll think here in town . . . that he's afraid Burness will raid our place."

"He must have a reason for holding the outfit off," Dick said. "Dad isn't very dumb. I think he has more brains than Webb and that sheriff put together. But as for this last turn of events. . . ." He pointed, but Clint already was gripping his arm and staring hard.

In the illumination from the windows of the Stampede, the figures of Red Tower and Hagen showed plainly. They walked briskly across the street and up to the jail, where they entered immediately. No others came out of the resort.

Clint nudged his brother. "They've gone in to see the sheriff alone," he whispered excitedly. "Dad and old Webb left him alone, 'cept for a deputy outside, maybe. Seems to me that it wouldn't be so bad if somebody did a little detective work. What do you think?"

"I'm beginning to think that's what's needed, and you and me can do that little thing, if we're careful."

"Come on," Clint said, taking his brother's arm. The two slipped quickly into a deserted side street and ran to a spot near the jail.

"That's Wilson's office," Clint said, pointing to a lighted window that glowed in shrubbery and trees near the side of the jail. "We'll slip over and I'll hold you up by your legs so you can sneak a look and listen. I can watch out at the same time."

"Why shouldn't I hold you up?" said Dick resentfully. "I'll bet I'm as strong as you are, Clint."

"I want you to do the listening, confound it. You can get more out of what you hear than I can. You were right twice tonight. We're losing time arguing."

Dick took a swift look around, and they stole to the space under the window. Dick found a foothold on a narrow ledge, and Clint held up his other leg. Clint used his left arm and hand for this purpose, and his gun came naturally and securely into his right. "All's clear," he said cautiously. "They're here," Dick whispered back.

Red Tower rapped sharply on the door of the sheriff's office, and awaited, with Jim Hagen behind him, for the invitation to enter. This was not forthcoming immediately.

"Who is it?" came the gruffly spoken question after a time.

"It's Red Tower," was the answer in a tone of importance.

"See you in a minute," said the voice on the other side of the door.

Tower turned to Hagen with arching brows. "Must be almighty busy," he observed crossly. "But there's no sign of anything doin' on the outside, except French milling around with some of his gang."

"Let that go," Hagen said impatiently. "Keep your mind on what you're goin' to say, and don't let him trip you, see?"

"I know what I'm doin'," Tower blustered.

"And now that we're fifty-fifty, I want to see that you do it right," shot back Hagen, with a dark look.

"When this foolishness is over, you'll go behind the bar and I'll do the bossin' same as ever," Tower declared, doubling up his fist and stepping close to Hagen.

At this moment the door opened, giving the sheriff a view of Tower and Hagen glaring at each other as a deputy passed out.

"Come right in, boys," the sheriff invited, lighting a cigar, "and close the door." He indicated two chairs close to his desk, when his visitors had entered, and then he looked at them curiously. "You boys got back as quick as you could, didn't you?" he asked pleasantly. He wore his hat on the back of his head and one leg was across his desk.

"It was lucky for me that I could walk back, or get back at all," Tower spluttered. "Jim, here, fetched me back on his horse when he found me over in the brakes, afoot and staggerin'."

"So?" Wilson glanced at Hagen. "You lit out to get him right after the show, eh? And you knew just where to go, eh? Or was it just luck? Was that it?"

"It was luck that I found him so soon"—Hagen scowled—"but I figured Burness would hit for the brakes and maybe start north on the river or cross somewheres and make for the line. Doesn't that seem natural?"

"It sure does. Burness would be a fool to travel east or south into open country where he could be spotted easy. Maybe he's making for Muddy Flat . . . that's an old hangout of his, but where'll he go from there? If you boys can give me any information, I'll sure welcome it with both ears wide open."

"Hasn't any posses started yet?" asked Tower vaguely.

"Nope. We've got to get our bearings, and act a bit slow with an old-timer like Burness. But I guess I'll be callin' on you boys to mingle with the chase soon. I'll need all the men I can get."

Tower shot a swift look at Hagen. They had agreed not to put the authorities on the right track for fear that they might have to join up with a posse, and, if Burness should happen to be spotted, his gang's first bullets would be directed at them.

"We're ready to go at the ring of the gong, Sheriff," said Tower. "I'm a little lame and bruised, but you can count on me. There's nobody in the country that would be tickled more than me to see him run down. He took my place for plenty, and then dragged me off with him so's I couldn't give the alarm. That's what I thought before I heard the explosion at the bank, and then I didn't. . . ."

"Yes, Red . . . and then?" the sheriff prompted smoothly.

"Then, Sheriff, I didn't know what to think, and things happened so quick I couldn't get my bearings a-tall, let alone knowin' what to do with a flock of guns ready to bore me."

"They didn't drag you by a rope, did they, Red?" the sheriff asked with an injured look.

"No, two of 'em put me on the . . . one of their horses, and one got up behind me. I didn't have any gun, of course."

"Why not?" The official appeared astounded. "You pack a gun at night in your place, don't you? I always thought you did."

"I usually do," Tower said, slightly irritated, "but I

had cleaned it, or laid it aside, or something, and I didn't have it on me. They rode off southeast with me, and I could hear the last of the ruckus at the bank, and then the whole outfit came rushing up to us, with Burness in the lead. Burness looked at me with blood in his eyes. I don't know why he should want to kill me, after cleanin' me out 'cept a small stake I've got hidden away, but that's what I expected."

"Should think you'd be shaking yet," observed the sheriff sympathetically. "You're as steady as a post."

"That shows I sell good stuff in my place." Tower nodded coolly. "I went to the place soon's we rode in and slung down a few snorts. Braced me up. After we'd gone almost to the brakes, Burness called a halt and told the fellow riding behind me to 'knock that rat off.' I thought that meant to shoot me for sure. I lunged ahead and he cracked his six-gun just above my right ear, and I went out completely before I hit the ground. Reckon they wanted to kill me without firin' a shot and makin' so much noise. Guess they thought they'd done it, for they rode off, and, when I came to, Jim, here, was bendin' over me. He had struck for the brakes, had got a glimpse of the gang, and then found me on the ground. I came back with him on his horse and, after a few drinks to straighten out on, came right here, with Jim, to report to you just what had happened."

"That's thoughtful of you." The sheriff nodded. He proceeded to light his cigar, which had gone out, and gazed softly at Hagen. "You lit out quick as you could, didn't you?" he asked slowly.

"You bet your life I did," Hagen affirmed vigorously. "I knew it would be some time before a posse could be started."

"Just how long did you think it would be?" asked Wilson casually.

"Well, it hasn't even started yet!" Hagen ejaculated. "And I've already found Red and brought him back, haven't I?"

"Sure." Sheriff Wilson nodded amicably. "It was mighty fast work, too."

"I'll say it was fast work," Tower agreed. "He probably saved my life, Sheriff, and I think he ought to get credit for it."

"Sure." The official tapped the ashes from his cigar. "Just how much do you figure your life is worth, Red?"

"It wasn't worth a whoop with that crowd and . . ." Tower bit off his words and scowled at his questioner. "I get what you mean," he said surlily, "and you can say what it's worth and be hanged."

"I just meant it was probably worth risking your life to save it," Wilson said dryly. "But you are the one to give Hagen credit, as I expect you've done. It was certainly great of him to get goin' so quick and to . . . er . . . rescue you so soon. Yes, I reckon you ought to give him credit. If I was you, I'd make him a pardner."

The way Tower and Hagen started and stared at each other was a dead giveaway. Then both looked at the sheriff in evident perplexity.

"After you left, Hagen, I had somebody in here from the place"—he frowned and gave each a sharp look—"and learned you'd left with about all the cash the bandits didn't take. If you find out who I obtained this information from, you'll both keep your mouths shut and forget it. But . . . er . . . wasn't it sort of thoughtful of you, Jim, to leave with all that cash?"

"It sure was," Hagen affirmed emphatically. "I

wanted to go lookin' for Red, and who was I to leave it with? I've always handled the cash when Red wasn't around . . . isn't that so, Red?"

"Of course, it's so, and the sheriff knows it. You've always known that Jim was my head man, haven't you, Sheriff?"

"Sure," replied Wilson, pursing his lips. "Naturally that money is safe then?"

"Certainly it's safe," Tower answered without hesitation. "And it's a good thing Jim acted as he did. It ain't much, but it'll make change until I can get more money here."

"Funny you would bank out of town that-a-way and keep so much cash in your safe," the sheriff commented. "Around fifty thousand, wasn't it?"

"I won't know till I reckon things up, but it'll be that much anyway. I always gave a man a fair play for what he wanted to bet."

Wilson waved a hand. "I'm not sayin' anything about the way you managed your business. As far as I could see, you held the pluckings down pretty well, and in two or three cases settled good-hearted in my presence. But you can't blame me for asking questions at a time like this."

"I don't want to speak out of my turn, but it seems to take a long time to get started doin' something in this case," said Tower.

"Now, we're comin' to the point," said the sheriff, rubbing his hands. "I was tickled stiff when I saw you boys come in. If anyone can give us a line on which way the Burness outfit went, it's you. And you can bet I'll be right grateful and keep what you tell me to myself. Not a whisper to a soul as to where I got my tip. Remember . . . not a whisper." His eyes brightened in expectation as he looked quickly from one to the other of the men before him.

Tower's eye was cold, and Hagen was looking at Tower as if he expected him to reply. There was an awkward pause, just enough to justify a suspicion that already had formed in his mind.

"I don't know," Tower said slowly. "And . . . I'm darned sorry I don't." His crestfallen look at the sheriff appeared genuine. "They dragged me away on a horse and ditched me when I was expecting a bullet in my head any minute. I was knocked out, and all I can say is that they were just goin' into the brakes southeast of here. I've got a hunch they went south, but I'm not sure and I wouldn't want to be responsible for sendin' a posse on a wild-goose chase." He looked up with earnestness in his eyes.

"Don't worry," said the sheriff, in a different tone. "There'll be posses for all directions. This is one time all northern Montana, and the folks across the line as well, are out to get a man for keeps. How about you, Hagen? You said you got a glimpse of the outlaws before you found Tower. You must have seen which way they were heading. And while I'm asking the question, why didn't you follow the band a ways when you saw your old friend Red was just shaken up and could be left for a spell?"

Hagen's eyes glinted, but he kept cool. "Sure I saw 'em . . . got a sight of 'em anyways . . . and they were headin' straight south through the brakes. I didn't know how bad Red was hurt, and wouldn't I have been the fool to chase into the badlands after that gang, alone? I was willin' to take a chance in the open, but . . ."

"I see, I see," Wilson said impatiently. "Well, you boys have given me some information, whether you know it or not. And I'm goin' to take one chance on their goin' south. Burness has got a lot of nerve and audacity and he's got away so many times before . . .

oh, we'll fool him, maybe. But you better get home, Red, and get some rest, after what you've been through, and I suppose you're goin' to look after the joint, eh, Hagen?"

"Sure, I am," Hagen said with a forced smile. "I'm at your service any time, Sheriff. So long."

As they started for the door, Sheriff Wilson suddenly spoke again. "There's something else that doesn't amount to much that I want to see you about, Red. Just wait a minute. You can go ahead, Hagen. Red'll be along in a minute, although I think he ought to go right home."

As soon as Hagen had left, Sheriff Wilson's manner changed. He strode quickly around his desk and confronted Tower. "Now, let's have it!" he shot at the resort man through his teeth. "Out with it, Red . . . I'm not playin' with you an inch farther . . . so get me straight on that."

Tower drew back, startled. "Why, what do you mean?" he stammered.

Wilson's right hand grasped Tower's coat collar in an instant. "I mean . . . if you want to put it that way . . . I mean that you're goin' to tell me the truth here and now, or . . . or you're goin' into a cell. But you're not goin' into a cell until I've given you a first-class, old-fashioned, ring-tail snorter of a beating." He waited as Tower's face whitened. "I'll make it easier for you," he resumed. "I'll ask you questions. Now, didn't that rat of a Hagen start away with that money, intending to keep it?"

"I . . . I suppose so," Tower quavered.

"You know so!" exclaimed Wilson, shaking the other like a rat.

"Yes!" cried Tower with a flash of defiance in his eyes.

"And he come on you by accident, wasn't that it?"

"Yes, but. . . ."

"There'll be no side-stepping between you and me this time, Red. Too big a trick has been worked here . . . much too big. Are you sure that outlaw took you away on a horse and then ditched you?"

"Absolutely," Tower affirmed.

"But they caught Hagen makin' away with what was left at the same time, didn't they?" Wilson asked in a softer tone, releasing his hold on the man first.

Tower saw a way to save himself. He could get Hagen any time. "Yes," he answered, lowering his voice. "Burness took what he had and his gun and turned us loose on the same horse."

Wilson stepped back a pace. "You've got more sense than I gave you credit for, Red. You had some kind of a fight on the way back, and maybe Hagen got the better of you, eh? And you made some kind of a deal, like the pardnership I spoke of? Better tell me, Red?"

"If you'll keep it to yourself . . . yes," replied Tower.

"And where did they really drop you, Red? I know Hagen wouldn't make for the brakes. He wanted to get away, and he took the one direction he thought Burness wouldn't dare to take. Which direction was it, Red?"

"East," breathed Tower.

"Just what I thought." The sheriff smiled. "You needn't join any posse, Red. I'll tell 'em you was hurt and can't stand it. Wrap your shoulder up or something and keep out of sight." He opened the door. "C'mon, Red"—speaking loudly and heartily— "don't take too many drinks, and take 'em hot, and get to bed as soon as you can. Good night, Red." The sheriff closed the door after his guest and went into his office, chuckling. He thought he heard a sound beneath the open window, and leaped to it just in time to glimpse two figures vanishing in the shadows.

He laughed softly. "I'd be concerned if there were not two of them," he muttered. Then he called two deputies from another room.

CHAPTER TWENTY-FOUR

When Andrew French entered the Stampede, a glance showed him that Miller and most of the Two-Bar F men were in the place and, as his foreman came walking up to him, he caught sight of Red Tower and Jim Hagen downing drinks at the lower end of the bar. The stockman and his employees ranged along the bar, signaling for drinks.

"Just got here," Miller told his boss in an undertone.

"Saw 'em tie up and come in," said Andrew.

"Went right down there and ordered likker quick as they could, with the barkeep breaking his back to serve 'em, and the rest of us staring," Miller went on.

"Got back mighty quick, wherever they went," was Andrew's comment.

"They don't seem to like it much, seein' us here," said Miller. "Oh, here they come."

Andrew French turned slowly as the pair approached. "Must've had a fast ride, boys," he said quizzically.

"Fast and hard enough, and wished on us at that," Tower said, glancing sharply at both of them. "Posse out yet?"

"Don't believe so," said Andrew. "The sheriff's looking after all that, naturally."

Hagen scowled. "Takin' his time," he said. He never had liked the Two-Bar F owner, and he knew French didn't like him.

"Maybe you boys can give him some information," drawled Andrew. "He's over in his office and I believe he's alone."

"That's what I wanted to know," snapped Tower. "Come on, Jim, we'll go over and see him. So long, Andy."

"So long," returned the rancher. Then, to Miller: "Something's up. Them two like me just like they love rattlesnakes. But they've got something on their minds and . . . say, Miller, take a peep outside and see if they do go right up there."

While his man was gone, Andrew spilled his drink on the floor. He looked about the room with a scowl, and, when he saw no empty glasses before the men, he turned back with a wink for the bartender, who was obsequiously attentive.

"That's where they went," Miller announced when he returned. He caught sight of the empty glass in front of the stockman, looked curiously at the noncommittal barkeep. "One ahead of me, eh?" He tossed off the potion in his glass with a gulp and grimaced. "First drink I've . . ."

"Don't finish it, Len," Andrew interrupted with a scowl. "I don't want you ever to lie to me, because I don't want to lose a good foreman. Let's sit down over here and wait till that pair gets back. I've a hunch the sheriff will begin to take action pretty quick, and I don't want you to worry none about my not lettin' our crowd trail along in any mad chase. I believe I know what I'm doing."

"If you don't, nobody else does," Miller said sagely. "I've been running with you a long time now, and I don't remember you ever makin' any big mistakes."

Andrew took his arm to lead him to a table. "I'd rather make a hundred little mistakes than one big one," he said in a confidential tone. "I have made some little ones on purpose."

Hagen was first to return, appearing a bit flustered. "Hagen, come here!" commanded Andrew French. Hagen frowned and hesitated, but there was no getting away from the look in the stockman's eyes, and there was no disputing he was a formidable power in the land. He went over to the table where Andrew and Miller were sitting.

"What's the news, Hagen?" Andrew asked with a direct look.

"Why, we saw the sheriff and had a talk with him, but . . . I don't believe we're supposed to say anything to anybody, Mister French." Hagen's tone was plainly deferential. He meant it to impress the rancher.

"I suppose," grunted Andrew. "Can you imagine anybody supposing at a time like this, Miller? Of course, not!" He glared at Hagen, who felt uneasy despite his desperate attempt fully to control himself. "Where's Red?" he demanded.

"He held back a minute with the sheriff at the door," was the reply. "He'll be right back over. Maybe he can tell you something."

"You both could tell me something, if you had a mind to," growled Andrew. "But you don't have to talk to do it. You tell everything by the look in your face. Get along." The last words were spoken in a tone of contempt. And Andrew did not miss the darting look of hate directed at him as Hagen strolled away.

Hagen's prediction was true, and Tower soon strolled in. He did not appear as composed as Hagen had. He attempted to ignore the presence of Andrew, until he was opposite the table where the rancher and Miller sat.

"What say, Red?" It was Andrew's voice.

Tower started, pretended to look about, and then walked to the table. "Nothin' much to say," he told Andrew. "But the sheriff might have something to say if you want to go over and see him. Our talk was confidential . . . he told me so himself, so . . ."

"Red, you'd make a poorer actor than anything else you can do," snorted Andrew, rising. "Come along, Len, and we'll go over and see the sheriff. One look at this fellow shows he isn't in too good."

As Andrew and Miller left the resort and started for the jail, they unexpectedly met Dick and Clint, who came out of the shadows near where Andrew had left them.

"We're goin' up to see Wilson," Andrew explained hurriedly. "We'll be right back . . . so wait for us down here."

"Why shouldn't we go along?" Dick asked coolly.

His father stopped, startled. "Why. . . we want to see him alone," he said with visible agitation. "Really, Richard, there are things that . . ."

"I know," Dick interrupted, "but because of our participation in this thing and what we know, we think we should be taken in on all of it."

"Clint must have put that in your head," said Andrew angrily. "There are some things that I do on my own hook. This happens to be one of them."

The jail door had opened, and two men had come

out and were hurrying down the street. All sensed that something was doing as a result of the official's interview with Tower and Hagen.

"You can come in with us if the sheriff says it's all right," Andrew decided petulantly. "Maybe you don't know as much as you think."

They hurried to the jail, with Andrew French showing, by his stride and manner, that he was mad. The door to the sheriff's office was open, and the interior showed no such peaceful scene as on the occasion of Andrew's previous visit.

The sheriff was standing, a grim look on his face, giving orders to a deputy. "Every man you can get," he was saying sharply. "All of 'em! I want the biggest posse that ever rode out of this town ready to start at daybreak. Horses and guns and the men to handle 'em . . . and you better get word to Webb while you're at it."

As Andrew stood in the doorway, after the deputy brushed past him, looking somewhat astonished, Wilson caught sight of him. "Come in," the sheriff ordered in a tone of command, "and those boys of yours better come, too. Hello, Len." He nodded to Miller.

"You act riled, Sheriff," Andrew observed, almost in reproof.

"I'm not riled," snapped the sheriff. "I'm just goin' into action." He turned on Clint and Dick. "You'll keep what you know to yourself," he said sternly. "If I wanted, I could throw you into a cell and forget where I put the key. You didn't put anything over on me."

"But you won't throw us into a cell, just the same," said Dick.

"Here, here, what's all this about?" thundered Andrew French.

"I want you to get your men out of town as quick as you can," Wilson said. "It'll only cause a misunderstanding if they loaf around here while I'm gettin' my posse together. Your sons will tell you what they were up to after you left, and that saves me explaining. Now get this straight, Andy ... there's been a big raid pulled off here, and I'm responsible. I'm responsible for maintaining law and order in this county, and I'm goin' after Burness right, and in my own way. Since you say it isn't necessary for your men to go along, get 'em out of town. If they stick around here, the men who are goin' will be askin' questions as to why your outfit is sticking here, and I've got no time to be answering questions."

Andrew's face was red and his eyes snapping. "My men will go," he roared, "but you don't have to speak to me in that tone of voice!"

"But I'm doin' it just the same!" the sheriff shot back. "And I've spared all the time I have for you, gents."

"Wait a minute. What's all this?" Norman Webb pushed to the sheriff's desk.

"It means that French is takin' his men back to the ranch," the sheriff announced severely. "You made a crack that you wanted to help get these outlaws, so, if you want to trail along, go get your trappings and your horse, and be here to join the posse at the first prickle of dawn. That's the startin' time."

"But you're acting like a wild man," Webb objected.

"Call me anything you want to, but I haven't turned my badge in yet, and you nor anybody else can get it!" thundered Wilson with fire in his eyes.

Andrew started to speak, but a deputy entered breathlessly at this moment. "We've got sixty-four men ..."

"I want a hundred and fifty!" roared the sheriff. "And I don't want any bank clerks or farmers or tea drinkers. I want men who can ride and shoot, and the tougher they are, the better. I'm takin' along nine hard ones that're locked up in this jail this minute. Get 'em!"

Andrew French, Dick and Clint, and Norman Webb left the room. Only the twin brothers were smiling.

A noonday sun hung, like a burning ball of gold, high in the zenith. The sky drew away in a clear blue veil, trailing its robes of green and deeper blue with their ruffles of white cloudlets circling the horizon's rim. The plain flowed gently, preening its saffron-tipped grasses, girdled with its flashing silver of river, proudly wearing its pink gems—which were the buttes. A scented breeze, prey to caprice among the trees, ravines, and billowing bench land, capered above the undulations of far-flung prairie. The air was sweet with the tinkling notes of meadowlarks at play. It was a universe of gold and green and blue ruled by the sun.

From three sides, the great posse closed in on the sleepy town of Muddy Flat, with its tumbled ridges behind and to either side of it, and its gray sea of dry gumbo in front, waiting a sprinkle of rain to become as sticky as glue, as slippery as ice.

Muddy Flat's single street suddenly was alive with horsemen; the thick dust rose in choking clouds; every resort and place of business was speedily fronted with a mass of riders—one shot, and the frail false fronts and dusty panes might have been riddled with bullets.

"On your guard!" came the roaring command of Sheriff Wilson.

The dust was settling as he dismounted in front of the largest resort. He swept inside with his gun in his hand, and men poured in behind him. Scarcely a dozen men were in the place. The look of expectation on their faces changed on the instant to concern. These riders were not Burn-'Em-Up Burness and his band back from a successful raid. Instinct told them they faced the law.

The sheriff stepped to the front of the bar. "Who's the boss here?" he asked the barkeep.

"Why . . . I'm workin' here," was the frightened answer.

"I didn't ask who was workin' here," said the sheriff sharply, "I asked for the boss. Get that dirty apron off, and get over on this side of the bar. Climb over!"

The man hastily untied his apron and scrambled over the bar, as a man came from the rear. "I own this joint, if that's what you mean," this man announced. "I'm Harrison. Who're you, and what do you want?" The man's small eyes gleamed with animosity. He was not tall, but was thick-set and of powerful build.

Wilson looked him over. "How long since Burn-'Em-Up has been here?" he demanded in a tone that called for an immediate reply.

"I don't know who you're talkin' about," Harrison flared.

A quick leap, and Wilson had him by the throat. He shook him like a rat, while his victim drew his gun. Wilson's own gun barrel came down upon Harrison's right forearm with a *crack* that was heard through the room. The gun fell to the floor as its owner howled in pain. He looked about in helpless rage, biting his lip.

"How long since he has been here?" Wilson repeated threateningly.

"He stopped in yesterday," the man said through gritted teeth.

"Take him away," the sheriff said to the men swarming the place, "and take this barkeep with him."

"You can't arrest me!" Harrison wailed. "I ain't done nothin'."

"You've run this place without a license for the past three years!" thundered Wilson. "You have your choice here and now of takin' your cash and lockin' up your dive and goin' peacefully, or I'll take charge of your cash and order the place wrecked, and tie you up so you can't wiggle on the way to the jug."

The sheriff turned on the others. "Line up here in front of me," he ordered. "Now, every man that's got an honest job and can prove it, step forward and tell me."

None so much as spoke.

"Take 'em along," Wilson ordered his men. "And search the place for more. Oh, he's goin' to close up and go peaceable, is he? Let him do it. See that they all have horses, and, if they haven't got 'em, borrow 'em from the livery. I'm goin' there next."

Within three minutes, Wilson confronted the liveryman, the one who had taken Bill Klein's horse the night the cowpuncher had ridden into town. "Where's this Burness?" he demanded.

"How should I know?" the man replied in a surly tone. "I'm just in the business here."

"What business?" the sheriff shot at him.

"Why . . . you can see . . . in the livery business," the man faltered.

"You mean you're makin' white likker and haulin'

it in here to be dressed up for the trade," snapped the official. "Don't think I don't know what's been goin' on in this town. I've let you fellows run hog-wild. I've given you just enough rope to hang your-selves and now I'm tyin' the knot." He turned to the men behind him. "Take him along," he commanded, ignoring the man's cries and curses.

Thus it went through the town. Sheriff Wilson en-tered every place, asking pertinent questions and ar-resting undesirables. The word sped quickly that the law had come, and many sought to hide or flee into the brakes. All were thwarted, and, in two hours, Wilson had arrested fifty-one, closed every resort in the town, seized the keys, and made Muddy Flat deader than it ever had been in its history.

When the sunset was blushing in the west, the posse halted on the plain north of the town. Wilson gave his orders crisply. Two deputies and forty men were to take the prisoners to Conroy under instruc-tions to "shoot to kill" if any of the latter attempted to escape. The sheriff with another deputy and fifty men were to ride west. The others, in charge of three deputies, were to ride into Conroy with all possible speed.

"And how about me?" Webb asked, sore from rid-ing, amazed by what he had seen and which he con-sidered a senseless move.

"You go into town with the others," Wilson com-manded most sternly.

"But . . . but where are you going?" Webb de-manded.

"I'm goin' about my business," was Wilson's grim answer. "This game is too strong for you from now on, old-timer. You're goin' home."

"I'll have your badge!" shouted Webb in a heat of anger.

"You've got it!" The sheriff laughed scornfully as he tore off his star and tossed it into the former stockman's lap. "Folks know me without it!" He gave a signal and dashed off into the sunset with his men.

CHAPTER TWENTY-FIVE

Outside the jail, Andrew French, Webb, Miller, and the two brothers, Dick and Clint, had stopped for a conference after the sheriff had delivered his ultimatum. Webb was more excited than angry, but Andrew seemed fighting mad. Miller was mystified and plainly ready for his orders. The brothers were eager, expectant.

The group automatically accepted Andrew as the leader.

"Are you goin' with that posse?" the Two-Bar F owner asked Webb.

"Why not?" Webb retorted. "Certainly I'm going. And what's the matter with Wilson? I'll tell you what's the matter . . . he hasn't had a big job on his hands in years. He's got old and now he's runnin' plumb off his head."

"Don't bother about Wilson bein' old," growled Andrew. "He's not so old that his brains aren't working. I know that old codger like a book, but he had a mean tongue in his head tonight . . . for no reason that I could see." Andrew thus disclosed why he was angry. He was mad at Wilson for having spoken to him so sharply. The sheriff had been blunt, that was it. Blunt to Andrew French!

"He insulted both of us!" Webb exclaimed. "He. . . ."

"Not me, he didn't," Andrew put in forcibly. "All right, Webb, go ahead and get ready for a hard ride." He turned to Miller. "Get the men together at once," he ordered. "The boys and me will go on to the livery. We're goin' back to the ranch."

As both Webb and Miller left, Andrew walked rapidly toward the livery with his sons. "What was the sheriff talkin' about as regards you two?" he asked Dick.

"We managed to overhear the conversation between him and Tower and Hagen," Dick replied. "That's why he was sore."

"Why wouldn't he be?" Andrew demanded angrily. "Eavesdropping, eh? That's nothin' to be proud of. What did he find out from that pair of double-crossin' hoss thieves?"

"I wouldn't think you'd want to hear it, if the way we learned it was so terrible," Clint put in belligerently.

Andrew halted and glared at his son. "I reckon you're responsible for more of those troubles than I'm givin' you credit for," he said.

Clint was roused instantly. "I'm willin' to take the responsibility for the whole thing . . . all of it," he flung back. "I'm ready to do more'n that. Instead of standin' by and lookin' on, I'm ready to start out after Burness alone."

"In which case, I'd have to go along," Dick said quietly.

Andrew French swore aloud. "I've a good notion to tell the two of you to try it," he blurted. "If I didn't want to see you again, I'd say go to it. You know the message Bill Klein brought back after he saw Burness in Muddy Flat. Burness is after me this minute. He'd give his right arm to teach me a lesson, as he looks at it. What did the sheriff find out, if you want to tell me?"

Dick stilled his brother by grasping his arm and shaking his head. "I'll tell you, Dad," he said. "I thought we ought to know for our own protection."

"I suggested it," Clint interposed.

"So we did eavesdrop, as you say," Dick went on. "Tower said the outlaws had taken him away by force so he couldn't spread the alarm or something. It doesn't matter. They rode him off on a horse with a bandit behind him. After the bank raid, Burness, with the main part of his force, caught up with them at the edge of the badlands, and Tower said they cracked him on the head and left him on the ground for dead. He said Hagen took what money was left in the place after the hold-up and started looking for him. By a lucky chance, Hagen started in the same direction as the bandits, got a glimpse of them entering the big brakes of the river, and found Tower on the ground. He brought Tower back on the one horse they had, and then they went straight to the jail."

"A dog-gone lie, every word of it," Andrew said vehemently. "But Tower held back for a last word with Wilson, didn't he? Hagen backed him up, of course."

"Sure he did. When Tower was asked to wait a minute by the sheriff, Wilson drew him into his office and put the works to him. Took him by the throat and threatened to give him a good beating and throw him into jail in the bargain. He meant it, and Tower knew it."

"Then Red Tower told him the truth, eh?" Andrew prompted.

"Red confessed that Hagen had made away with the money that was left, and intended to beat it for good. He ran into Burness and his gang out east of Conroy . . . the one direction Hagen figured he wouldn't take, because of the open country. Tower confessed that Burness kicked them out after taking Hagen's gun. Tower and Hagen got in a fight, and Hagen got the better of the encounter. Then they made peace on the basis that hereafter they would be partners in the Stampede. After that they rode in with the first story agreed upon between them."

"Suffering coyotes!" Andrew ejaculated. "Why, Burness wanted 'em to come back with the story that he had gone east to put the sheriff off the track. He hasn't any intention of goin' east, nor north, to my notion. He might go south, but I doubt it. Here comes Miller with the men. Let's get on to the livery. It won't be long afore daylight, and our place is at the ranch."

Within a quarter of an hour, the Two-Bar F owner and the others had ridden out of town, but not before they had seen plenty of signs of the forming of the big posse the sheriff was assembling. At dawn, when the posse was starting on its fast ride to Muddy Flat, they were well on their way to the French Ranch.

When they were finally on Two-Bar F range, Andrew gave his directions to his foreman. "Put out some look-outs up and down the valley," he said curtly. "Otherwise, I want every man in the outfit at the ranch house, and out of sight. Gun 'em up and have the horses handy and be at the house for supper and further orders."

"That's plain enough," said Miller. "I got you."

He left with the men before they reached the house, and Andrew and his sons rode on home.

At sunset Sheriff Wilson and his men were streaking across the plain toward the band of trees that marked the course of the river. "They'll all wonder why I cracked up Muddy Flat," he told his deputy. "I thought I might as well make a job of it while I was there, for I really didn't expect to find Burness there . . . although there was a chance. We've got a hard bunch with us and I'm not afraid to meet up with him any time. In fact, I wouldn't be surprised if we did meet up with him, and this very night. Pass the word to be alert and to meet shootin' with shootin', if it should start."

Although he had had no sleep the night before, and had ridden far and hard, Wilson still appeared to be as fresh as any man in his posse. With him were several prisoners he had deliberately taken from the jail, after explaining what he wanted them for. They had been eager and enthusiastic in accepting the terms.

"And if any or all of you knock one of those outlaws out of the saddle with a bullet, I'll see that you go free. I give you my word," he had concluded.

When Webb had said Wilson was acting like a wild man, he had almost been right. For never, in his terms of office as sheriff of that county, had Wilson been so wrought up. The fact that he had expected Burness to make him a call someday, and that he had come while Wilson was absent from town, positively infuriated the sheriff.

Night fell soon after the posse had gained the river and turned upstream, due west in the direction of the Two-Bar F Ranch, Paradise Valley, and the foothills of the Rockies.

* * *

Andrew slept most of the day. Clint and Dick slept a spell, but were too restless to stay in the house. Late in the afternoon they went out and found the bunkhouse crammed with men. They were smoking, reading, sleeping in the bunks, and three games of poker were in progress at the tables in the center of the room.

The men looked up, instantly alert, as the brothers entered. "Anything new, Duke?" one of the men asked eagerly. "We're raring to go."

Dick grinned. "There are a lot of people back East who wouldn't dare call me Duke," he observed with a twinkle in his eye. "But I suppose I've got to stand for it on my own father's ranch."

"Or on any other ranch when we happen along," said another cowpuncher, and laughed.

"But we won't stand for the men on the other ranch startin' it!" another called from a bunk.

"Well, that's pretty good," said Dick. "If you boys keep on acting this way, I may stay on a spell."

"Wouldn't hurt our feelings any," said one, "nor the old man's, either, I'll bet."

Clint was grinning through all this. "I gotta watch him harder than ever this time," he drawled. "Anybody notice he's packin' a gun?"

There was a roar of good-natured laughter at this sally.

"Anyway, I'm enjoying this visit more than any in more years than I'm willing to admit," said Dick soberly.

"That's because you've mixed more with general activities this time," said one of the men slyly. "You're beginnin' to belong, see?"

"That settles it, Dick," said Clint. "You're solid with 'em."

Dick had gone to the bunk where Bill Klein was lying. "How do you feel, Bill?" he asked.

The cowpuncher's face twisted into a horrible grimace. "Awful," he said. "Wouldn't I love to be out on the range in the hot sun and the dust, with the sweat runnin' into my eyes . . . wouldn't I? And here I've got to stay penned up, with just a little airing in the shade twice or three times a day, and read and sleep and eat three square meals with dainties from the house thrown in. It's awful hard, Duke, to have to die by inches this way. But it's better than dyin' by yards or rods, at that."

A great howl of laughter greeted this, and Dick laughed himself. "If I didn't know you pretty well, old scout, I'd think you were faking," he said soberly.

"He ain't doin' anything else but!" shouted one of the men. "But don't tell the old man, for we're all standin' behind him so's he can get a good rest." There was more laughing and bantering.

Then Bill's pal, Ed Munsey, spoke up. "Do you know what that poor dyin' creature got me to do?" he said solemnly. "He's cleaned his gun and got me to have his hoss ready to go with us when the time comes."

A cheer followed this announcement, and then Dick held up a hand. "Maybe we hadn't better make so much noise," he suggested. "There might be a spy around, and he would know there were a lot of men here."

Whether intended as a joke or not, the men sobered instantly. Dick could see that the possibility of a fight of some kind was uppermost in their minds. They exchanged glances, and a silence fell over the room. For possibly the first time in his life, Dick realized what a tough, competent, loyal crew his father had gathered around him. Any man present would fight at the drop of a hat for the Two-Bar F or anybody on it. It gave him a thrill. Shortly afterward he and Clint left the bunkhouse.

The talk at supper was sparse. Andrew French was in an almost glowering mood. After the meal, he went out to talk to Miller on the front porch. It was already dark. Dick and Clint were left to themselves and promptly took their horses, as had become their custom, and went for a ride up the wide sweep of Paradise Valley, wherein had been gathered the great herds of the Two-Bar F.

"I don't see any sense in bringing all these cattle in here," Dick told his brother. "I don't think after all he got in the Conroy robberies, that Burness would attempt a raid on our stock."

"He might do it under the impulse of . . . of pure cussedness," Clint ventured. "You know, Dick, I've never seen that coyote pull his gun, but I've got a sneaking notion I could beat him to the draw."

"Then forget that notion," said Dick shortly. "He's bad enough not to experiment with. All these cutthroats and bad men don't respect him and crawl around on their hands and knees before him for nothing."

"Yes, but the average cut-throat, as you call 'em, or bad men, aren't fast at hip work," Clint pointed out.

"It would tickle me if you got the gun business out of your head," said Dick without a trace of annoyance in his tone.

"Oh, well, we won't talk about that end of it," Clint replied. "But it's an important end in this present business, just the same. And listen, Dick, if we should get mixed up with Burness, for the love of Mike, don't go for your gun. With a crowd like that, you're wearing an ornament, and I've a hunch this affair is goin' to wind up with some hard and fancy shooting."

"Do you think I could ever get to be much of an expert in that line?" asked Dick whimsically.

"No!" was the blunt reply. "You didn't take to it at the start, and you haven't practiced. A man may be born a natural gunman, but he might as well be a woodchopper unless he continually keeps in practice."

Night had fallen some time since as they rode on up the valley with the shadowy herds about them. The stars hung on the peaks and high ridges like the candle clusters on a Christmas tree. A cool wind blew down from the higher reaches, scented with balsam. It was a weird, shadowy domain, peaceful and silent.

Suddenly the stillness of the night was shattered by sharp reports down the valley in the direction of the ranch house.

"What's that?" Dick cried as they cautiously reined in their mounts.

Clint was so taken by complete surprise at the sound of the shots that he sat stunned in his saddle. "It's a raid!" he shouted, his voice carrying up and down the narrow valley.

"They're raidin' the ranch, and here we are 'way up here. Come on, Dick, we've got to get back, and quick."

They started down the valley at breakneck pace, and soon saw a number of men riding furiously up the valley toward them. "Hold your fire!" Clint called. "They may be our men."

They slackened their pace as the riders raced toward them. Both held their guns in their hands. They were somewhat bewildered at the sudden turn in events, and the shooting below had stopped as abruptly as it had started. As the riders approached, they waved at them. "Up the valley!" one shouted in a high voice.

Clint could not recognize the voice, but he decided to take no chances, and whirled his horse. "Come on, Dick," he cried, "there's something doin' up above! Follow me, and ride your head off."

He dashed ahead with Dick following, and, as he rode, he veered to the left toward the timber on the south slope of the valley. He wasn't at all sure that the men behind belonged to the Two-Bar F outfit.

"Straight ahead!" came the ringing command.

With that, Clint knew the riders were hostile. There had been about ten of them, as far as he had been able to make out. An ambush! Burness had attacked the ranch, and these were members of the band. But it could have been done so much easier. And why had the shooting at the ranch house ceased so suddenly.

"Come on, Dick!" he shouted. "We've got to ride for it!"

They pushed their horses toward the timber. "They're after us!" yelled Dick.

"Whatever you do, don't shoot!" Clint called. "There are too many for us."

Just then the air was split by a sharp report, a gun flamed from behind and a bullet sang above their heads. A second later a dozen reports broke, and a rain of lead sped past them.

In this emergency, Clint's first thought was of his brother. If he had been alone, he would have made for the trees ahead, shooting as he rode, speeding for the friendly shadow of the trees. But with Dick, he . . .

"Halt!" came the sharp command from behind. "Halt, or we'll pull down our fire!"

Clint knew what that meant. Unless they stopped, the riders behind would cease firing over their heads, would lower it, and . . .

"Stop!" he shouted to Dick. "Whatever you do, don't fire!"

"Drop your guns!" came the sharp order as the riders closed in about them. "Pick up their artillery," the leader told one of his men. Then Clint and Dick both knew what was up.

In the light of the stars, they caught sight of the diminutive figure, the pinched features and the small, snapping eyes of Limpy Lowell. They were in the power of Burness.

CHAPTER TWENTY-SIX

As night fell, Sheriff Wilson and his posse neared the Two-Bar F Ranch. Wilson wanted to consult with Andrew French alone. He and his men were keeping a sharp look-out along the timber by the river and to the west and south. In his heart, the sheriff had no expectation of encountering Burness and his men this soon, if at all. From what the stock-man had told him about the warning Burness had sent to him after he had defied the outlaw by sending him a message by Limpy Lowell, Wilson considered it only a fifty-fifty bet that Burness would strike here to get his revenge. For, since the time of the sending of the warning, Burness had raided the town of Conroy successfully and made away with a large sum of cash, enough, the sheriff thought, to ease any grudge he might have had toward French. Still, the sheriff could take no chances. His pride was smarting under the lash of the outlaw's raid.

When they had almost reached the lower camp of the Bar Two, a gun flamed against the darkness and a sharp report broke the stillness into many echoes. There were two more red flashes and reports, and then his men followed his instructions to the letter and sent a crashing volley toward the point where the firing had come from. The swift-moving shadows of several horses and riders were seen, and a second volley roared in the night.

But Wilson had perceived that the riders were few and were making straight up the incline toward the Two-Bar ranch house, where lights shone dimly. He recognized instantly that these riders were not members of Burness's band, but look-outs that French had stationed.

"Stop firing!" he shouted at the top of his strong voice as he swung in a curve ahead of his men. "Stop firing! Those are Two-Bar men. Follow me, and not a shot unless I fire first."

He swung his posse toward the ranch house, where, even at a distance, signs of activity at the ranch were visible. Lanterns were bobbing, and Andrew French's voice came down to them in a rumble.

"Tell 'em I'm goin' to signal," Wilson roared to his deputy, "and to hold their fire till I give the word!"

Then, as they raced their horses up the long acclivity, Wilson raised his gun and fired three shots in the air, so that the flashes of his gun would spurt upward.

As they neared the house, they saw an unbroken line of men in front of the house and on either side. "Stay back," he ordered his deputy. "I'll go on alone. Looks like French has got every man in his outfit up there, and they're too hard a bunch to take chances with."

He went forward alone, just as Dick and Clint, far up the valley, were starting down, lured by the firing—only to be captured. As he drew near the porch of the ranch house, he was recognized.

"It's Wilson!" Andrew shouted. "What was the

idea in comin' up here and sharpshootin' at my men?" he demanded in an irate tone.

"Because your men didn't have sense enough to hold their own fire," Wilson returned angrily.

"They was ordered to fire when they saw men comin' as a signal," French roared in reply.

"And my men had orders to fire if fired upon," said Wilson coolly. He stamped up the porch. "Lot of good it'll do us to be sky shootin' to signal to the Burness gang if they're around here," he said grimly. "Send a man down there to bring my posse up. Then I'll see you alone."

"Bring 'em up, Miller," French ordered crisply. "You might have known I'd have look-outs down there," he stormed at the sheriff as he led him into the house. "What's up? Is Burness headed this way . . . doubled on his tracks?"

"Suppose your housekeeper would lend me a cup of coffee?" Wilson asked mildly, smiling at Susan Enfield, who was watching from the dining room door. "And maybe they'll scare up something for my bunch out in the cook house."

French nodded to the housekeeper. Then he stared searchingly at Wilson while the sheriff put his hat on the table, sat down in an easy chair, and mopped his face and brow with a big blue bandanna. "This is the second chance I've taken today," he announced.

"It's hardly a time to be taking chances . . . foolish ones," said French. "You knew I could protect my property and my ranch."

"Perhaps you can, and perhaps you can't," purred the sheriff. "I happen to know more about this man Burness than you. I've had experience with him and his methods before, although you knew nothing of it, and I'm not goin' to bother to tell you now. Listen. Burness is goin' to do one of two things. He either will do his best to make a clean getaway with his plunder . . . and it's enough to tempt him to do so, for he took plenty . . . or he's comin' here to try to get even with you for sneering at him and scorning him twice. I'm taking the chance, however, that he's comin' here."

He ceased and thanked the housekeeper for the coffee, cold meat, bread, butter, and mustard that she put on the table before him. He began to drink the coffee and eat at once.

"What other chance did you take?" asked the stockman curiously.

"Don't you remember that Red Tower and Hagen came back first with a story intended to cause me to believe that Burness had headed south?" said the sheriff as he made his meal. "Later Red confessed that Burness had dropped him east of town. He knew I would wring the truth out of Red. He took a chance on my goin' east. I thought this out and took a chance on him goin' south. I went south with every man at my disposal. If he saw us goin', his way was clear to race up here while the coast was clear. We hurried to Muddy Flat and he wasn't there. I cleaned out the town, broke up the bars, and sent half its population to jail, guarded by a third of my men. They're herded in jail afore now. I sent the other third to town in case he might turn about and try to free the scum I jailed. Then I came here in a way he couldn't very well see me. I want that man, and I'm goin' to get him."

French frowned. "I hope he comes," he growled doubtfully. "I've men on the watch where they'll do the most good. He can't surprise us."

"Where are the boys?" Wilson asked casually.

French started. Then he called loudly to Miller. The foreman came up the porch and appeared in the doorway shortly.

"Where are Dick and Clint?" the stockman demanded.

"Why, they're out for a little ride up the valley, I expect. That's what they said they was goin' to do."

"And you let 'em go!" Andrew thundered.

"They said they took a ride every evening," replied Miller. "I had no orders to stop 'em from takin' a ride if they wanted to, and they would have laughed at me if I'd tried. I haven't been told to order 'em about, 'cept to keep 'em from leaving the ranch. If they tried to leave the ranch, I reckon the look-outs would follow orders and send 'em back."

"As if they'd listen to a look-out!" cried French. "Send some men out to look for 'em at once. They usually go up the valley."

"And where'll I send the men to look for 'em," retorted Miller in a voice that rippled anger. "They didn't go down from here, that's certain. If they went up the valley, they know what they're about. Those boys are not fools. If I've got to comb the valley for 'em, it'll take every man I've got." He turned away, biting his lip.

Andrew stared at him in amazement. Then his face clouded darkly and he spoke harshly: "You're turnin' down orders, eh? You'll do as I say, you fathead, or you'll quit. Those boys may be in danger."

"For that I should quit," returned Miller calmly.

"And I wouldn't blame you a bit," the sheriff announced.

For a moment there was a heavy silence, and the faint reports of shots came to their ears, shots in the upper valley.

"The look-outs!" exclaimed Miller. "They've met

up with the outlaws. I'll get the men mounted." He ran out with this.

But Andrew and the sheriff looked steadily at each other.

"It might be the look-outs," Wilson said doubtfully.

Andrew shook his head, face going pale. "It's the . . . the boys," he said hoarsely.

The sheriff now was roused to quick activity. "We don't want to take all the men up there," he said sharply. "If it's them, they might be doubling back this way. I'll go up with Miller with half of my men and half of yours. Half our outfits must stay here, and you stay here to order 'em to shoot to kill if hostile riders should appear. There's five thousand cold in it for the man that drops Burness. I had the right hunch. I'm goin' to send for the rest of my men from Conroy. Now be as you've always been in time of hot trouble, Andy . . . keep your head."

He was out the door before Andrew French could reply, and Susan Enfield came into the room. "It may not be them at all, Andrew," she said soothingly. "Let these men younger than you are direct things. There'll maybe be hard riding and swift shooting. Miller and the sheriff know how to run these things. You know Clint's too fast to let them get him and Dick. Maybe they're helping the lookouts. Don't be in such a fuss when we don't know what it's about. And it's night, man, and Burness would shoot you on sight."

Andrew spoke in a hard, but almost despairing voice. "No, Susan, I can see it now . . . he wants to hit at me, at my very heart, through the boys, and that would be worse than bullets . . . worse than death." He sank suddenly in his chair, weak with shock and fear and anxiety.

The courtyard and rear of the big ranch house was

a scene of extraordinary activity. Riders were catching up their horses and mounting. Dust rose and swirled about them. There were shouts and curses, and the voices of Wilson and Miller roaring orders. One lean rider, mounted on a mustang that possessed the speed of a race horse, streaked eastward, bound for Conroy. Then there came the pounding of two-score and ten horses bound up the valley. Others were in the shadows of the barn, the haystacks, the bunkhouse, and the big ranch house.

Bill Klein appeared in the doorway of the living room, booted and spurred, his heavy cartridge belt and gun buckled where they belonged, and an extra gun thrust into his belt on the right side.

"Miller told me to stay here and take your orders, sir," he said in a ringing voice. "I'm able to do that, at least . . . and I haven't been a range boss for nothing. There's about fifty men cached near the house, and, if they try to strike in two places, they're goin' to find it hard in both."

"That's right," Andrew said, rising. He walked to a corner and brought forth a repeating rifle. "If any riders show up, make sure they're hostile, and then pour the hot lead into 'em for keeps."

Klein's eyes shone. "It's the old man himself that's ordering," he said as he turned to the door, "meanin' no disrespect."

Instead of becoming angry, Andrew seemed pleased. "You feelin' all right now, Bill? What's this I hear about you havin' heart trouble?"

"What! Me?" scoffed Klein. "Somebody's been handin' out a pipe dream. The boys have been kiddin' a lot about me hangin' out in the bunkhouse with this hand. I could have done lots of things with this hand. Miller didn't do any kiddin' when he gave me this job tonight."

"Go ahead." Andrew smiled. "Now, what's this?"

There was a commotion in the yard in front of the porch. "Let him alone!" ordered a harsh voice. "That's Mister Webb, a friend of the big boss."

A few minutes later Norman Webb entered to find Andrew frowning. "What's goin' on up here, Andy?" he asked anxiously. "Did Burness raid your ranch?"

"Well, maybe he's up this way and maybe he ain't," French evaded. "Did you go out with Wilson this morning?"

Webb snorted. "Of course, I did," he said. "He chased down to Muddy Flat, which was foolish, as I told him. He smashed or locked the saloons and then took a bunch of no-good prisoners and sent them to be locked up and fed at the county jail. Sent the posse into town, all except what he took with him, and wouldn't let me come along. Threw his badge at me. I told you he was too old to be sheriff. He's crazy! I went on into town, ate and got a fresh horse, and come up here. I met a feller riding like the wind on his way to town. Steered around me. Guess he's got a message. What's happened, Andy? I won't quit this thing . . . not with you in the mix-up, I won't."

"Sit down, Norman," said French in a different tone. "Susan! We got another visitor. I guess you know him. Bring him some coffee and a bite."

While Webb was taking his coffee and a snack, Andrew told him what had taken place, and hinted what he feared.

Webb finished eating and looked at Andrew earnestly. "He wouldn't dare to do it," he announced. "Not in a million years. You always did jump at conclusions. C'mon, let's play cribbage."

"It . . . it doesn't seem right," Andrew protested.

"And it doesn't seem right for you and me to be here. We ought to be out. . . ."

"What could we do?" Webb asked wisely. "There's better riders and gunfighters than us out now looking after things. Our turn will come later."

After an hour of play, thundering hoofs in the courtyard brought them to their feet, their cards scattering on table and floor.

It was Miller who came in, and both men saw he had serious news. "It must be him . . . Burness," the foreman said grimly without preliminaries. "They shot down one of our men who was on guard. He was able to tell us there were just a handful of them before he died. We couldn't find Clint or Dick, and we think they're chasing 'em. Wilson's spreading the men up there, laying a trap. I'm to take the rest up when they come from town. That's all I have to report at present. Wilson will send news of anything that happens."

"Spreading a trap!" cried Andrew, his face white. "For who?"

"For Burness," came the answer, sharp and cold as ice.

"He's settin' a trap for me!" shouted Andrew. "They've got the boys! Tell Wilson to bring back the men. No . . . that won't do now. It's too late. But I personally will take charge of the men comin' from town." His face purpled as he sank into a chair and waved his foreman aside.

Chapter Twenty-seven

Pansy had watched her father prepare to join the posse that was being raised by Sheriff Wilson before the dawn. Her heart was filled with misgivings. Norman Webb swore occasionally as he donned range clothes and boots for the ride to come. He cleaned and oiled the gun he hadn't used since he had quit ranching. The girl was almost afraid to speak to him. She knew something fearful was to happen.

"Where are you going, Father?" she asked finally.

"I'm goin' out on a social ride with that fool, Wilson," was Webb's disgusted retort.

"You're really going out with a posse, are you not?" persisted the girl.

"I reckon that's what one would call it," snapped her father. "Sending every man he can raise in one bunch. He's an old fool. We're goin' to start at dawn."

"But you don't have to go, Father," his daughter protested.

"Oh, I don't?" Webb said angrily, scowling at Pansy. "Well, I'm goin' just the same. I'm as much responsible for law and order in this town as Wilson is . . . more, perhaps. It's my duty. I do have to go. Where's my range hat?"

Pansy gave up in despair and went for the hat. For some reason she couldn't explain, she had no fear for her father's safety. He was not so fast on a horse of later years; he was not so quick or sure with his gun. Younger men would be in the vanguard if there was to be real trouble, and one of those was sure to be Clint French. She thought she had been through with him, but now that death might be hovering in the offing . . .

"Here's your hat, Daddy," she said cheerfully when she brought the hat to him. "Do you mind if I ask you a question? Oh, it isn't about you, you old bear." She put her arms about his neck as he shoved his weapon into its worn holster.

"Just like a woman," he observed, looking down at her. "And you are a woman now, Pansy. Women are always asking questions." He stroked her hair. "Well, what is it?"

"Is Clint going with the posse, Daddy?"

He released her with a very queer expression on his face. "Aren't you goin' to ask if Richard is goin', too?"

"Of course, he'd go where Clint goes, so . . . I . . ." She faltered and looked at him steadily.

"Well, he's not goin'," Webb said with a convincing nod. "He and Richard and Andy and the whole Two-Bar outfit are goin' back to their ranch. Now, does that make you feel better?"

"You don't mind my asking about my friends, do you, Father?"

Norman looked at her a long time. He loved this beautiful daughter far more than life itself. And how beautiful she was. Such eyes and lips and hair. The slim grace of her young body. And if anything happened to him, what . . . well, nothing would happen. But if she should marry? He had never thought of her as married. But here was that elusive, effeminate charm that men would die for and kill for, and go through the very fires of purgatory for. It was as if she had grown up before his very eyes in a few moments.

"Why are you looking at me so strangely, Daddy?" she asked, a bit startled.

"Pansy, my little sweet, you are all I have," he said gently. "You are young, full of life, and beautiful. You must be careful about men, sweetheart." Then he kissed her impulsively and quickly made for the door.

"Take care of yourself, Daddy," he heard as he hurried out.

Pansy was worried despite what her father had said. She was wondering, too, about the way he had looked at her, and what he had said about being careful about men. She flushed as it came home to her that she was thinking so much about Clint French. She hadn't been kind to him, but, then, he hadn't been kind to her, had he? She didn't know. She rather thrilled at the thought that he was intensely jealous of her. As for Dick French—she paused and thought. Then she shrugged her shoulders and tossed her head and had the housekeeper prepare her a light breakfast.

Pansy was among those who watched the big posse ride away. She saw the Two-Bar outfit was not among them. If they hadn't gone back to the French Ranch, they might be circling around to meet the posse, or they might have gone on the manhunt in a different direction. She didn't understand why Andrew French would refuse to join the chase, unless he had had words with the sheriff. By the way her father had spoken of Wilson, calling him a fool and deriding him, she assumed he, too, had had words with him.

She walked thoughtfully back to the house and moved about but little during the day. She tried to read, but this attempt was a failure. After all, her father might get hurt, might even. . . . She put this thought aside with a shudder.

It was just sunset when, from her chair on the front porch, she heard the loud, thundering impact of scores of hoofs. In a moment men and women, boys and girls, were in the street, hurrying into town. The posse had returned. So soon?

Pansy hastened down the street, but saw her father riding toward the house. He motioned to her to go back, and she turned and ran to the house. She waited until he had put up his steaming horse, given directions as to its care to their man, and then met him in the back yard.

"Daddy! I'm so glad you're back!" she exclaimed, throwing her arms about him and giving him a kiss. "I'm so glad that you needn't tell me anything, unless you wish." Her last words were said wistfully.

"Danged nonsense, the whole business," Webb stormed as they walked to the house. "Went down to Muddy Flat, where anybody with a bird-seed brain might know Burness would not be. Of all places to look for him! In one of his hangouts, which would be the last place he would go. Wilson tore the town to pieces and brought back a lot of no-goods and put 'em in jail for the county to feed. Didn't find out a thing, the fool!"

"Well, come on in, Daddy, and get washed up and have a good supper," Pansy said cheerfully, patting his shoulder. "As long as you're back again and all right, I don't care what happened."

Webb washed and ate supper without taking off the rough clothes or boots he had worn on the ride. He was more than taciturn during the meal; he was brooding. Pansy noticed this, saw that he was not satisfied with what was being done, but forbore asking him questions.

After the meal he went out and instructed the man to saddle a fresh horse. This did worry the girl. He went into the house and buckled on his gun and got his hat. Of course, Pansy didn't know that the entire posse hadn't returned, that the sheriff had ridden west with many men.

"Father, are you going out again?" she asked a bit sharply.

"Now listen, girlie, we've got a manhunt on our hands," he replied sternly. "Not just today, or possibly tonight . . . we may be engaged on this matter for days. And I am not goin' to stay behind. You must be brave. You were born on the range, and range women are brave and patient where their men folks are concerned. You mustn't worry, and you must not go out on the streets. I am saying this for your own good, as well as mine. I cannot worry about you and attend to whatever business I may have in hand at the time. I cannot stop it, and you must do your share by being optimistic and brave."

There were tears in Pansy's eyes as she kissed her father. "All right, Daddy. It's . . . it's just new to me, that's all . . . I mean this outlaw business. Don't worry about me."

Norman Webb pressed her hand and went out the rear door.

When his horse's hoof beats had died in the street, Pansy put on a warm jacket and went out, also. It was now long past dark. She hastened to a point where she could keep in the deep shadow and see the front of the jail. Many men were about. She saw men go into the jail and come out, but, after keeping her vigil for more than an hour, she had not seen her father or the sheriff. Then she did a bold thing. She walked to the corner, and, when a young man, heavily armed, was about to pass her, she accosted him.

"Is the posse going out again?" she asked in a natural tone.

"Why, they ain't all come back yet, miss," was the respectful answer as the youth touched the brim of his cap. "They haven't ordered the rest of us out yet, but maybe we'll get orders soon."

"Is Sheriff Wilson back?" asked Pansy, surprised at his answer.

"Nope, he's still out with a bunch. Don't worry, we'll get the gang we're after." There was a note of pride in his voice.

"I hope so," she said. "My father is out, and it worries me."

"Ain't you Norman Webb's girl?" he asked, looking at her closely.

"Why . . . yes," she stammered. "Yes, I am."

"You needn't worry about him. I think I saw him ridin' out west, like he was goin' to the Two-Bar. He'll be all right."

Pansy thanked him and made her way straight home. When she got there, she found that her father had not returned. She sat down on the porch to think. The sheriff and a bunch hadn't returned. Perhaps they had gone out to the Two-Bar Ranch. Her father had followed. Then, had there been trouble out there? Had the bandits attacked the ranch? Had someone, perhaps, been hurt out there? She remembered her father had said something about range women. She was range born.

She kept thinking for what seemed hours, until

she started up. There was a stir in the center of town. Men rode swiftly down the street. She could hear shouts and cries. She waited for no more. She stole upstairs and donned her riding habit and boots. She thrust a small, pearl-handled revolver in her jacket pocket. Clint had taught her to shoot, she recalled with a swift intaking of breath.

The house was asleep. She hurried to the barn, quickly saddled her fast mare, Betsy, and led the animal into a vacant lot, under the trees near the main street. Her father was right. She was a range woman.

She watched in the shadows, and within fifteen minutes every member of the posse left in town galloped past her—going west. Pansy looked after them. Were they going to the Two-Bar? It was early morning now, still dark. She felt that she had to find out where the riders were headed. She *would* find out.

She went out into the street and walked boldly up to the jail. The street was not filled this time. She went into the jail and turned to the sheriff's office.

"There's nobody in there, Miss Webb."

She whirled to see a man at a desk in the outer office. It was the turnkey, although she didn't know it.

"Oh," she said in a calm voice. "Can you tell me where those men are going . . . the riders who just left town?"

"Why . . . er . . ." The turnkey hesitated. Something told him he should not divulge any of the sheriff's office business to this young lady. He decided to play safe. "I don't exactly know, miss, and I couldn't tell you if I wanted."

"But I just want to know about Father," she insisted. "I am worried about him, and, if I know where he has gone, I will be relieved. Was he with those men?"

"I'm sure I don't know," replied the turnkey

truthfully. "But you have nothing to worry about. You should not be out at this time, and, if you don't go home, it may be necessary . . ."

"You needn't bother," she interrupted haughtily, and flung herself out of the jail. She knew what he had meant. It might be necessary to send her home under escort. The impertinence of the man!

She saw the lighted windows of the Stampede and immediately was obsessed with an idea. She knew Red Tower but slightly. Her father had never said anything definitely against the resortkeeper at home, and he was a gambler. Moreover, he knew everything that took place in town. Red Tower knew where the posse had gone, and he was just enough of a sport to tell her outright. He might consider it an honor for her to ask him. It was worth trying, anyway. Her mind made up, she hurried to a side door of the resort, where she was in the shadow of the building. She might be able to signal him or signal someone who would tell him that she wanted to see him, which would be just as well. She opened the door slightly and peered within. The place was deserted. But both Red Tower and his man, Jim Hagen, were there behind the bar. Then what she saw and heard held her spellbound.

"Why didn't you go along with the posse?" Tower was asking. "It would look good for the place to have someone along."

"Why didn't you go yourself?" Hagen said, sneering. "You had plenty of sleep. Look better for the supposed-to-be-boss to go, wouldn't it?"

"Nobody knows anything about our partnership yet," Tower said, snarling. "And I'm still runnin' things here, even if you do get in on the cut. I'm not in condition to ride out there to the Two-Bar, and then maybe have to ride in the hills till kingdom comes, and you know it."

"I think we'll announce our partnership tomorrow, after what you've said." Hagen scowled, shooting out his jaw.

"I don't think we will," said Tower sharply. "You can get out of here now and I'll look after the place."

"Not till I've made up the cash," said Hagen, leering. "I wouldn't trust you. . . ." He stopped, taking a step toward Tower. "Why, you rat, you've got a gun, eh?" He leaped toward Tower, and a gun *cracked*.

Hagen staggered back and fell behind the bar. Tower leaned and deliberately fired again.

Pansy closed the door and leaned faintly against the side of the building for several moments. Then she ran across the street to where she had left her horse, mounted, rode out into the street, and turned west with the first faint glimmer of dawn at her back.

CHAPTER TWENTY-EIGHT

As Pansy rode westward at a moderate pace, which would give her time to think, her heart was in a tumult. True, she had accidentally learned that the posse, and her father, had left for the Two-Bar Ranch. Then Burness and his band of outlaws must be in Paradise Valley. But that other—the cold killing of the man Hagen filled her brain and her being with a chill. Even after he had shot Hagen down, Red Tower had leaned over and fired a second shot to make certain of a sure job. Range stuff! It was a cowardly thing to do, and she would certainly tell the sheriff about it, thought the girl. Then, after a time, she decided she would tell her father first. She had to put this horrible scene out of her mind.

She had her father and Clint—yes, Clint!—to worry about, without letting what she had seen in the Stampede unnerve her and occupy her thoughts to the exclusion of everything else. Her father would be very angry with her for going to the Two-Bar. But she would put his anger aside. She was a range woman and she was going to her father and her man. It sounded foolish, but, after all, it was true.

Would Clint be angry with her, too? She would

turn his anger aside, also. She couldn't blame him for being jealous. If she couldn't handle him in such a situation before—before?—what would she be able to do with him after—after? Her thoughts trailed off in confusion, and her cheeks bloomed with roses as the daylight spread over the land. Although she was riding alone, she was not afraid, even though she knew a desperate band of outlaws was abroad.

The dawn blushed as rosy as her cheeks, then came a flaring crimson, and at last the great golden crown of the sun. Pansy looked back with an expression of pleasure. When she looked ahead, she started, and the smile died. A horseman was bearing down on her like the wind.

Her first instinct was to turn and ride as fast as possible back to town. But she was nearly halfway to the ranch. Then her fears were swept away. This must be a member of the posse hurrying back with a message or for some other reason. Then she saw a rider off to the left, and still another off to the right, ready to close in upon her. Friends or foes, she was fairly caught. Her head went up. She felt quickly of the little but efficient revolver in her jacket pocket and pushed on.

The rider ahead came on with a rush. He was a big man, mounted on a superb horse. His big hat was drawn low over his eyes against the bright rays of the rising sun. He pulled up with a suddenness that caused his horse to rear, and swept his hat in a circle.

Pansy saw his face was dark, his eyes black, and his lips thick. He wore a bushy, black mustache that needed trimming, and a thin growth of black beard. Something about him suggested the quarter-breed, Indian or possibly Mexican. As he smiled, his teeth showed white and even, and he almost appeared handsome.

"Ah, miss, out with the morning sun, which is no brighter than your eyes," he said in a moderate voice as the other two riders closed in, and Pansy felt the chill of fear. "Out with the meadowlarks, and I'll bet their notes are no sweeter than your voice. Good morning, Miss Webb!" His hat swept low, and he replaced it on his head firmly.

"Good morning, but . . . I . . . believe you have the advantage of me," said Pansy, seeking to regain her high spirits.

"Of course, I have, miss," he said, the smile gone. "But all you have to do is be quiet and do as I say. You will not be harmed."

He had deliberately mistaken her meaning, and was informing her she was a prisoner. There was only one who might be expected to act in such a bold manner, to take such a chance. Burness!

With this thought, Pansy's eyes brimmed with contempt. She felt absolutely unafraid of him. She would not hesitate to shoot him. She lifted her head haughtily. "Am I to take it that you're the killer and bandit they call Burness?" she asked disdainfully.

"I couldn't take that from a man," the outlaw said with a faint smile, "but from you, milady, it is a compliment." His voice changed. His eyes flashed unexpected malice. "Whoever I happen to be, miss, you are goin' with me if I have to rope you to the saddle. I mean just what I say. It isn't far . . . where we are goin' . . . and soon you will be with your friends again. Before the sun is at high noon, I would say. Will you come?" He put the question sternly.

Pansy considered. This was Burness, all right. If she didn't go, he would have her roped to the saddle, as he had promised. In which case she would have no chance to use her gun. She knew he intended to use her in some scheme. She might learn what he was up to, get away, and sound the alarm. She took no stock in his promise that she would be with her friends by noon.

"All right." She nodded. "I'll go."

"And there's where you show more sense than your dad ever had," said the outlaw. "It isn't his fault, understand . . . for he was born that way. Tell him I said so next time you see him. Now, follow that man."

One of the riders started toward the river, and Pansy rode after him. Behind her came Burness, and after the outlaw chief came the third man. They rode at an easy lope, southwest toward the river, and Pansy was relieved to find that they really were not riding away from the ranch. In a short time they reached the north bank of the river and entered the shelter of the trees. Pansy had noticed the tracks of scores of horses, all heading for the Two-Bar. And here was the very man they sought, behind them. Surely they could not have overlooked his band if they were hidden along the river. Could it be possible that Burness was here alone, save for two men?

The rider led the way up the river for two miles or so and then plunged through some bushes and slid his horse to the water's edge. The others followed, and, when they were at the bottom, they turned in under a hanging bank, a cavity large enough for themselves and horses, with a dirt roof, a sandy floor, and a fringe of overhanging green growth and thin roots through which they could peer out at the opposite bank and up the river. A small, natural hiding place, well concealed, easy of exit, but into which none could enter without being seen, and, if there were more than one, they must come singly.

They dismounted, and Burness rolled and lighted a cigarette. He ordered saddle blankets for Pansy to sit on. "Here we will have to stay until it is time to go up to the ranch," he explained to the girl almost apologetically. "May be an hour, may be two, but I hardly think it will be any longer than that." He smiled.

"To the ranch!" Pansy exclaimed, incredulous and wide-eyed.

"To the Two-Bar, to be more exact," said the outlaw, nodding.

Pansy's spirits fell. Had this man raided the ranch before Andrew and the others had returned, or had he caught them napping and carried off Andrew, Clint, and Dick? Something terrible must have happened if he actually proposed to go up there this morning. He certainly wouldn't dare to go up there if the posse were there. But the posse may have turned off before reaching the ranch, or they might have been ambushed. She was almost frantic, but did not show it.

"I suppose they will be waiting for you," she said pleasantly.

"We will see presently," replied the outlaw. "I've been waited for on more than one occasion. I've even been welcomed. Funny part of it is, I think I'll be welcome in this case . . . at the end."

Slowly the confident, cruel, masterly personality of this notorious bandit and desperado made itself felt upon the girl. She now saw the inexorable brutality of the real man. A killing meant no more to him than a soft April shower. And he possessed a maniacal cunning.

"Who do you think will welcome you?" she asked casually.

"Ha! We will see about that, too," the outlaw replied, and laughed harshly. "You better sit down and rest a while. I'm tired of talkin' . . . to you." He went outside with the two men, and they talked in soft tones at the edge of the river, out of earshot of Pansy. Burness's broad back was turned toward the girl. She looked at it as if spellbound. It seemed to grow broader and broader—a target that would be hard to miss. She felt the gun in the pocket of her jacket. That broad back fascinated her. She could shoot straight at a greater distance than this. She could draw her small pistol stealthily and send a bullet crashing into the middle of that back in an instant, and she could wound, if not kill, each of the other two. With their leader dead, would the other two have the nerve to shoot her or even lay a hand on her? Their first thought would be of flight, if she let them get away.

She pressed her right hand against the gun, so near, so easy to reach. She had spent hours of practice at the very thing she was considering doing now. She was steady. She knew she could do it, and she would have no remorse for having shot such a monster in the back. He turned once to look at her, and what she saw in his eyes nearly brought about the very act she was seriously contemplating. But something held her back. Instinctively she felt that the death of the bandit would in some way have a bad result for her father and Clint and the others. Perhaps he had them in his power. Did he really intend to go up to the ranch? She decided to wait and see.

At the end of an hour there was a rustling on the blind trail above the hideout. Burness and the others leaped within the overhanging bank, jerking out their guns. Pansy tensed. If the newcomers proved to be friends, she was determined to shoot Burness to death. The outlaw never knew how close to death he had been at the hand of a mere girl that morning. His own egotism and contempt for women had caused him to overlook searching his fair prisoner.

A minute later a rider slid to the bottom of the trail and flung himself from the saddle. Burness and the others hurried out to talk with him. The man was smiling.

"What's up, Warren?" Burness asked sharply. "Talk low but fast."

Warren looked past the trio, and his eyes lifted as he saw Pansy. Then he turned to the others and spoke rapidly in an undertone. When he had finished, Burness said: "That's good. Now you boys know what to do. Go ahead, and, if anything does happen . . ." He lowered his voice so that Pansy could hear no more.

The two men who had been with Burness, and Warren, now led their horses up the sandy trail to the upper bank. A silence settled down, during which Burness rolled and lighted a cigarette and scowled at the girl. He lighted his smoke, stood with his big legs far apart, and spoke slowly and distinctly, as if he were teaching a child.

"It's our turn now, miss, and I want to tell you something so you won't be so foolish as to make any mistakes." His eyes were cold, his voice was hard. Pansy knew the true Burness was talking, and, although she was inwardly apprehensive, she did not show it outwardly.

Burness apparently did not expect a reply. "We are goin' to get out of here and take a ride up the river through the trees. When we reach the Two-Bar lower camp, we are goin' out in the open and ride up to the ranch house . . . you and me, understand?"

Pansy gasped and went white. "What has . . . happened there?" she managed to get out in a very faint voice.

"Nothing has happened at that particular spot as yet," said the outlaw. "Whether or not anything does happen there will depend on you."

"On me?" the girl faltered.

"Exactly. On you. You are merely to ride with me up to the house, talk a little, laugh maybe, but, if you yell, it'll start the works goin'. When we reach the porch steps, we will go up on the porch, and then you can do what you please . . . yell, cry, go somewhere, say anything you want . . . but you must be steady on the ride up."

There was real fear in Pansy's eyes now. "You're going . . . to . . . kill who is in . . . the house?" she asked breathlessly.

"On the contrary, I'm not goin' to kill anybody," Burness said sternly. "Andy French will tell you or anybody else that after we have met. Do you think you can compose yourself and ride up there with me? Say so. If you can't, I'll ride up there alone . . . and that won't be so good for you." His eyes snapped fire, and his lips tightened.

Pansy tried to assemble her scattered thoughts. This brute was going to see Andrew French. He promised not to kill anybody. But she must ride up to the house with him. Why? Then a light broke through the clouds of doubt and conjecture and perplexity. He wanted her as a shield, so that he wouldn't be fired upon going up the hill, to surprise and puzzle Andrew, possibly her father—but she could spread the alarm before he could shoot them and get away.

"I'll do as you say," she said in a low voice.

"You'll remember my orders and not go to pieces?" he asked.

"Yes," she replied, looking him in the eyes without flinching.

"Then we'll go," he said grimly. "You'll note it's not noon."

They led their horses up the sandy trail and mounted in the trees on the north bank. "Just ride ahead on this hard trail," said Burness, and the girl proceeded to obey, with Burness riding behind her.

The sun was high over their heads when they came out at the Two-Bar lower camp. Pansy rode on the outlaw's right, to her surprise, as they proceeded up the long climb to the house. Before they were halfway up, they could discern activity about the abode of Andrew French.

"Faster!" Burness ordered, and they increased their pace.

The mouth of the valley was clear of men, and only three were in sight at the house. As they neared it, they saw Andrew French with a rifle across his arm. At the side of the house was Bill Klein, who Burness had met, wounded, and sent back with the message of warning to the stockman. With Klein was his old partner, Ed Munsey. The rancher had remained behind when the big posse started on into the hills. There were certain papers he wished to put in shape before he joined the chase. Klein and Munsey were to ride with him. Webb had gone on with the others.

As they approached the porch, Pansy felt something hard in her side. She twisted and looked down. Burness was gazing at Andrew on the porch as the rancher lowered his rifle. Pansy grew cold all over as she saw Burness's gun at his side, pointed toward her. Her face flushed with anger. Burness had gained the ranch by using a woman for a shield. The beast!

Burness flung himself from his horse at the steps and covered Andrew instantly. "If there's any trouble," he cried hoarsely, "you'll go first. I've come here peaceful to talk to you. Are you willing?"

"Come in," Andrew invited, his face pale. "Keep your guns down," he ordered Klein and Munsey, "and take Pansy around back to Susan."

Inside the cool, comfortable living room, Andrew French and Burness faced each other. "Nice place you have here," the outlaw observed. "Not that I came here to talk about your dump," he added.

"It was a coward's way to come," said Andrew. "Behind a woman's skirts."

"I had to make sure of not bein' pot shot," said Burness. "I had to talk to you, and, when you've heard what I've got to say, you'll be mighty glad I got here." He was looking about the room, and now he suddenly whirled on the stockman. "Don't try any tricks," he warned with a heavy scowl. "If I should not get back to a certain place there are two young men you'll not see again."

"My sons?" Andrew asked unsteadily.

"Exactly," replied Burness. "And you know I don't lie, French. Give the word so I can have a sandwich and a cool drink of milk. It's hot. If you think I'm foolin' . . . look." He drew like lightning and tossed his gun on the table.

Andrew walked unsteadily to the dining room door and called instructions to the housekeeper. "It's . . . it's a dastardly thing for you to do," he told the bandit. "You'll get even with me through the boys, is that it?"

"You're forgettin' two things," Burness returned

calmly. "You sent one of my men back with a black eye and a message to me sayin' as much as that you could get me whenever you wanted to." Burness laughed derisively. "Why, all these posses and your outfit thrown in can't get me, you old fool. Your brains have dried up. The second thing is that I'm an out-and-out bandit, train robber, killer, rustler, and general all-around outlaw, and I want the money."

Susan brought in a lunch, her face and manner cool, and put it on the table. Burness began to eat, standing, looking at French.

"You've called yourself the right names, save that you're a rat to boot," said Andrew. "I'm willing to believe you when you say you have Dick and Clint in your power. Now what do you want?"

"Before I tell you that," Burness said with his mouth filled with the food he was rapidly gulping down, "I want you to get it into your head that I've got Clint and Dick . . . I guess that's his name . . . dead to rights. They're guarded by five of the toughest men in my band. We made a big haul, and those men have instructions to do a certain thing . . . I won't be hard on you . . . if I'm not back by tonight. I have entrusted some of the swag we took in Conroy to two I can trust. I have the rest myself. If those men are to get a cent cut-in, they must obey orders. I don't think they'll fall down on the job, do you?"

"What's your proposition?" Andrew asked hoarsely.

"You carry more cash in your safe than any rancher on this range," said Burness, gulping the last of his repast and draining the glass of milk. "I want all you have, and, if it isn't more than twenty thousand . . ." He shrugged. "In addition to that, you're to call off the men and I send the chicks scooting back to you unharmed."

"And . . . if I refuse?" Andrew could hardly get the words out.

Burness laughed and leaped like a tiger to regain his gun. "Then I'll have to shoot my way out, startin' with you. I think I can make it. Come on, I'm in a hurry. Take your choice."

"Come in the office."

Once in the office, Andrew opened the cash compartments and watched Burness stuff his pockets with the bills. Having finished, and looking satisfied, Burness said: "Come out with me to the porch and tell those men not to molest me, nor to attempt to follow me. You can shoot me down, but, French, you will break your heart in a million pieces. And be sure to call in the men."

Shortly afterward, Burness rode down the hill, while Andrew motioned back his men.

CHAPTER TWENTY-NINE

As soon as Burness was out of sight, Andrew French called for Pansy. The girl had been crying, and Susan Enfield came in with her.

"There, there, Pansy," said Andrew in considerable excitement. "Now you must tell me how you met Burness, and all about it."

"I could have shot him dead," moaned the girl, "that's what gets me. I've got a gun . . . Clint taught me how to use it . . . and I had two chances to put a bullet in that coward's back. I could have got the others, too, I think. And I didn't do it . . . I didn't do it."

"It's a good thing you didn't," Andrew said, putting a hand on her shoulder. "Now you must tell me about it, Pansy. You must tell me everything, you understand? Did he take you from your house?"

"No, no," said the girl quickly. "When the men all left town, including Father, and I learned they were coming up here, I couldn't stand the uncertainty any longer. I started for the ranch. That cowardly brute caught me about halfway here. He had two men with him, and they took me to a cutbank along the river and held me captive for two hours or so. Then

is when I could have shot him. I had two chances . . .
three, four, or five chances . . . to shoot him."

"You must forget about shooting him!" Andrew
cried impatiently. "That would have been the worst
thing you could have done. Do you know he has
taken Dick and Clint prisoners, and that, if he
doesn't get back to where they are, they'll be killed?
Now you see how important this whole thing is?
You must tell me quickly."

"Clint a prisoner?" Pansy gasped. "How . . . ?"

"That'll wait," Andrew said sternly. "Now, after
they took you to that place on the river, what took
place after that?"

"We stayed there an hour or more. I sat under
the bank, and Burness and his two men stood outside and talked. I couldn't hear what they were
talking about, but Burness seemed in good spirits.
Then another man came. Burness called him Warren. After they had heard what this man had to say,
Burness told them to get along . . . that they knew
what to do."

"Yes, yes," muttered Andrew. "This Warren must
have been up this way watching the house, and
went back with the word that the posse had ridden
away. Go on, my girl, go on."

"Then Burness told me flat that I was to ride with
him up to the house. Said I was to compose myself,
talk or anything, but ride with him to the house. I
thought he was using me as a shield, and that I
would be leading him into a trap up here. I never expected he would get away alive. But I suppose he
came to bargain for Clint and Dick's release. He's a
monster, Mister French. He'll kill them both!"

Andrew was quick to reply. "No, he won't Pansy.
Don't say that. I think I've half stopped it already. I
have one more move to make, and I'm goin' to make

it quicker than greased lightning. Now, you stay here with Susan and everything will be all right."

"Where's Father?" asked the girl.

"He's all right," replied Andrew, strapping on his gun belt with its holster and huge weapon. "He's out with the men." He drew on his coat hurriedly. "I'm going up the valley, Susan," he said to the housekeeper, "and you look after Pansy."

He hurried out, calling for Klein and Munsey.

"They've got Dick and Clint prisoners," he explained hurriedly. "Burness said if he wasn't back where they are tonight, his men had orders to . . . very bad orders." The old stockman's face was gray. "I bought him off, and now we've got to call off the men so he can release the boys. And we've got to hurry. Listen, Klein, I've got to leave a trusty man here with the women. I'm goin' to leave you . . . not that Ed Munsey, here, isn't trusted, too. But you've got a better head, whether Ed likes it or not. And if any of our bunch shows up, especially Wilson or Miller . . . which they probably won't . . . send 'em out in a hurry to call off the bloodhounds. As soon as Clint and Dick are back, we can go after 'em again in earnest and show no quarter. Understand?"

"Is that what Burness came here to tell you?" asked Bill Klein.

"Yes, and we can't waste any time. Ed, get our horses out."

"He's lyin'!" exclaimed Bill with an oath. "I wish I had shot him in his tracks, like I intended. I'm a fool."

"You'd have been a fool to do it," Andrew put in. "Why, I could have dropped him with my rifle when he was riding away instead of holding you two back. Ready, Ed?"

At this moment Pansy came running out of the house. "Mister French, there's something else!"

"Yes, yes," said the stockman eagerly. "What is it, Pansy?"

"I thought I'd wait and tell Daddy, but I don't see any reason why I should. Everyone has to know it some time. When I was trying to find out where the posse was going, I looked in the side door of the Stampede, thinking Red Tower would tell me. Oh, I know I was excited. Tower and that man of his were quarreling behind the bar, and, before I could close the door, the man made a rush at Red when he saw he had a gun, and Red shot him. Then, when the man fell, Red leaned over and shot him again. Oh, I . . ."

"Don't worry," Andrew said soothingly. "We . . . the sheriff . . . expected that very thing to happen. They're no good. You go back in the house and get something to eat, and rest till I come back. I'll bring your dad back." When the girl had left, he said significantly to Bill: "That's one of 'em gone down there. Reckon Wilson will tend to the other. All right, Ed, let's go."

Within a few minutes the stockman and his hand were racing up the valley on two of the best horses the Two-Bar could offer, and the Two-Bar was famous for its horses. Late in the afternoon, guided by men they met, they found Sheriff Wilson high on the right ridge at the head of Paradise Valley.

Wilson favored him with a tired smile. "We've got 'em," he said wearily. From behind him, Norman Webb nodded in triumph.

"Got who?" French demanded.

"The whole outfit," replied the sheriff. "They're in that cup above the head of the valley. Paradise Dome is behind them, and it's so steep a fly couldn't crawl up it. They've got to come out on this side or the other, and we'll shoot 'em down like rats.

Miller's on the other side. We're just waitin' for Burness to get back before we start the slaughter." The sheriff licked his lips in satisfaction.

"But the boys . . . Clint and Dick!" Andrew fairly shrieked.

"They're in that old cave, you remember, just below the cup. You can see the ledge in front of it from here. We've seen 'em, and could close in and get 'em out, but we want Burness himself, first."

"Call off the men!" cried Andrew. "Burness saw me at the house. I paid him off in money, and he said, if he didn't get back to his men, Clint and Dick would be killed. They're prisoners up there, I tell you. I'll pay the bank loss myself . . . I'll turn over my ranch . . . but I want my boys! Call off the men, Wilson. I order it. I command it! It was part of my promise, and, if I don't live up to it, Burness will live up to his!"

The sheriff looked at him keenly. "Burness was bluffing."

"He wasn't bluffing!" cried Andrew. "He came to the house, and from the minute he arrived, he was in my power, and he knew it. He threw his gun on the table. When I asked him what he would do if I refused, he said he'd try to fight his way out, but if he didn't get back. . . ." Andrew swore. "Call off the men before it is too late. And Burness must not be molested. I gave you the tip that he'd more than likely come up this way to get even with me. That's how you were able to set your trap. I'm entitled to consideration. I've got more than money at stake."

"Come over here and let me get this thing straight," said the sheriff impatiently. "You come, too, Webb. Meanwhile, I'll send word to Miller over across not to bother Burness right away. I've got 'em sewed up, anyway." He turned away to give his instructions, and then joined Andrew and Webb aside.

Andrew explained in painful detail the events of the day.

"I still believe he's bluffing," said the sheriff with a scowl when Andrew had finished. "And how's he goin' to know if I've pulled off the men if I do pull 'em off? If he has got that pair of young scamps, he'd probably take 'em along until he was sure he was good and away. My men are pretty well hidden. I couldn't get 'em out on short notice, anyway. We'll let him get back and see what move he'll make. He wouldn't bump off those boys on a bet . . . you ought to know that, Andy. Let me tell you something. He's got the best part of the Conroy loot himself. Those three men with him have probably got the rest. And he got more'n twenty thousand from you. I'd bet my last dollar he and those three men that were with him are shootin' for Canada this very minute."

"It may be all you say," said Andrew, "but I don't want to take any chances."

"We won't," the sheriff said grimly. Again he gave instructions, and a number of men stole away.

"Just leave it to him, Andy," said Norman Webb, gripping the arm of his old friend.

"How come you've changed so sudden?" Andrew demanded, surprised.

"I've seen things," Webb said, nodding his head. "I slipped the sheriff's badge back in his pocket when he didn't know it."

"Well, I'll be . . . !"

Andrew's exclamation was cut short by a shout. "Look!" cried several men, pointing to the ledge in front of the cave below the cup in the mountain. In the mellowing light of the sunset they saw several figures, and then . . .

* * *

After their capture, Dick and Clint had been taken up the ridge, south of the valley, higher and higher, and then forced to ride along a narrow ledge northward until they reached a point at the head of the valley and directly above it. Above them loomed the great Paradise Dome.

"We're at the cave," Clint whispered excitedly to his brother.

"You don't need to whisper," Limpy Lowell said in his mean voice. "Talk right out loud. Nobody'll hear you except our men, and they don't care what you say. Take him into the cave, Clint. You know where you are. But you didn't think Limpy knew, did you? Limpy knows more than you think. Get in there!"

Limpy's gun was out, and with him were three hard-looking members of the Burness band. Clint realized they hadn't a chance in the world against the four men, unarmed as they were, and he surmised that the men had their instructions as to what to do in the event that he and Dick should attempt to get away.

So they entered the cave, the very cave Clint had shown his brother a day or two after Dick had arrived at the ranch. Clint had to hold Dick, for the latter was fighting mad.

"If I hadn't been along, you'd have gotten away from that bunch," he said bitterly. "Why didn't you leave me, Clint? It would have been better for me to have been captured than both of us."

"Wise up to yourself," Clint retorted grimly. "We would both have been riddled with bullets. We're up against a hard proposition."

"All right, you pets," came Limpy's voice from the front. "Chat away, but don't try any tricks. There's four of us here, and we have our orders."

"If it was just you, you little rat, I wouldn't stop a minute," Clint said savagely. "I wouldn't even take a club. I'd take your gun away from you and rub your nose with its barrel. Then I'd kick you off the ledge."

"Why, you . . ."

"Oh, shut up," said one of the other men. "We're not here to talk. We've got 'em cold, and what's the use raggin' 'em? If you don't stop struttin' around and shootin' off your mouth, Limpy, we'll gag you. We're not here to listen to you."

There followed a significant silence outside the cave.

The brothers sat down, rolled and lighted their cigarettes. "Limpy doesn't even stand good with his own crowd," whispered Clint. "And don't forget this, Dick . . . he's yellow. I know the little rat."

The two carried on a whispered conversation. The cave was dry and warm. After a time they doubled up their coats, used them for a pillow, and fell asleep.

Meanwhile, Burness and his three picked men were circling to southward to take up their station along the river. The band was cached in the cup above the cave, and Burness had no idea of leaving his men. He was yet to see the big posse sweep up from Conroy toward the ranch, and when he did see it. . . . There were men who carried money among those cached on the mountain. And Burness was a fighter. He would no more have it said that he abandoned his men and fled than he would have cut off his right hand.

It was broad daylight when Clint and Dick awoke. As they stepped to the entrance of the cave, a man sitting on the ledge with his back against a rock rose suddenly. It was not Limpy, although the diminutive gunman was crouched on the opposite side of the entrance with another guard.

The man who had risen spoke in a gruff voice. "Here," he said. "Here's something for you to eat and some water. Take it and keep your trap closed."

"Thanks," said Dick, taking the package of food and the canteen of water. "Nice sociable gent, you are. We'll just take this and maybe eat some of it to oblige you."

"I said take it and shut up!" commanded the guard.

"Why don't you take a nice jump off the ledge to improve your disposition," Dick suggested. "Imagine a bum like you sassing a gentleman of the range. You're the one to keep your mouth shut, you lout. And if any of you scum try to get into this cave, we'll beat you up. Chew that with your greasy tobacco, and clean your teeth next Christmas."

The others laughed as the guard's face reddened. Then he sat down. "Talk all you like, bo, but don't it look nice outside with the sun shining and the birds singing and everything?"

"You talkin' about birds singing," scoffed Dick to his brother's delight. "Why, you never saw a bird without wanting to shoot it, and your work is done in the dark, not with the sun shining."

The guard remained silent.

The brothers ate their breakfast of cold meat and bread and drank some of the water. All day long they bantered their guards. Every time one started to reply, he got the worst of it. Once Clint and Dick stood in the front of the cave, pointing out spots of interest.

"Looks nice, eh, Clint?" said Dick. "Won't be long before we'll be down there with decent people. If these brainless saps knew what was coming to them, they wouldn't even wait for their horses . . . they'd run for it."

So it went all day, until the first pink flush of sunset. Then came a sudden and startling interruption. The brothers hurried to the entrance and saw one who could be no other than Burness striding along the ledge toward them.

"Here's the chief!" Limpy Lowell called out.

"Get 'em out of there!" the outlaw commanded. His face and manner showed he was in a towering rage.

"Which one of you brats is Clint French?" he demanded when the brothers stood before him.

There was no answer, for Dick had insisted that under no circumstances were they to reveal their individual identity.

Burness looked from one to the other of them, trying to decide which was which. He turned to a man behind him. "Give them their belts and guns," he ordered. Then, to Limpy and the three others: "Stand back, and, if they make a move to shoot before I say, let 'em have it!"

He watched closely as the brothers buckled on their belts and hefted their guns. Both belts and holsters were worn, and the two handled their weapons the same. It was impossible to tell them apart. Cries came from either side of the mountain. Burness merely sneered. "We'll tend to them later," he said through gritted teeth. He took a silver dollar from a pocket. "I want to give this upstart Clint a chance first to show what he could do," he said in a harsh voice. "Now you'll come by chance. You're comin' out here in front of me, one by one, and shoot it out with me, understand? Go for your gun, or you won't ever have another chance." His eyes were blazing. He handed the dollar to Clint. "Spin it. Heads you're first, tails you're second. Spin it!"

Clint spun the coin, and it landed tails up.

"Step aside," commanded Burness. "Watch him, you men." He handed the coin to Dick. "Spin it. Heads you're first, tails you're second. I'll allow one tie, and then change my tactics."

There was a flow of hope in Clint's breast. If Dick would only tie up and draw tails. He was trying to think as Dick spun the shiny coin.

The coin flashed in the dying rays of the sun, spun on the rock of the ledge, and came heads up.

"Step out!" roared Burness.

As Dick stepped out, Clint leaped ahead of him. "I'm Clint!" he shouted, and the shout was drowned in the roar of guns.

Burness slid down on the side of the rock, shooting wildly. Clint's aim had been true. Dick was stunned. Then he caught sight of Limpy Lowell raising his gun. In a trice—something he always said he could never do again—Dick jerked out his weapon and shot Limpy down. Then he swung a backhander that struck the man behind him fully in the chest and knocked him off the ledge. A horrible cry came up from below. Clint's gun spoke again, downing the man who had come with Burness. But a shot from the other guard struck Clint in the shoulder, knocking him to his knees. Then Dick's weapon spat its second message of hot lead, and the guard plunged on his face.

Then men were shooting from above and on either side. As the light faded, a blaze of shooting darts of fire swept into the cup. Wilson had sprung his trap.

Dick picked Clint up in his arms and carried him northward along the ledge while Andrew French and Norman Webb ran to meet them and took Dick's burden.

"Are you hit bad, Clint?" Andrew cried.

"Naw, but I'll be laid up a week or two," Clint gasped. "I got him, Dad, I . . ." Then he fainted.

CHAPTER THIRTY

It was a big and jubilant gathering in the Two-Bar F ranch house that night. Andrew French strutted about, supervising the dinner served to all comers, and smiling as he hadn't smiled in years. Norman Webb seemed a different man, more like the commanding stockman he had been for so many years. Clint was propped on a couch where he could see what was going on, and Pansy Webb was sitting beside him. His left shoulder was swathed in bandages, and Dick had to roll his cigarettes.

"Too bad you never learned to roll them," he told Pansy, with a sly wink at Clint.

"Yes, sir," Andrew was telling Norman Webb, "Dick got two of 'em. Threw one of 'em clear over the ledge so, when he plunged on the rocks, he didn't know what hit him. An' me . . . I'd been afraid for him to carry a gun. Man, the money Burness had on him. His shirt was so packed with big bills it's a wonder to me that Clint could plug through 'em. Yes, sir, it is."

"I've a good notion to go back into the cow business," said Webb. "I'm kinda sick of living in town."

"Well," drawled Andrew, "by the looks of the

way Pansy greeted Clint when we brought him back, an' what's goin' on over there by the couch, you'll have to live in town alone by and by."

"*Hmmm,*" grunted Webb. "Well, if it turns out that way, she'll be gettin' a cowman, anyway."

"That's the talk!" roared Andrew. "Hear that, you folks over by the couch? Norman says if things come out like it looks they would, Pansy will be getting a cowman, anyway."

Pansy blushed furiously, and Clint patted her arm with his good hand.

"Looks like somebody was getting ahead of me," Dick observed, scowling at his brother. "But he had to get wounded to do it. That always gets 'em . . . a wounded man they like."

Clint grinned. "Why, we've been positively engaged for an hour," he drawled. "So I guess we're ahead of him, eh, sweetheart?"

Pansy laughed happily, and then looked slyly at her father, who was beaming his approval.

"Susan!" roared Andrew. "Looks like you was goin' to have help on the ranch soon. Clint wouldn't live in town on a bet, and Pansy's tired of it down there, so . . ."

His words were drowned in the laughter of those in the room.

At this moment all looked up, for there was a clatter of hoofs in the courtyard, and Miller could be heard above the din, yelling his orders.

Shortly afterward, Sheriff Wilson came into the room. His clothes were dusty, and there were dusty wrinkles about the corners of his eyes. But his eyes gleamed ever so brightly.

"Well, we cleaned 'em out," he announced, taking the chair Dick pulled up for him, and putting his big hat on the floor. "Cut 'em to pieces, brought some prisoners along to take into town tomorrow, and left a bunch of men to round up the stragglers. Got most of the money, too . . . besides what Burness had. You did mighty fine work, Clint, and you, too, Dick." He turned to Andrew with a twinkle in his eyes. "You know, I was beginning to think that pair wasn't good for much."

Everybody laughed again, and he was told the news about Pansy and Clint. "Shucks," he said, and frowned. "I've seen that comin' a long, long time. I was merely wondering how long it would take."

"Aren't you goin' to congratulate us?" Clint complained.

"I suppose it'll cost me plenty for a weddin' present," drawled Wilson, "and, after all, congratulating engaged couples is like sayin' 'Happy New Year' to my guests in jail. Don't mean nothing."

"You did a fine job," complimented Norman Webb.

"And that goes for me, too," said Andrew heartily.

"What're you goin' to do with the prisoners that're in jail from Muddy Flat when you get this bunch down?" asked Webb curiously.

"I'm goin' to take the Muddy Flat bunch to the county line and tell 'em never to come back," the sheriff said soberly. "And Muddy Flat is through as a bad town. So's Conroy, for that matter."

"Did you hear about Red Tower killin' Hagen?" asked Andrew.

The sheriff looked up quickly. "No . . . but I expected it. He saw his chance when we were all out of town. I'm just goin' to let him tell his story when I get back, and then I am goin' to say . . . 'Red, I don't feel like I can trust you. You've lied to me too many times, and we're not goin' to lie around here any more. I'll give you just three days to sell your joint and get out of town. Now go along, and don't forget the time limit.' He'll get out, all right."

"And a mighty good riddance!" Norman Webb ejaculated.

"Yes, I figure on cleanin' the county up right, see that these prisoners get started for prison, and then I'll be through. I've already turned in my star to Mister Webb. I don't think he'll have any trouble from now on. Anyway, I've been sheriff too long."

"Your star. You didn't turn in any star to me," blurted out Webb. "You've taken it off and put it in your pocket, like you always do in such bad cases. I'll bet your star is in your right coat pocket this minute."

A hush came over the room. Wilson gave Webb a queer look and instinctively thrust his hand into his right pocket. When he brought out the star there was a cheer.

"What'd I say!" cried Webb in triumph. "Our sheriff would be a pretty picture without a star, wouldn't he, boys?"

"Well, Norman," said the sheriff, grinning. "I know you put that in there. Looks like I've got to spend the rest of my life being an ornery sheriff."

"Being the best we ever had," boomed Andrew French.

There were boots on the porch, and Bill Klein saluted. "Here's a telegram for Mister Richard French," he announced.

"How'd it get up here?" asked Clint. "Did old Mose ride all the way up here? This is gettin' to be an important family."

But Dick already had grabbed the telegram and was tearing it open feverishly. He looked at the signature. "It's from Janet!" he cried, and started to dance.

"Who's Janet?" Clint asked.

"They're coming!" exclaimed Dick, reading the message. "Listen . . . 'Mother and the rest of us are coming out in two weeks. I'll wire when we're starting. Love, Janet.'"

"Love, eh?" said Clint, rising on his good arm. "Who's Janet?"

"Janet, my dear brother," said Dick, raising his eyebrows, "is the girl I'm going to marry. When I asked her to do that little thing and to visit us out here in the wild and woolly, she said, if they came, she would marry her dear old Richard. And, whoopee! She's coming. Who's ahead now, Clint!"

"Susan!" roared Andrew. "Susan, we're goin' to have more help, and this time it's Richard!"

About the Author

Robert J. Horton was born in Coudersport, Pennsylvania. As a very young man he traveled extensively in the American West, working for newspapers. For several years he was sports editor for the *Great Falls Tribune* in Great Falls, Montana. He began writing Western fiction for *Adventure* magazine before becoming a regular contributor to Street & Smith's *Western Story Magazine*. By the mid-1920s Horton was one of three authors to whom Street & Smith paid 5¢ a word—the other two being Frederick Faust, perhaps better known as Max Brand, and Robert Ormond Case. Many of Horton's serials for Street & Smith's *Western Story Magazine* were subsequently brought out as books by Chelsea House, Street & Smith's book publishing company. Although virtually all of Horton's stories appeared under his byline in the magazine, for their book editions Chelsea House published them either as by Robert J. Horton or by James Roberts. Sometimes, as was the case with *Rovin' Redden* (Chelsea House, 1925) by James Roberts, a book would consist of three short novels that were editorially joined to form a "novel." Other times the stories were serials published in book form, such as *Whispering Cañon* (Chelsea House, 1925) by James Roberts or *The Prairie Shrine* (Chelsea House, 1924) by Robert J. Horton. It may be obvious that Chelsea House, doing a number of books a year by the same author, thought it a prudent marketing strategy to give the author more than one name. Horton's Western stories are concerned most of all with character, and it is the characters that drive the plots rather than the other way around. It is unfortunate he died at such a relatively early age. Many of his novels, after Street & Smith abandoned Chelsea House, were published only in British editions, and Robert J. Horton was not to appear at all in paperback books until quite recently.